Already the air was ge
dimming. He stepped
volume to cope with the
was pounding. Mike co
He started heading over
numbers admitted a feeling of happy concern about the fire
restrictions being ignored but a voice boomed out from behind
him. It was his partner, high on the stage with a microphone
looking the natural MC. There was a surge from the crowd. The
band was known.

"Oh, some you heard them before maybe? Well, I wan you
give a big up for the music crew. Big up, ya hear me?"

Down in the crowd Mike watched the whole event, chuckling.
Things were working out.

BACKSTREETS

Also in the BACKSTREETS series

SLACKNESS

BACKSTREETS

BIG UP!

JONATHAN BROOK

B🌳XTREE

First published in the UK 1994 by
Boxtree Limited
Broadwall House
21 Broadwall
London SE1 9PL

The right of Jonathan Brook to be identified as Author of
this work has been asserted by him in accordance with the
Copyright, Designs and Patents Act 1988

10 9 8 7 6 5 4 3 2 1

Cover art – Faisal/M. Bishop
Cover Design – Martin Lovelock
Series Editor – Jake Lingwood
Series Production – Joya Bart-Plange

Phototypeset by Intype, London
Printed and bound in Great Britain by
Cox and Wyman Ltd, Reading, Berkshire

ISBN 0 7522 0925 6

A CIP catalogue record for this book is available from the
British Library

Thanks to MOOK

One

The room was a wash of soft brown in the dying light of the afternoon. There were no curtains to block out the glare but the glass was stained with the residue of tobacco smoke, so any light breaking through was filtered. Bouncing off wood gave it the final touch and this room was largely furnished in the stuff. Even the floor still showed it was timber, despite the efforts of a million shuffling feet to obscure it with filth.

On the walls there were some dusty pictures and a few chrome fittings to light them. It was too dark and they were too covered in grime to make out the details from where he stood at the bar but he knew what they portrayed. He remembered them from the time he was in this room a few years ago and the recollection made him smile. Each frame contained a scene from some ancient brothel, probably Roman, with figures in robes reclining across cushions and rounded women attending. As youths this had greatly amused Curtis and his friends. They had only seen the humour of sex in the art. He stepped over to one of the frames and examined the picture. Another few years of exposure to the bar's foul air had obscured the detail even more but he could just make out the design. He flopped into one of the tan sofas that lined the wall, rolled his head back and stared at the scene. It showed a fat man at play with two women, spread across a low couch. This time he could relate to the picture in a way that was different and Curtis felt a surge of confidence. He had come through to adulthood and the memory of a youth's attitude made him chuckle. Maybe there had been changes in the last two thousand years but he was still likely to be doing something very similar to the picture's content this evening, though it would not involve handing over any money. This time he also noticed the ambition of the player in the scene. He got up and paced back to the bar, muttering.

"Man have to be gymnast to pull that off."

Usually, no matter where you might be in West Park, you could always hear the low rumble of traffic floating up from the highstreet but this room was silent. The air was heavy, like a weight pressing down on his shoulders and he became aware of the sweat forming on his brow. Thinking he might cool down by sitting, he pulled up a stool and rested his arms across the bar, watching his movements in the mirror that ran behind a long row of bottles. He made sure there was no dust on the bar top that might stain his cuffs.

It surprised him that the place was so well stocked with alcohol, as everyone knew the club was dying. Where he sat was for private guests. The room below was the main club and you only got invited up if you had the right friends.

Curtis had always known people and had been here in this room a few times but that had been back at the start of his clubbing days and he had found the atmosphere a bit stale, favouring a good blues. By the time he was really into clubs this place was going down. In good times it was jumping and for a few years it had been the main club spot in his patch but the hall was big and old style. If it wasn't full, then it felt cold and people started to drift to smaller, harder clubs. Places where you felt like you were in a crowd. The club had stayed open but fortune had turned into a slow death and nothing they put on seemed to make any difference. Few people even thought of coming out here these days.

That was the beauty of it all, according to Ben and Mike. He smiled again at their plan and lit a cigarette. Smoking helped to kill time. Exhaling, he saw the plume of smoke rush and then settle in the still air, rays of soft light playing at the edges. It hid his face in the mirror.

They were down there right now and if they listened to his advice they would just be on the point of walking out. Ben should be on his feet, tapping the desk and sighing. If they were really crazy enough to take this place on, then the price might as well be right. By now Hargreaves would be open-mouthed, appalled at their suggestion. He was constantly appalled. The sweat would be dripping into his lap, turning the white shirt he always wore a shiny grey. Curtis hated that. He could tolerate a bum as long as there were no pretensions. Hargreaves thought he was smooth. His pasty little face would be all screwed up and his breathing quite audible. One day his heart would just pop with all the bleating, and the shocked expression he was so fond of pulling when he talked money would be stuck on his face for eternity. For now he would mop his brow and whine away.

"Guys, guys, see my side of it. I have to take something from the door. What's my margin otherwise?"

A thin, reedy voice. His hands would be waving in the air in a wild attempt to convince them of his point but they would ignore him. They knew he would settle for the bar; he had no choice in the deal.

"Well, me walkin, then. Come, Mike."

Curtis heard the raised voices from below, Hargreaves making a last bid for his cut of the door. The three friends had discussed the play coming over in his car and he knew how the act was going. Ben would be up for the money in a few minutes.

Despite what he thought of the idea they could still have the loan. He had never known them so excited, Ben particularly. Anyway, there was a chance it might work out for them and he was always ready to help if he could. Cash was not a problem for him these days.

There was a sound behind him and he turned to see Ben emerge from the steps that brought you up into the middle of the room. He was dressed in loose denims and walked with a slow, easy rhythm.

"Well, you look relax, Ben. Mind, that nothing new. It go good for you?"

Ben flashed him a wide smile and laughed. "Safe, man. Long as you have the money for me?"

Two

West Park was groaning in the heat. Summer had come early and for two weeks the sun had blazed the city. They were stuck on the highstreet in a long train of cars, the air-conditioning whistling.

"Crack a window, C. It's too warm back here." Mike was in a heap on the rear seat, wiping his face. He was only wearing a thin T-shirt and some knee shorts but his back was wet with perspiration.

"Nah, Mikey. It stinks out there. Anyway, we're not moving, so all you gonna get is fumes."

Mike didn't reply. It was true that the heat had brought the smell of trash onto the streets. He stared through the glass at the traffic and wondered if he could make it to a shop and get a drink before they started moving. He had a persistent thirst but it was not only from the heat. Teaming up as a partner with Ben made him sweat more than the air temperature did.

"Well, we all set, then." Ben sounded smug. His frame was relaxed in the leather seat. "One week till the first night, so we have plenty to do. When we see the band, Mike?"

"We can drop round anytime you want. I told Sophie we'd bring her the deposit over, soon as we were definite."

"We go round straight away, then . . ."

"So you walking, Ben?" Curtis had cut in before Ben could beg the ride. "It not enough I lend you the money for your big business dealings but you want me as chauffeur too. Boy, you think I enjoy sittin park like this."

"No, I mean . . ."

"So you can take the tube, then?" Curtis was talking slowly, with an amused lilt to his voice. He forced a space in the traffic, pulled over and killed the engine. They all climbed out of the car, sluggish in the heat.

"So we might see you later for a drink."

"Yeah, I just getting a few things an' then I'll be round my place. Bell me." Curtis backed away from them on the pavement, heading for the open doorway of a grocery shop.

"Right, later. Oh, an' C, thanks for the loan. You help us out a lot."

"Yeah, thanks, Curtis. Come and check out our opening won't you?"

Curtis nodded and walked into the store. What a concept! Mike and Ben running a club night and booking bands. Let's face it, they were barely out of their school uniforms. They had even persuaded some maniac to lend them the money.

Then he realised that they'd all been at school together and they were really all about the same age. He had to smile. Maybe he couldn't be thinking of them as his little brothers for too much longer.

The carriage was packed and Ben had to fight down the urge to get off before the doors hissed shut. He rarely used the tube. On the occasions he went into town he would either be driven or take a bus but the rush-hour was looming and it was a relief to escape from the surface heat.

They were crammed together in the centre of the train, surrounded by a colourful range of people. There were some penguins in suits, sitting next to a bunch of freaks from Sheltham who were probably going to score somewhere. Ben was glad to be moving on from that game. Next to them were some office girls, chatting about a promotion they should have got and a few stern figures absorbed in magazines. The train shuddered and started to move and he stared at the ripples the movement made in one of the girls' plain black skirt.

"Are they never gonna modernise these fuckers?" Mike was screaming in his ear, cutting through the clunks and scrapes the wheels made on tired track.

"Yeah, yeah." There was a lot floating through his mind. The past few months had been hectic. After his initial idea about setting up a club, Mike had talked him into trying it as a weekly residence. They had sat in Bliss that night getting smashed and come up with a plan, agreeing to be partners. Ben had always been interested in the live scene, so he could handle the bands, leaving Mike to take care of the system and DJ work. At that drunken stage it had all been easy, no risks and no outlay but the work had piled up. They had to scout for bands, recruit some help with the equipment and raise capital. That was when Curtis entered the equation. He had been good about it though, no hesitation.

The biggest hassle was the venue. At first Maxine's was the obvious choice, but that ruled out a straight forward residency. Despite months of trying, Mike had never managed to get a DJ spot for even half an hour at Maxine's, let alone a whole night. This was probably because he was white and there weren't too many white ragga DJs. Whatever the reason, there were people who had Maxine's sewn up. They would have to look around for another option. Ben had never guessed West Park had so many broken-down clubs. They had tried everywhere, even bingo halls and the local social, until Curtis suggested talking to Hargreaves. He was the manager of an old dance hall and the place was close to folding.

Ben and Mike had never been inside the building. They had only passed by it a few times. It was in the south of West Park, set back from the road and surrounded by a high fence which meant only the domed top was visible, a dirty, green copper. On either side there was a row of condemned terraces, windows and doors boarded up. This part of the patch was almost a wasteland.

Their first reaction to the building was revulsion and they told Curtis to turn the car round. Once inside the fence you were facing a huge, brick edifice with small towers on each corner. Faded flags crowned them. There was an immense porch like the gaping mouth of a stone colossus and a board next to it, presumably to advertise coming events. It was bare.

It took Curtis a while to convince them it was worth entering but once inside they were sold. The period look of the frontage was ugly. It belonged to another era of design that had not been flattered by the passing years. However, this was not true of the interior. It was the same age but the style still worked. Indeed, the very fact it was antiquated made it atmospheric, perfect for a club.

Walking through the porch they entered a large reception

area with a small bar on one side and an area for hanging coats facing it. From here you could see the main hall through a revolving glass door. They pushed through, one at a time.

Everything was lined in wood. It was all of the same hue, a soft chestnut. It stretched down either wall to a high stage and made up the whole of the dancefloor. That was when he had the idea for the name.

"We call it the Chocolate Box, Mikey."

"You what?"

"The club name. Well, all this wood look just like chocolate to me. It perfect, man."

They walked down to the stage and Ben clambered up. Behind him was an ocean of scarlet, a curtain reaching up to the shadows in the roof. He could see the length of the room, back to the glass door. It was a big space, ideal for a live show.

"How many you reckon?"

Mike looked around, trying to guess how it would look, full of people. "Nearly a thousand maybe."

"It's the one, innit?"

"Man, but look at the roof. The sound'll get lost up there. It has got character though."

They were in love with it and it had been hard putting on the act for Hargreaves. He complained about them keeping all the door take but gave in, just as Curtis said he would. The circles Curtis moved in knew about how well clubs were doing. Now it was down to them to make the place work.

Hargreaves got four hundred for a month, to cover four shows. They got Saturday night, which was what they had wanted, and had access during the day to set things up. Ben was a bit anxious. He had enjoyed the drunken plotting but all the running around was getting like work now. His social life was suffering. There was the money too. The band wanted eight hundred and the other expenses were adding up, so Curtis was down fifteen hundred already. He had tried to work out the door take and what they would have to charge but it made his head ache. Mike could deal with that.

"This is our stop, I think." Mike was making for the doors and Ben had to rush after him before they hissed shut. "You asleep or something?"

"No, Mike. I'm just trying to work out some details, you know."

"Details like, if we flop, yeah, and how we're going to pay Curtis back. Those sort of details?"

"Well, you can always get your paper-round back, can't you."

They laughed and pushed into the crowd at the base of the escalator.

Fifteen minutes of mad racing beneath the streets moved you to another world. As they came out onto the pavement they joined a swirl of people rushing between the canyons of offices and department stores. Every one of the multitude looked as though they had a purpose, places they had to get to and for a certain time. This was not the case down in West Park. The pace was more mellow and you could always observe at least some of the locals hanging out, chatting in groups along the highstreet and outside the lines of houses. Even though Ben had seen it a thousand times, the atmosphere here perplexed him and he gazed at the scene for a few seconds before setting off with Mike.

What he found hard to understand about those who relished this way of life was their "drive". Getting up at eight and working all day was hard enough for him to consider but he knew that a lot of people actually enjoyed it. This was beyond his realm of comprehension. "Cha! Think I need a drink, man. These city people make me tetchy."

"Relax. We're here anyway."

They were still on the same wide thoroughfare, standing in front of a small, metal door. It seemed alien in this environment. All along the road there were huge, glass-fronted blocks with boutiques and electronic stores at the ground level. Some of the doorways had tiny trees or plants adorning them. The scent of money hung in the air. It was present in everything: the buildings that looked like they were dusted down every day, the cars that slid past, even the clothes the pedestrians wore. And this area was not the most central money district, it was just north of the most affluent stretch. There was money in this town, nobody could question that.

The door they faced was insignificant in comparison with the other entrances. The agency was paying for the location and could only afford the most humble premises. Next to the frame was a plaque with several names engraved on it and buzzers next to them. Mike pushed the one that had "Shark Music" written by it.

Sophie came down to let them in. There was a slight scuffle between them to be the first to follow her up the staircase. The office was way up on the top floor and both of them had discovered the pleasure of watching her wriggle up the incline.

When it was hot outside, Sophie liked to wear a skirt but it was such a minimal mini that it was more like a wide belt around her waist. The lead man on the stairs was sometimes blessed with a celestial view. She was about twenty and had an outrageously attractive figure, with legs the same colour as honey. They followed her up the stairs like panting wolves.

"Good job you came with the deposit. I wasn't getting paid this week unless something came in." She had a warm, open tone to her voice, like all good PR people. Ben thought she liked him.

Mike was of the same opinion. "No hassle with the band then, making the date I mean?"

"Oh no. They'll be there. I was thinking I might come along myself, see what you two are up to. I heard your ad on the radio. 'The Chocolate Box', like the name."

They had come into the small room that was the office and she walked over to her desk as she spoke. Ben smiled at the praise. There were three desks in the room and all the usual office junk. Today she was alone but there were usually two guys there, talking on the phone or staring up at the band posters that covered the walls.

"Great, we'll put your name on the door, then."

"Right, sure. Sorry. I'm in a rush today and I have to make some calls."

They took the cue and Ben handed her the cash Curtis has given them, stuffed in an envelope. Mike thought it was more official than a roll of loose notes.

"So, boys, see you on the night."

They left her with assurances she would enjoy being there and crashed back onto the street. It was still hot but a breeze was heralding the coming night and the air felt less oppressive. They headed back towards the tube.

"Girl sweet on me Mike, I tell you. She cute."

"I thought we might have to sign something at least." Mike was talking to himself, trying to remember they were involved in a business venture here and not the regular game. It was hard with Ben around. Besides, he could not deny to himself that Sophie was alluring. "It could be me she finds attractive, you know? Did that ever occur to you?"

"Well, no, Mikey, it hadn't, now that you mention it."

They came to a halt just before the noisy entrance hall of the underground and exchanged smiles. There was never any real malice between them.

"So you make a play for her on the night, I do the same and may the bes man win."

Mike thought about the potential embarrassment of a rejected pounce. "I accept the challenge. May the best man win."

Ben was glad to be home. He lay back on his bed, pulling deep on a joint, thinking about Sophie's charms. The recent workload had forced him to curtail his usual pursuits and he was missing the joys of womanhood. Mike's outburst made him chuckle. He had heard about the scene with Celia some months ago and as far as he knew the situation was still the same with his friend's virginity. It was intact. Mike making moves on her had not annoyed him. It was an open game in Ben's eyes, as he had no real attachment to her anyway. His dealings with her had been some time ago. No girl he had been with was worth falling out with a buddy.

It was the summer now and his last run of sex had been a few months ago. He would have to stop working so hard.

There was a sound at the front door and he jumped off the bed. His father would want to know how the day had gone and Ben didn't want him in his room with the aroma of hash so strong. One of the side benefits of his new activity was that the moaning about finding a career had stopped and he did not want to ruin that. Getting caught smoking would be disastrous. It was no secret that he smoked but it was tolerated only as long as it was hidden and did not have to be faced. His father could handle it that way.

As soon as he announced the plan, Pops had become consumed with enthusiasm, relieved that his son had found his path at last. The risks of the enterprise were ignored. Every day there would be a little chat about how things were proceeding. Overcome with price, he was even telling his friends about the deal. For a while it had amazed Ben to see this change but he understood now that his father had only wanted him to be busy, involved in some constructive activity. They had been getting on with each other lately.

He stubbed the joint out and kicked the ashtray out of sight under the bed, then went out to the top of the stairs. As he stepped down onto the top step he heard the sound of conversation drifting up from below and he paused for a second, trying to identify the twang of a girl's voice. It was nobody he knew. *So him bring back strange woman to the yard now*. He smiled and took the stairs three at a time, eager to see the guest.

His father stood in the centre of the kitchen, holding a fat suitcase with both hands. "Ben, so you in, boy. We have some family staying for a week or two. You meet Ruth before, I think."

He could hardly miss her. She took up most of the room, short and very wide, wearing a huge blouse and impossibly tight jeans on tree-trunk legs. Her face was bright and soft, covered in a massive smile. He put her around the late teens. A whisper broke from his lips. "Girl mampy, sah!"

"What you say, Ben? You meet before, yes."

He managed to regain his composure. Maybe she had a gland problem or something. "Uh, no, I don't think so. I'm Ben." He stepped over with his hand out to shake but she leaned forward and wrapped her arms around him in an alarming bear-hug. The air was squeezed out of his lungs.

"I love meeting family." She had a sweet, rich voice, coloured by a strong accent. He guessed it was Midlands but was too busy trying to break off the embrace to place it exactly.

His father butted in. "Ruth here for a while with some

work. She your cousin from Birmingham and I tell her you won't mind showing her the sights and things."

Before he could express his horror the suitcase was being dragged up the stairs.

"She take your room so you better move your stuff now if you need anything. The sofa right to sleep on fo a while."

It was getting worse by the second. "But Dad, you know what I got on. I . . ."

She was shifting her bulk up the staircase, his father hidden from sight in front of her. Before she swung round the top though, she tilted her head back and beamed at him. "I so grateful, Ben. I know we gonna get on jes fine."

He stared up at her, speechless. There was only one chance of escape from the appalling prospect of escorting a country mampy round the patch and he whispered to himself again. "Ben, man. You gonna have to throw yourself into your work, rasta."

Three

The week started off busy and just got worse. Neither of them had guessed at the amount of work they would have to put in to make the club happen. Mike had hassle from his boss at the record store for taking time off but still managed to get the use of the shop van and the rusty heap proved invaluable. Curtis had dropped out of sight, knowing he would only get roped in as a taxi driver. He was spending more time with the boss man Carl now that he was big in the team and when he wasn't with him his girlfriend Amanda had first priority. Curtis was in deep.

So, the van was their only transport and there was a lot to shift over to the club. Mike borrowed most of the PA gear from friends who were electronics buffs but they had to hire a few cabinets to boost the volume and that meant getting people to help with moving it all. Calling in these favours paid off though. They soon had the best local system and Mike passed many hours checking the acoustics, flooding the hall with bass.

Ben had some friends who were drifting through art school and he recruited them to manage the decor and design a backdrop. All these people wanted expenses and material costs so Mike had to blow some savings he had sworn never to touch. Money cares not what promises you make to yourself. They even had to find Curtis at one stage and hit him for another five hundred.

The main hall was interesting enough as it was, so they just arranged for some more lighting and concentrated on the backdrop. This was a neon blue with "Chocolate Box" written in huge orange letters. Most people found it garish but Ben loved it. Then they moved upstairs. Here they had installed a separate music system and filled the room with soft lighting, giving it the look of a film set from a forties movie. The music was more jazz for this room and they nicknamed it the "Basement" because of this atmosphere. Downstairs got straight reggae and revival stuff but the top room was more for hanging out.

Mike had teamed up with an Asian kid to do the sounds. Dressed in hippy gear, with a fuzzy growth of hair on his chin, he called himself Alfred and walked round in a daze most of the time but he had a good rep. He was on a wage, which amused Ben. They could bust on the first night.

They refused to take the easy route and that was their strength. Though they both had real worries, they had not compromised with anything to save money. That had been the principle right from the beginning. Do it, then do it all. They worked well as partners. Mike worried, Ben calmed him down.

With all the demands on his time Ben managed to avoid his social duty with Ruth. By mid-week he was at the club.

all day and night and had no time to get home. Anyway, his father was still impressed by all the hard work. Ben dealt with the flyers, printing them through an agency and then distributing them. He put posters up all over the patch, often exchanging insults with the competition and he had to take care of the radio ads. Hargreaves rarely put in an appearance but when he did he was only critical of their work, sure they would flop. Mike started to look a wreck until Ben told him Sophie might be put off by it. The joke lifted his spirits and he started grooming himself again.

By Saturday morning they were ready. They had a small party in the upstairs room to thank everyone for their help and then the partners went home to change, agreeing to meet at eight. The doors were opening at ten and the club would run through to three.

When Ben rolled in at nine he found Mike in the Basement, flicking through his record choice. Alfred was warming the system up with some beats downstairs and the sound was bouncing round the walls, while the bar staff lazily cleaned glasses and wiped down the bar.

"Thought we said eight."

"No hurry, is there?"

"No. It's gonna be a graveyard anyway. Have you seen it down there?"

"Well, we no a open yet."

"Oh, well that's a relief." Mike had a troubled gleam in his eyes, trying to be sarcastic but in truth, desperately worried. Both he and Ben knew that failure now could cripple them. It was not the money. They had worked hard and a collapse would colour them as disasters generally, not just as club-runners.

"Ease down, Mike. Place fill up, I tell you."

By ten-thirty there was nothing but space in the vast hall.

None of their friends had arrived. The band had failed to show for their equipment check and were due on at midnight. A lonely drumkit sat in the middle of the stage. Mike was running round the club like a scared rabbit and Ben started sipping brandy to steady his nerves.

At eleven they retired to the Basement again and sat waiting for news, like expectant husbands. Mike's face was chalky white. Then just before twelve, as they were sinking into final despair, a vision appeared at the top of the Basement stairs.

She was only in a plain red blouse and black cottons but Sophie would have looked desirable in a mail bag. She stared at them for a second, then a whimsical smile spread out on her lips. The band were shuffling up the stairs behind her. "They had problems finding the place."

There was a river of people on the stairs. They flooded the room, pushing up to the bar and swamping the tables.

Sophie sat down next to Mike and Ben, carried forward by the deluge. A roar of feet and shouting came up from below them. "The bouncers weren't letting anyone in till the band had turned up. I think the manager was scared about the refunds. Not surprising with the crowd you've got out there."

Mike and Ben gazed at each other in silence.

"Await. You say there is people out there?"

"Yeah, it's packed." She had a soft voice and they had to strain their ears to hear her over the din but Mike rushed to the stairs and fought his way past the traffic of people. It was a sweet sight as he turned into the hall.

The walls were hidden from view by the crowd. Already the air was getting smoky and the lights above were dimming. He stepped into the throng. Alfred had lifted the volume to cope with the increase of noise and a slow reggae beat was pounding. Mike could feel the floor quiver with vibration. He started heading over to the entrance, eager to check on the numbers admitted and feeling a happy concern about the fire restrictions being ignored but a voice boomed out from behind him. It was his partner, high on the stage with a microphone. The band were busy around him, preparing their instruments.

"So you get in at last? We sorry about dat indeed, an' we havin' words with the management to make sure we get no repeat problem."

Ben was quite drunk and his face shone with confidence. He lifted his voice to a shout and swaggered across the wide stage, looking a natural MC, though he had never been in front of a crowd until this moment.

"But we havin' no more delay. Tonight we have the debut show here down at the Chocolate Box an' me just here to say hello from the club. We going on till three but to kick off, we have a little band for you . . ."

There was a surge in the crowd. The band was known.

"Oh, some you heard them before maybe. Well, I wan you give a big up for the music crew. Big up, ya hear me?"

The drummer cut in with a beat, drowned out by the crowd as two singers strolled on and took position. Ben backed off, clapping his hands and beaming at the band. Down in the crowd Mike watched the whole event, chuckling. Things were working out.

That first night they had a better attendance figure than any other club in West Park. The audience at Maxine's was halved. It was an older clientele than they had expected, as it was strictly a driving night out but there was still some youth there. The place was heaving.

Alfred was a class DJ, perfectly predicting the tastes of the crowd throughout the evening but keeping his own style as well. When he came off, Mike took over and treated the listeners to a string of obscure tracks, establishing his specialist knowledge. Ben hung around the bars getting smashed and being the socialite. He had enjoyed the role of MC, though it was totally impromptu and they had already decided that the club should have no obvious organiser. All he had to do was to keep the band happy and entertain Sophie. This he found painless until Curtis strolled in at two o'clock with three white guys he had never seen before. He immediately refunded their admission from behind the bar and gave up his table, which included Sophie, who seemed charmed by Curtis and his style clothing. Ben thought he and his pals looked like Italian Mafiosi these days, each wearing a dark suit. They were drinking French brandy, on the house, but he had no worries about expenses. As the club wound down around quarter to three, the box-office girl came up to the Basement with a small bank sack. Alfred was finishing the night on the decks so Ben and Mike were having a quiet drink with Curtis. Sophie had left before anyone had the chance to pounce but promised to make it a weekly date in her calendar, she had had such a good time.

The sack landed with a clunk in the middle of their table and the girl made Mike sign for it. The three guys with Curtis had said little all evening apart from the odd muttered word to one another so Ben was left to chat with his friend, both of them feeling the effects of the sweet spirit. Mike busied himself with checking the notes, which were a heap just in front of him. After a few minutes they noticed the counting was still going on and eyes turned to the piles and his computations.

Mike looked up at Ben. "Ben, there is some serious money here, man." His face was glowing and he blew out a sigh. "Each pile's a grand."

There were four clumps of paper on the table by his drink and a smaller pile he had not finished with. Ben dropped his mouth open and stared. As he looked on, relishing the

sight of his own wealth, a sleeve brushed the table-top and
Curtis wrapped his fingers around two of the wads. Ben
noticed that a missing digit did not prevent his friend's
dexterity, as one pile was neatly pressed against the other,
then folded. Curtis had conquered the disability of his
gangster wound a while ago. The hand closed slowly then
divided the remaining piles. One was pushed over to Mike
and the other in Ben's direction. The sight of their earnings
being so cruelly removed fascinated Ben. Curtis handled
the money like it was a pack of cards.

Mike grabbed his pile and stuffed it into his shirt pocket
before any more was collected. "Well, you knew we'd settle
the loan, Curtis." He laughed at the scene, Curtis taking
their candy away.

Ben managed to break his forlorn look and turn his eyes
away from the depleted money and to Curtis who smiled
back at him. His damaged hand still hovered over the table,
clutching the cash. Ben was amused now, he had no other
choice. It was just sad Curtis had been there to collect at
the very moment the take had arrived. There was no wriggling out of this one. "Money come, money go. Least I was
rich for a moment."

Even the impassive threesome sniggered at his words.
Ben slowly made for his solitary pile but as he reached
down, Curtis revolved his hand so it was palm-up just
above Ben's cut.

"Now, B. You forget a little ting maybe?"

Ben stared at him in shock. Surely he was paid back in
full? He had two grand in his clutches after all. "I don't
follow you. Wha go on here?"

"Well . . ." Curtis split Ben's pile in half with one flick of
his hand. "Seems to me there a debt you still have to settle.
A little draw I set you up with."

Ben's face was a study in sadness. He had forgotten the
lump Curtis had given him. "But, C, that so long ago an'

I . . ." The money was already being dragged slowly back across the table, through the maze of drinks and cigarette boxes. He looked on, like an angler losing his prize fish.

"Think of it this way, B. Time an' money is beyond the control of any man. This only your first night an' you made five hundred and a bit. You put in the work an' you get pay. I only get my twenty-five hundred."

Everybody was laughing except Ben. He had a glass to his lips to cover the scowl. "You lucky I don't ask for me ten per cent interest, boy."

Even Ben had to chuckle.

Four

Ben opened his eyes and remembered he was in the living room. The television was barking in the corner and he could see Ruth's bulk jutting out either side of any easy chair just in front of where he lay. When he had checked to make sure he was not having a bad dream he threw the blanket off the sofa and stood up.

"What time is it, Ruth?"

"I think it round ten or something."

She did not turn from the TV and Ben mouthed silent insults to the back of her head. It had been light when he got in from the club and he could still feel the alcohol poison rushing through his blood. His eyes felt like sandpaper.

Things were not going too well with Ruth. She had found

work as a secretary, and was supposed to be looking for a flat but he saw little evidence of it. His father liked her cooking and that seemed to be a deciding factor in her staying.

Everything in his life was perfect. He was making real money for the first time as the club got stronger. They were in their fourth week now and Ben actually had money in a bank account. His father had nearly fainted when he showed him the plastic. He had no debts and over a grand in his jeans pocket from the night before and was rapidly getting known as a founder of the "Box", as it was abbreviated. This meant his dating potential was vastly improved. He had started eating in restaurants. All this was exactly what he wanted and he was very happy apart from one thing. He was waking up on a sofa every morning because a tug boat was sleeping in his bed. He couldn't even get into his room anymore, not that he would recognise it anyway. It had been feminised. The girls he was meeting would not be impressed by a sofa in his living room for a love nest or waking up to Ruth watching television. Words to his father on the subject were ignored and Ruth didn't seem to care if he was unpleasant to her. Her skin was thicker than a rhino's. There was only one answer. Since he had some money now his attitude had changed slightly. Ben only saw the future carrying on in the same way so he viewed his new prosperity as a permanent development. He pulled some clothes on, went out to where the phone lay and punched some familiar numbers. The drone of the TV in the background strengthened his resolve. There was a click at the end of the line.

"Talk!" Mike must be feeling worse than he was. He never sounded so gruff on the phone.

"Happy, man, we gettin' a flat. Today if we can. I come straight round."

"Yo! Ben. What do I want a flat for?" He was waking up a bit now.

"Cause it time you get away from your family rowing, an' treating you like a kid still all the time. You got the money now too. We get ourselves the bes bachelor pad in the Park, man."

"Maybe that's not such a bad idea, you know."

"I tellin' you. Get ready. I be there in a bit, yeah?"

"No, we have to go down the club. There's a band who want to set up some of their gear down there today, remember? Alfred's turning up too, wants a chat. Anyway, there's something down there that'll interest you. I'll pick you up in a while, yeah?"

"Sweet, yeah."

He replaced the phone in the cradle and went into the kitchen. Mike had confused him and coffee might clear things up. He was feeling severely jaded. At the back of his mind he knew he was putting less effort into the club than Mike and this thought troubled him for a moment. He would start handling the bands on his own and let Mike deal with the sounds. That way his investment was protected. The smell of coffee grounds filled the kitchen and he started thinking of more appealing topics as he slurped the antidote.

Mike drove fast and Ben decided to click his seat-belt in. It was a signal that he did not trust the driver, as he never wore them usually, but Mike ignored it. He had spent the bulk of his profits on the car and was still at the stage where it felt new to drive. They flashed by the crumbling buildings that surrounded the club and through the gates, stopping with a screech just at the entrance.

"You is dangerous behind the wheel, you know. Anyway,

what happen to the 'practical vehicle' talk an' all that bullshit?"

The car was a two-seat sports and heavy on fuel. It was only a few years old but already scratched in places from previous drivers. Strips of rust broke through the ice-blue paintwork.

"It's a hatchback." Mike was protesting. He was claiming petrol from their expenses and had initially planned to get a small van so they could move the equipment they needed. The job at the record store was long gone, now Mike had money in his pocket. He had quit after the first night. The van he had borrowed disappeared at the same time. "I think it's perfect for the board directors' limo, don't you?"

They walked through the hallway laughing and into the main room. On the stage a few musicians were experimenting with the limits of the PA, getting the levels ready for their show at the weekend. Sound checks on the night never went smoothly. Alfred was at the side of the stage lost in his headphones, trying some records he had just got hold of.

The hall had a busy atmosphere with all the activity so the two friends headed for the Basement, rather than disturb the others. Ben was eager to find out what Mike had been referring to and they could talk up there.

Mike flopped in a sofa whilst Ben wandered behind the bar searching for a beer. "Hargreaves said there's some rooms above here which he lets out."

Ben stuck his head over the bar. He had found a bottle of beer which he opened and took a swig from before responding. "Ah, that better. What you say? Rooms here. Him never say nothin' to me."

"No, he only mentioned it to me when we had that week getting ready, cause we were here all the time. Door's open if you want a look."

"Yeah, man. Why you say nothin' to me before?" Ben moved from behind the bar, excited by the discovery.

"Well, I never knew you was after a place, did I? Come on, then."

In the far corner there was a small doorway. Ben had not been aware of it until now as it was well hidden in the brown tones of the room but Mike pushed through and he followed up some stairs. It was dark but after a few steps he saw him open another door, lined by a flash of daylight, and they walked into a room.

It was the same shape as the Basement except the roof was sloped on one side. This cut down on some of the space but it was still huge. Three doors led off the main wall and Ben hurriedly nosed into each one. The kitchen was tiny and fairly broken-down but he noticed it led through to the bathroom where there was a washing machine. Either side of the kitchen were the bedrooms, large boxes, each with a high window looking back on the dome of the building. The view of green metal was surreal enough to be interesting. There was a rough cream carpet and some plain furniture; two chairs, a table and a couch.

"What you think, then?"

"I think we have the housewarming after the next show."

They came down the stairs and found Alfred sitting in a sofa. He was looking confused as ever, dressed in baggy denims and a purple rave shirt. It was not clear whether this spaced look was due to him being on something or if it was the norm. But he did always have this expression on his face, like someone who has woken from a deep sleep only seconds ago. Neither of them had seen him taking anything, not that it would be a problem with them. Mike expected a DJ to take uppers. Alfred spoke with a hippy drawl, stretching the words out and sometimes pausing for a few seconds, which was frustrating if you were in a hurry.

The thin tone of an educated background was also present in his speech.

Alfred had dealt mainly with Mike and Ben had yet to have more than just a brief conversation with him. What he had heard was tedious anyway as they always talked about the decks or some aspect of the sound rig, so Ben turned for the stairs down to the hall. "So, Mike, I find the man and we take it, yeah?"

Both of them were excited by the prospect of their own place, although Mike had some minor reservations about sharing with Ben. At least things happened around his friend though. "Sure, I come with."

"Uh, guys, could I speak to both of you together like?" Alfred lifted himself out of the sofa and stretched like a sleepy cat.

Ben hung at the top of the stairs. "Make it quick, then."

As though to aggravate them Alfred said nothing for an instant and then hit them with the speech, moving his hands sluggishly to emphasise his words. "You guys, you know . . . you guys, this place is healthy. I like it an' I think the vibe's right and everything but, well I have to say it, no lack of respect to you but, well I want a bit more cash for what I'm doing."

Ben had squirmed throughout the monologue and as it finished he paced back to the stairs, glancing at Mike. "Double his money?"

"Safe."

Both of them made for the stairs, leaving Alfred more bemused-looking than ever, his mouth a little black hole of surprise. He called to them as they began to descend. "Well, if it was so easy for you to pay me more, then why did I have to ask?"

Mike shouted back at him from the foot of the stairs. "Cause we're bastard capitalists, Alfie."

*

It was set. Mike and Ben had their own pad, nestling in the attic above the club. Hargreaves charged them a little over the normal rate but they could afford it. The profits from the club had transformed their paying power and they were getting advance ticket sales now. Through the week the flat took shape and looked habitable. They put posters up and littered the floor with magazines and the circular stains from coffee mugs. The two had never been happier.

Five

Kimps pushed his thumb through the peel of the orange and deep into the flesh. Twisting with his other hand he split it into two rough halves and then licked his fingers. He picked up a tumbler from the table, took a half in each hand, then squeezed the juice from them with one clench. When the last drops had fallen into the glass he dropped the crumpled shells on the table and walked over to the window.

He could hear the sound of the pool beneath him: shouts and splashes from dozens of kids. Through his window there was a panoramic view of the scene, to accompany the din. His office overlooked the rectangular stretch of water. There were other noises coming from the gym and exercise hall, the clanking of machinery and grunts of people trying to lose a few pounds. The centre was busy due to the summer heat.

Kimps was sweating. "Harvey, this place makes me sick."

"Yes, mister Kimps." On the other side of the room his assistant was flopped in a sofa, fanning his face. Kimps had not turned from the window and Harvey knew he was trying to scare him by not looking at him. It wasn't working.

"And you make me sick, Harvey."

"Very sorry about that, mister Kimps."

Kimps slowly turned his head so Harvey could see one eye staring back at him. "All I have is this lousy fucking pool. It's nothing. I have only one plan and leave you to deal with it for a month, and you fucking blow it." He was speaking quietly, allowing his voice to assume menace with the restraint. When he was angry the light touch of an American accent became more pronounced.

"Yes, if you listen to what I have put into motion though . . ."

"I don't want to listen to you, Harvey." Kimps sighed and sat down at the table, his back to the window. "You should listen to me." The words were left to hang for a second whilst he sipped at the juice, then he continued. "I told you I would be gone a month, yes? You know I have my family there. My father has been trying to establish something other than this fucking gymnasium for the last year, ever since I got sent here, so I tell you to keep an eye on the club and . . ."

"I've put something into action though . . ."

"Don't interrupt me, dick! Just listen for a minute." He was rubbing his brow now with frustration. "All I've wanted is to get something else together apart from this place. My father set me up here because he wanted me to learn clerking, you understand. But I do not enjoy the smell of people working out or the sound of kids pissing in the pool. You can deal with all this, Harvey, when I move on. So I want no irritation with this other venture. We've been buying the land up round there for a long time. But I come back yesterday and all I hear since then is about this new fucking club. If that place doesn't sell, then we're left with fuck, you understand. Pops will be very pissed off."

"It's just a couple of kids. I've dealt with it."

"I hope so. If not, I'll play golf with your balls." Kimps very rarely altered his facial expression. He was adept at maintaining the mask of cool disinterest, so Harvey could not fail to notice the glare. "I want the club broke, Harvey. It represents something dear to me. It means a way out if I can pull it off."

Harvey nodded. There was not much to say to him in his present mood. He sat it out for a few seconds trying to look meek.

"Whatever you do, make it good. I'll see you in the near future."

Harvey stood up and made for the door. Before he opened it Kimps had gone back to staring dreamily out of the window.

Amanda lifted a knee and stroked the skin of her calf, feeling the heat. She could see Curtis dressing through the arch, slowly buttoning a shirt. "It's going to be warm, I think."

"Yeah, I know."

"Make sure you don't forget our dinner date tonight, will you."

"How could I? That's gonna be a scream, for sure." There was a smile on his lips but he sounded tired.

She knew him well enough to know this was only a symptom of his mood. The phone-call had angered him. The shrill tones had been ignored as they were entwined in sex but the voice on the answer-machine was demanding. "Pick up, boy. You have a job today." It was the flat growl of Carl. Curtis expected the sound of a hang-up but Carl just waited, saying nothing into the machine and he was forced to leave her. It had not been easy.

They had been together for five months now. The honeymoon period of bliss was over and the days of endless eye-gazing were gone. He had thought the familiarity might kill the affair but the initial wonder had been replaced by a deeper bond between them. They had entered the telepathic stage. Curtis had not touched another body. His lust for her remained and his first attraction, the way they interacted in the mental arena, had matured into respect. Curtis had never felt this for a girl before. This was the reason for his anger. He did not want to break from her touch in response to a phone-call but had no choice. Carl was still boss. At least until Curtis was finished with the things he was checking, anyway. Now he had been summoned like a jester to the king and had to gaze at her on the bed whilst he prepared to leave. Framed in the arch her body was perfection.

Light filled the flat from the wide bay windows. The extreme sun of a month ago had abated slightly but West Park was still unusually hot and the glare of the morning set out the contours of her shape distinctly. She could feel a film of water on the soft mound of her belly as she stroked her body, wriggling free from the covers. Amanda knew he was watching. Her hand dipped slowly to a thigh and made soft brushes on the skin. It was too much. He rushed across the room and launched himself onto the bed. She blew soft sounds of encouragement into his ear as he fumbled at his waist and crashed into her. "So, I'm still your sweet seductress, Curtis."

Carl was sitting at the bar in Maxine's clenching a brandy

glass. His eyes were concealed by the usual shades but Curtis could tell he was seething, as his frame was taught on the stool, motionless.

"Me ave a problem wid the car, sah. I sorry me late an' that." He sat down next to him. Curtis had not meant it but his words had sounded arrogant, his displeasure at being disturbed coming through in his tone.

"You sorry, you say?" Carl had not moved. He stared straight ahead over the bar.

"Well, I was a bit busy too. Had a little ting to deal with, you know."

"You mean you fuckin' some girl? That what you mean. Fuck the car bullshit."

Curtis did not like the way he was being called a liar. He liked even less the fact it was true but he decided to try and calm the situation. There was no point getting in a row with the man. "So wha you want anyway?"

That broke it. Carl backed off the seat and slammed his fist down on the bar, shattering the glass. Droplets of his drink and shards of glass filled the air. Curtis felt his cheek burn.

"You talk to me like you the ras man, well fuck you. Give me story an' I sit wait here for you, you think I is fuckin idiot?"

"I think I'm cut."

"Right you is fuckin' cut, you lucky I don't cut you proper."

Curtis dabbed at his cheek and felt the blood, hot on his face. Carl lurched forward and grabbed his lapel, pulling him down to his shoulder, talking softly at his ear as Amanda had done only half an hour before. "I is the man, an' the day you forget that, is war, you hear me, ras war between you an' I. So don't fuck wid me again, boy."

For an instant he thought of pushing the older man away and laying into him, turning his face into a bloody mess.

But Curtis was wise and knew there was no sense in fighting with him. He was not ready for that yet. "You is the boss man. I work fo you, no mistake."

"Aright, my friend. Now we can talk." His tone was relaxing now he had vented his rage and he sat down again. Curtis watched him reach over the bar, pull out another glass from the pile and fill it from his flask.

"Fix up you face, boy, an' we talk. An' one of you others . . ." Carl turned back into the room where a few of the team sat in silence. "Tidy up this fuckin mess."

Six

People were just starting to come in but Mike was still up in the flat getting ready. He was grooming tonight. After the run of success with the club, his ego had reached sufficient strength to contact Celia. The girl was the closest he had got to body friction and he wanted another chance. A nervous phone-call to her shop and she had agreed to meet him tonight, at the bar. There may even have been a tinge of excitement in her voice. Ben had not been consulted so as to avoid the inevitable endless ribbing. Anyway, he would not mind them meeting.

His watch showed it was time but before moving toward the stairs he splashed aftershave over his neck. *That makes em growl, boy.*

It was filling up but there was no sign of her. Recovering

from a second of disappointment he ordered a beer at the bar.

"So hello, Mike." It was Alfred, sprawled next to him at the bar. They had a guest DJ on tonight so he was doing his spot later. Mike didn't want to be busy at the decks.

"Yeah, how you doing?"

"Fine, real sweet man. I've been cruising today, went . . ."

Mike did not want to get stuck in one of Alfred's drawling chats. He liked the guy but tonight there were other things on his mind. "Look, Alfred, I'm meeting this girl in a minute and it's a bit, you know, delicate."

"Ah. Sweet. You an' Ben busy, yeah?"

"Come again."

"Well, I saw him splitting a while ago, couldn't stop, meeting some girl, I think."

"I don't know what he's doing, haven't seen him much today. Anyway, the thing is . . ."

"If you got a girl coming, maybe I can help you out."

Mike was curious. He had been examining the new arrivals at the stairs and not really concentrating on Alfred and his rambling but now he turned to him. "I don't follow."

"See, the reason I'm a mellow dude an' you cats is always running around is cause I have a little booster time to time. Keeps me calm, you know."

Mike was staring into his eyes, puzzled. It was hard not to laugh at the DJ's hippie-speak.

"Perfect for entertaining a chick."

"Really?"

Now his attention was assured and Alfred knew it. Mike had to accept his own ignorance of women and was prepared to listen to any suggestions.

"I can let you have a tingle, seeing as you upped my money an' everything. I think you boys is safe really." He put a lazy hand into the flowing silk of his shirt and pulled at something, then put his hand out as though to shake.

Mike shook and held onto a tiny paper wrap as they broke off.

"Have a good time on me."

Mike glanced at the parcel. "Nah, I don't do powders but thanks all the same."

"Easy . . .', He was whispering now and Mike had to strain his hearing against the soft cry of a saxophone playing in the background music. "Make an exception with a girl. That's my advice. She'll appreciate the gesture." Before Mike reacted he had slid off the stool and ducked into the crowd.

As Mike saw his back vanish, there was a brush at his shoulder.

"So you finally make the effort to call then." It was his beach-scene, self-abuse fantasy, Celia.

Ben was about to suffocate, his collar was so tight.

"So, Ben. What wine you recommend?"

On the way in, the girls had gone first and Curtis had tapped his back before they reached the table. "You show a label there, boy. Can still smell the bag."

Ben had been forced to go straight to the bathroom, determined to restore his decorum and then discovered there was nothing showing. Curtis knew him too well.

"Red or white if we havin' fish?"

Curtis was testing his patience. Sophie sat next to him, hardly managing to keep in a squeal of laughter. He didn't want to look a fool at the table. "Why, white naturally. Maybe a Muscadet."

Curtis sniggered although he was quite impressed.

Sophie swept in with her soft voice. "Isn't that a bit sharp, Ben?"

"Hmm, maybe. We could go for the Sancerre."

Curtis had to laugh out loud now. It was obvious

Amanda had been doing some coaching whilst he raced back from Carl's errand. She was glowing with contained humour.

He looked at Sophie sitting by his side for a moment and decided she was certainly beautiful. He had noticed her at the club that time and was conscious that he had not forgotten what she looked like. To Curtis, some women had a grace of movement more attractive than any attribute of their figure. When this was combined with eyes that had seen the cold humour of life, they reached a pinnacle of attraction in his estimation. Sophie was getting close. She wore a long, simple dress, an emerald shine that was moulded to her body. Ben was doing well if they were sleeping together. From what he could tell so far, that was not the case. One glimpse of Amanda was enough to remind him how lucky he was though.

She was more mature than the other girl. In a plain black shirt, pearl buttons and some jeans she was still stunning. He flicked her hair back, relishing the line of her cheek.

"Hey, I think we should order before they close. It's quite late, you know."

A reference to his delayed arrival naturally. He started planning how to make her happy when they got back.

"You know what you want, Sophie?"

They were on the floor, Mike trying to keep up with her body twisting around him. He was not fond of dancing, being painfully aware of his clumsiness but she had led him down from the bar and he saw no way to refuse. Besides, she was helping him, hugging his body and guiding the flow. It was hard to concentrate.

Celia looked better than he remembered, dressed in the usual lycra but somehow sex seeped from her figure tonight. She was scaring him.

"I'm more a listener really."

She smiled and stepped to his side, so his thigh was between her legs. "Show me what you want to do, or you wan listen?"

He felt a surge of fear. All around them couples were tied together in the dance and he could see girls on their own just showing moves. Seeing them sway made him aware of what she expected. He was sweating. It might be best to level with her. "I'm a bit of an amateur, Celia. Maybe we could grab another drink or something else upstairs. I've got a room up there."

The girl froze against him, as though she was facing a difficult decision. "We never did finish what we started last time I saw you, did we?" Grabbing his hand she pulled him through the crowd and made for the stairs, then he guided her to the stairway and up to the flat. "You sure we won't be surprised?"

He nodded and indicated his room with a hand movement. If he was interrupted like the last time he was with Celia he really would be a hopeless case.

"So, you been wid a girl yet?"

The straight question alarmed him and he answered like a guilty schoolboy. "No, you were the only time I . . ."

"Me, so that mean you is still a virgin."

She looked out of place in his room. Although he had cleaned up it was still littered with magazines and record sleeves. To avoid her stare he cleared a space over to his bed and fiddled nervously with the hi-fi. A small reading lamp was the only light and the cream walls and floor were softly lit by it.

His seduction plan was so clear to her she started to giggle, spotting that the music was already in position when he hit Play. "Mister Romance, you have any other surprises?"

"Actually I do." Now he went to the foot of the bed and

lifted a small square of glass onto the sheets. From his pocket he produced the wrap and positioned it on the glass. Finally he found his wash bag and took out a disposable razor. "We can break a blade free to cut it."

She sat down by the kit and smiled up at him. "Well, Mike, you know how to treat a girl right in some ways."

Pleased by her reaction he snapped open the wrap but her fingers took it from his hand.

"First thing first."

He was sitting by her on the bed. Every muscle tensed as she took hold of his fingers and brought them over to her leg, allowing him to stroke up to her flat stomach.

"Jes touch me for a minute." With him caressing her gently, she folded the wrap and put it back on the bed. Then, like a cat under his touch, she lay back on the bed and lifted her top, dropping it to the floor.

For the second time he stared at her breasts, then with no hesitation moved down the bed and began kissing them roughly.

"Easy, boy, be gentle."

He ignored her, carried by some desperate energy and started pulling at her leggings, increasing the brutality of his kisses.

Celia was not ready to be rushed though. She ran her hand down to his waist and gave him a light slap.

He fell back against the wall, blowing air through his lips. "Why d'you do that?"

"Cause I am the boss, you understand. You learnin' from me an' I think you a bit eager at the moment. Got to calm down a bit."

Now the hand that had attacked him expertly slid his belt open and he felt her push into his jeans. He was embarrassed by her grip.

"It alright, boy, I make you come an' then we can take our time."

"But I won't be able to . . ." He was already close. Just rubbing against her had almost been enough and now she spared him nothing of her prowess.

"We have something to get you movin' again, remember." She nuzzled his chin with her lips, then kissed him hard, blocking his hands with her arm against the wall. The feeling of restriction excited him even more and she felt him swell. "You nearly there, Mike."

He let out a tiny sob and then tensed. The spasms at his legs shocked him; he expected her to be appalled but she just smiled, gripping him even tighter.

"Now we can start for real."

His strength was gone and he lay panting, watching her back off the bed and wriggle free from her remaining clothes. This done, she came over to him and started removing his jeans and shirt. He was immobile and like a child let her free his shoes and socks. The last barrier he dealt with himself, worried by the dampness and she retreated to the top of the bed. When he turned back to her, made anxious by his nudity, she was between the sheets.

"Come then, Mike."

Gingerly he lay next to her and was amazed by the softness of her body. Already he felt the first shiver of arousal.

"Now we can use this." The wrap was between her fingers.

"I'll get the glass."

"Hold on, loverboy."

Since they had first entered the flat her face had shown amusement and superiority. Now she was stopping him from leaving the bed and he felt a slight irritation with her. "Well, I don't want to dab it."

"You don't have to, I do that."

Before he could utter a sound of protest she was sliding down the bed, kissing first his chest and then his stomach. He was ready for her touch and felt her firmly pulling down on his skin. Her head began to sink and he stared up at the ceiling, thanking the gods for this moment, but before he felt the first warm rush of her mouth he heard the wrap rustle and closed his eyes. As she rubbed the drug into him he felt a cold tingle. Mike thought he was going to die with pleasure.

He was thinking how she would react if he reached for her hand. In the dark of the car it was hard to make out the line of her body and he didn't want to grab the wrong part of her anatomy, it might panic her. Her gaze was fixed on the lights streaming past the window.

"So Sophie, what you do? I can drop you somewhere if you want."

Curtis had leaned back from the wheel to speak. What was he saying? Ben had assumed they would all head for the club and at last he would have the chance to speak with her alone. Maybe Amanda had suggested he offer, out of politeness. It had taken enough planning to organise the meal and there had been no opportunity to speak there. She was looking thoughtful now, weighing up the night's choices.

"If you could drop me at a tube, that would be great."

Disaster. How could there be no hint of interest?

"Nah, I take you home. Can't go on the tube at this time. Where you live?"

"No really, it's over the river."

Curtis hesitated but Amanda shot him a sidelong glare.

"Then we going over the river."

She turned to him. Was that a smile? Maybe this was working out and they had all conspired to get him back to her place. There had been some quiet chat earlier between the girls and they obviously got on with each other. They had even swapped numbers.

The car took a bridge and headed into a fashionable riverside area, small streets with tall houses. The brick of West Park was replaced by elegant pastel stonework. She instructed Curtis on the route and they were soon outside her home, one of a row of townhouses.

"Nice place for a flat."

"Oh, I've got the whole house."

Nobody said anything. The house was probably worth a few hundred thousand. Ben recovered and gave her an expectant grin.

"I'd ask you in but I'm terribly tired. It was nice to meet you both." She was talking to the front but turned to him at the same time as she fumbled with the door handle. "Thanks for the meal, Ben. Give me a ring at the office sometime."

She was gone, leaving Ben devastated on the back seat. Curtis waited until she waved from the top of the stone steps leading to her door and then tore off. Ben was speechless. His share of the meal had cost him sixty notes. His expression was not missed in the rear-view mirror.

"You sure got some things to learn, boy."

He stared at the dashboard vacantly. "I thought things were workin' out, thought she was hooked when she said yes to going out bro."

Amanda sighed. "I think Sophie may like you, Ben, but you can't expect every girl you take out to invite you in for a quick bedding, can you?"

"Why not? If she like me it make sense. Anyway, how you know she like me?" There was humour in his tone. Ben was not completely unaware of the march of feminism. Before Amanda could answer he cut in again. "You gal think you have all the obstacle in life. Well it tough being a guy at the moment I tell you."

"Speak the truth there, Ben."

"Not you as well?"

Amanda was giving the driver a perplexed smile.

"Well, he have a point, you know. There are complications in all this."

"So you think Sophie should have raced up to the bedroom with him right now?"

"Now, did I say that?"

Ben was not keen on the attention shifting to Curtis and tried to interject but Amanda was on a roll and cut him dead.

"Now, listen, I know she likes you because I am female too and know all the signs . . ." They were sniggering at this. Age-old, feminine wisdom. "And know all the signs of imminent affection, so relax, Ben. Just let her get the idea slowly. As for you . . ." She gave Curtis a light tap on the crown of his head.

Ben was worried how his friend would react but saw a broad smile on his face. Like tickling a Doberman.

"Yeah, I know. I should know better an' everything else. You wait till we reach, gal."

She laughed and Ben relaxed. He had not spent much time with the couple but had seen Curtis slap a girl if she wound him up. There was something different about this one, like he was pacified, content.

"We drop you at the club, B. Want to finish the conversation at home if that all right with you."

"Curtis . . ."

There was a playful lilt to her voice and thinking the couple were now absorbed in each other he fell back into the soft leather.

"Oh, and Ben."

She had turned again to speak with him and he leaned forward, adopting the tone of a harassed butler. "Yeeees."

"I know she likes you . . . because she told me she does. Give her a ring."

Seven

With neither partner floating round the club Alfred had assumed control. He was up in the Basement trying to persuade the cashier it was safe to give him the night's take. This had become a regular event at the end of the evening and there was always a swollen bank bag handed over but the girl had to get a signature and Alfred didn't qualify.

"Now, you know I work here, don't you. I mean, you seen me on the desk this evening . . ."

"I've told you already. I need one of them to sign."

She was pretty, if a bit plain. Ben measured her form for a few seconds as he stood at the top of the stairs.

"Oh, at last. He's been hassling me for ten minutes."

The upstairs bar was thinning but there were still two or

three tables of people chatting, enjoying a stiff drink before leaving. Ben had been thinking of Sophie and Amanda's words but the sight of Alfred diverted him. The DJ looked more out of it than usual. His face shone with sweat. The girl looked panicky. "Alright, settle down the two a you." He had been neglecting his golden-goose investment again. "Alfred, you know is I or Mikey who have to pick up the bag."

"I was just helping out cause Mike split hours ago, you weren't here an' . . ."

"Yeah, safe."

The girl gave him a receipt form and a pen and they sat down at a table. Alfred was generally out of his head but that didn't stop him being trustworthy in Ben's eyes. He was no real threat. Now he was making apologies as Ben filled out the paper and smiled at the girl.

As he stared at her eyes, pausing again with interest, there was a blur of movement at the corner of his vision. The three of them were still seated at the table, Alfred babbling, but Ben's instinct told him this was not just someone brushing past him or getting up to leave. Despite his casual outlook on life, Ben had grown up in an environment where you had to be aware of danger and if he had a feeling about something he would act on it, instantly.

Without taking his gaze away from the girl he threw himself back from the table, dragging the money with him. There was no doubt in his mind now. Alfred and the girl had been startled by his violent movement but they were not from the streets. If Curtis had been with him then he would have been standing by his side by now, ready to fight. He would have seen the threat.

"You gonna get cut if you fuck us, kid. Put it over."

There were two of them, lean and wiry. They were older than him, white, cheaply dressed like football fans in their casuals. One of them had a blade buried in his wrist.

"Do it, git. Now."

Ben didn't like the idea of surrendering without a fight but there was a bony hand outstretched for the money and he had little choice. Two on one was bad enough but there was the knife to deal with as well and they would use it. He had met up with their breed before. Alfred was no use. He was hyperventilating with fear and nothing had happened yet. Everyone else in the bar would keep still. Ben had learnt that people don't like getting involved in confrontational situations, just the same as they walk around the body of a drunk lying in the street. It's not worth the risk and most times you don't get thanked for it anyhow.

He was close to the stairs but the exit was blocked by one of them. The other was circling round the table with a hand still out, his muscles tensed under a thin T-shirt and jeans. Ben was static, calculating his chances, trying to find an out.

"I theenk you have need help, yes?"

The sound was so alien all three of them stared across to the bar where it had drifted from. Draped over one of the stools a well-dressed black guy was grinning at them, baring a flash of teeth. He must have had his back to the table as Ben had not noticed his presence beforehand. The accent intrigued him. He rarely dealt with anyone outside West Park, let alone the country, and the voice was even stranger coming from a black man.

"Fuck off, Frenchy. This ain't your piece."

The youth slid off the stool and softly laid his glass on the bar. He was so relaxed Ben thought he might be backing off but he paced over to his side in a lazy glide. His frame was slight, wrapped in a baggy, powder-blue suit. He was about Ben's age, with short cropped hair and a fragile face: a bit pretty in a feminine way, not the sharp-edged profile of the street.

"So, you insult me. Now it is my struggle also."

There was confidence in the tone of his voice but Ben couldn't see any reason for it in his physique. He made Alfred look sturdy. "You best back off, man. I thank you all the same but is wise thing I deal with them myself." The new player might just make things ever harder if he got in the way.

"No, no I insist." Quite indifferent to the risk from the knife, he took a step round the table, past Alfred who was cowering in a heap in his chair.

This incensed the knife-man. He lunged forward. The arrival of the foreigner was a nuisance; already he had taken too long over the job. "Ralph, handle the other soot."

Immediately, the other man made a move towards him but froze just as Ben was bracing for the attack. He was staring across the table.

His friend was making wild stabs with the knife, lashing at the air. There was no contact though. Nimble as a ballerina, the man with the strange French accent dropped and turned, the wide grin on his face provoking increasingly frenzied strikes. Gasping from his exertion he had to pause and Ben's saviour chose this moment to act. Somehow calm and unruffled from the attentions of the knife, he deftly jumped right next to his opponent, swept an arm to his chest and gently pushed him. It looked ridiculous to Ben, this soft nudge but as he gaped the knife-man toppled backwards, letting out a surprised yelp. He crashed to the floor. In the same graceful way he had evaded the sweeps of the knife the youth hopped over to the flailing arms of the man on the floor and seized one of them. There was a crack like a dry branch breaking underfoot, then a pitiful howl of pain.

To his credit, the other thief did not run. With animal fury he crashed by the table away from Ben, pushed Alfred out of the way and ran straight into the triumphant youth, trying to knock him to the ground. This time he had not dodged to one side, though Ben was sure he could have evaded the charge but took the full impact face-on. He stood firm, hardly registering the force on his body. Before the other could throw a punch he reared up and sent four or five blows into his face. Ben could not distinguish the individual strikes, his arm was a wave of movement. The nose went in a spurt of blood and the man dropped to his knees, reaching out for support.

"You keep the blood away from my suit, you cretin."

Ben smiled at this. The youth looked seriously worried about the bleeding man staining his clothes, worried for the first time in the battle. He stepped back and spat a few words of his own tongue at the sinking man before kicking him over. Both men lay crippled, their limbs entangled.

"They are finished, I theenk, my friend. Alonsee. You must buy me a drink for my trouble."

"Well, I think that a good idea. Be with you in a second."

The barman had called for the outside security and two of Hargreaves's men were strolling up the stairs. They were middle-aged, portly. "Everything back to normal, is it?"

"You speak like you is working a fuckin' cinema. I should sack the both a you."

Rather than concern, their faces showed smugness at his outburst. "Only Hargreaves can sack us. You don't run this place, you know."

"Well, throw these out the back. Cha. Is only kwashi a work here. Take them out the road and turn them loose, ya hear, me no want policeman shut we down."

The knife-man and his partner were pulled down the stairs and Ben returned to the bar. Alfred had scurried off somewhere and the other occupants of the room were leaving now, so the room was almost empty.

"So, wha you drinking?"

"I desire a beer, thank you."

Ben ordered two beers, then turned back to his guest. "You fight good, boy. I thank you."

"You may call me Lucien." He put out his hand for Ben to shake.

"Ben. So you is a black Frenchman. I never see dat before."

"No. I live in Paris but I am from the Cameroon first. And I live here now."

"Well, I owe you one."

He was still smiling and looked elegant in the suit, but not like the other Africans Ben had met. There was a style look to him, like the pictures of fifties jazz musicians he had seen in Mike's magazines.

"So what bring you down West Park?"

"The music. I come to see you or this Mike. But you not here so I wait. I was here some weeks ago when you had a good band, a very pretty girl singing."

"Yeah, I remember that night it cork. But what you do then, in music I mean?"

"Oh, I rap my poetry. I play here with my production . . . my band, sorry."

Ben was taken aback. After watching him fight he was amazed to hear him mention poetry or rapping but it did fit with his appearance. "Sure, well you have a tape we can listen to?"

Lucien burst into laughter and reaching forward gave him a hearty slap on the back. "You make me happy man, yes a happy man. Was you who ask me to come and play here, my friend. I am well known in this town."

Eight

Ben stared at his watch. It was just past noon and he had to sigh. Sophie should have been lying by his side right now, the pear curves of her skin lurking under the covers. He reflected on how seldom things went according to plan. Anyway, all was not lost. There was still Amanda's message of hope.

He climbed out of bed and dressed, throwing on a base-ball hat to shield his eyes from the inevitable sun, and stumbled out to the living room. The night before was still foggy in his memory but he remembered getting fairly drunk and a cup of coffee would bring back the details. First thing was he had to check with Mikey about Lucien right away, as he had told him to turn up for a sound check round about two. This meant they had to get the sound equipment ready and it would take at least an hour to rig the stage. He had thought of waking his flatmate the night before but the snoring audible at his door had put him off. Mike could be hard to wake.

"What time is it?" It was the voice of a dying man, a faint croak. Mike's head was stuck around the corner of the kitchen door at a mad angle, looking as though it was separate from the rest of his body. He stared lustily at the jug of Java Ben was making.

"Fuck me, boy, you look terrible. Whappen here, then?"

"Oh, all sorts, man." Though suffering from the obvious strain of an acute hangover Mike was beaming. He looked like he'd stumbled over a gold brick.

"Await, how come you look so fresh on top, boy?"

"Well, there was a development of a kind last night, you see . . ."

There was a sound behind him and Ben peered round his friend's body to see Celia, rubbing the sleep from her eyes. She was dressed solely in a long T-shirt that brushed the top of her bare thighs and Ben could see she hadn't spent the night on the couch. Both of them had the morning-sex look; tousled hair and flushed skin. Ben blew out a long rush of air. "Wo, boy. Mike, you lose your cherry, then?"

"Morning, Ben. Charming as ever. Hope you have a coffee for me, then?"

Ben was roaring now. "So Celia, you can stay away from him? You have a scorecard for me to read?"

"Don be so cruel. Anyways, you might be upset with the results, boy."

Mike looked delighted but it took Ben a few seconds to work out her meaning. "Girl still have a tongue on her, then. In all senses . . ."

"Why you have to be so vulgar about it? Pass me the milk there, will you."

The lovers clumsily prepared their drinks and shuffled out of the kitchen, into the lounge.

Ben followed them, chortling loudly, and sank into the sofa next to Celia. "It had to happen wid some poor girl, I spose, but I never thought you two would get it together."

"Yeah, yeah. How did your date go, then? Alfred told me you were out with someone." Mike was gazing into his coffee while Celia flicked through a magazine.

Ben hit him with the artillery, keeping his voice casual. "Oh, I was out with Sophie. Had a meal and went back to her place."

A vicious attack on the hungover Mike, who tried to maintain his expression but was obviously envious. He could not pretend Sophie was of no interest to him. Celia had been his initiation but Mike had told himself he was in with a chance. This meant the bet had been lost. "So how was it?"

"Mike . . ." Celia was scowling at her lover.

"I'm only asking how it was. Honestly, move with the times, girl. We can talk about these things these days, male bonding an' all that."

"So Mike turn into an agony aunt now, is it?"

"I wanna know how it went. I mean, was it . . . consecrated?"

"Come again."

This was too much for the girl, who threw her magazine to one side and stood up. "You two can talk about your conquests without the blessing of female ears, I think."

"Celia, I was only asking him . . ."

She was pounding her way back to the bedroom.

"Boy, not only you go with a woman for the first time but you have your first row too. Is progress in the flat."

"Listen . . ." Mike looked round to make sure Celia had gone in the room, out of earshot. He was standing, intent on following her and making peace, but first he lowered his voice to a whisper and stared at Ben inquisitively. "Did you fuck her, B?"

"You ask me a question like that? It sensitive, these thing."

"You hear what I asked you?"

"Well, it not quite happen yet . . ."

"Aha. So I'm still in the running, then." Mike had a sickeningly smug look on his face. "Yes. I have to make a call or two, I think. To a certain blonde-haired lovely. Was you who made the bet, remember."

"Oh no. No, Mikey. The girl already say she likes me. Bet over, rasta." He was following him across the room, arms in the air to indicate his protest. He wanted no interference from Mike. "I mean, have a heart, man. You not into her anyway, are you?"

Mike froze in thought for a second. "After my discovery last night, what do you think, Ben? Don't you think I have some catching up to do?"

Now he was pushing the door to his room. Ben felt flustered. "Await Mike. I have to tell you. There some French guy turn up last night, help me in a fight, say he coming at two today."

Mike turned round, looking alarmed. "Lucien was in a fight? You know who he is, even?"

"Well no, but he seemed a sound guy, pitched in, you know."

"He's one of the top draws on the scene, Ben. I booked him ages ago. Time you started putting some fucking work in round here an' got to know the score."

Ben ignored the flare of temper. He knew Mike was going through a strange period right now. "Look, I is happy for you, man, an' I know you has new hormones floating round your body but I need you to set up the system. So tell the girl a dig up an' we can get to it, yeah?"

Ben didn't like the look that spread across Mike's face.

"Last night I discovered my dick, boy. It's my turn to lay up in bed all day with a girl, don't you think? You can set up the PA, time you learnt. I have more important business to attend to."

The door was pulled shut and after a moment he heard the soft murmur of a girl's laughter.

"No ras, Sophie, fuckers pulling knives on me an' now I got some crazy poet turn up, an' the electronic lynch pin a the whole operation wanna fuck all day. Mikey . . . I prefer you as a virgin, boy."

Curtis hit the accelerator and pulled round the line of stationary cars. Ignoring the bellow of a horn from an oncoming truck he went up to fifty, then pulled dead into a tiny gap just before the lights, without a sound from the brakes. The car behind him tried to box him out but he nudged the bonnet forward, in little hops until he had the space. He reached down to the radio volume and twisted it right round. It was a track he liked.

After dropping Amanda off at work he had stopped at Maxine's to collect his money. The fracas with his boss had been forgotten and he had a roll in his jacket pocket. Curtis was off the wage now. The way he had handled Red, and double-crossing Ash had been rewarded by a profit-share deal and Carl just stuffed a wad into his hand once a month. Sometimes he didn't even count it until he got to the bank, where the cashier would pick apart the pile of notes he handed over and write the figure on a slip of paper. The sum was always big enough to make him smile.

He was careless with the money for two reasons. Firstly he always had been. Money was there to burn in any way he desired; that way you never allowed it to be your master. The second reason was more complex. He viewed the cash from Carl as incidental, merely a stepping stone to something else. In a way it almost shamed him that he was still working for the man, and treating the money casually let him kid himself it was not a leash, as he still longed for his own set-up. He had enough in the bank for his immediate wants but knew it was a stagnant activity working for someone else.

To move into his own deal he would have to go through other players, not just go it alone straight away. He had failed that way before. That was partly why he was rushing now, shooting the lights and jumping traffic. He was late for a meeting at Bliss.

Stefan stood up to greet him as he came in. He wore the usual suit with razor lapels and Curtis noticed the flash of his watch, a two-grand timepiece.

"Man, I sorry. The traffic's just a bitch at this time a day." He insisted on getting the drinks and reiterated the apology. Curtis didn't want any hitch in his relations with the trio.

"Don't worry yourself about it, Curtis. There's no hurry." Stefan spoke with the swing of the street, despite his appearance. Manicured hands caressed his brandy glass.

"So where the others?" He had only seen them all together, "The Board", as they were known. "They're over at the den. That's where we're going now." Stefan sank the drink and moved off his stool, reaching down for a briefcase on the floor. "That is, if you have the admission charge."

"Yeah, no problem with money." So he had finally got the invitation. This was what he had been working on for the last two months, humbly courting the three.

"It stands at two hundred, right now."

"Safe."

Outside the bar, Curtis walked toward his car but Stefan caught him by the arm. "We can walk it."

He had only heard talk of the den. At first he thought

it must be some dumb rumour going round but after meeting Stefan it was confirmed. He and the other two partners on the board had set up a club, an exclusive club with invited membership only, and the clientele represented every major player this side of town.

Curtis knew little about the three. He had heard they were from out of town, made some money in robbery and invested it in setting up the den. People didn't talk about them much and they said even less themselves in the times he had been out with them. He had been approached and vetted and the money pick-up he had made in their presence down at the Box had probably been a last assurance of his status.

Now they walked along the highstreet and took a turn. It was a road he knew well, lined with the finer examples of West Park's domestic architecture. The houses were set back from the pavement, hidden by trees in the gardens. It was the nearest the patch had to an avenue. Stefan paused at one of the gates.

"Not here, man? So close my yard."

They walked up a thin path, shadowed by the house. It led up to the main porch but the guide veered left and circled the building, then made his way down some flaking concrete steps to a low door. The street was close but here in the rear of the garden and with trees along the perimeter they were completely hidden from view. Before Stefan got to the bottom of the steps the door opened and two men checked their faces. Curtis followed him through the opening.

"It's a house rule, I'm afraid."

They stood in a small hallway, lavishly decorated in red fabric and gold-edged mirrors. Curtis sensed the front man stepping behind him and lifted his arms so he could start the frisk.

"There are a few rules." Stefan handed his coat to the

other man and opened a small hatch behind him, set into the wall. There were two rows of metal squares, each with a keyhole and handle. He pulled one open. "No watches. No electronic equipment of any kind. No violence and no meeting with any of the help outside the walls of the den. You understand? Any breach of the rules and membership is terminated." He dropped his watch into the drawer and pushed it shut, then opened one for Curtis. "And of course, the entrance fee is payable each and every time you enter the den, no disputes. We are free to raise or lower the charge as we wish. We also have sole power of admission selection."

"An' what can I expect for two hundred pound?"

The other doorman had produced a signing book and money box. Curtis pulled out some notes and counted out five twenties and two fifties. Stefan seemed to ignore his question. "Cash only, no refund, twenty-four-hour access. And what you get, my friend . . ." He stepped forward and the far door of the hallway swung open. "Is everything you want and whenever you want it."

They went through to a low-ceilinged lounge, dimly lit by standing lamps in the corners. As his eyes adjusted, Curtis could see the shapes of people relaxing round the room. It was more like a waiting room than a club and his first reaction was one of disappointment. It reminded him of a tacky sex-salon parlour, the kind you could frequent for a few notes in the centre of town. There were girls carrying silver trays and the air was thick with smoke. It was blow though, not tobacco. Stefan was still by his side and took him by the arm. "This is the reception area. Come through to the bar, I'll show you around."

There was a walk-through arch in the wall opposite, similar to the one in his flat. This was not at all what he had hoped for and he was on the point of expressing his anger to his guide as they sauntered across the deep carpet.

However, the sight through the arch made him hold his tongue.

"You see some of our guests like the relaxed look of next door, especially if they just want to find a girl or meet someone. The bedrooms are all upstairs. We lease the whole house. Me, well I prefer this sort of mood."

The bar hugged each long wall of a massive room, a huge chrome snake. Stools lined it and almost every one was occupied. It was a gallery of infamy. Every big player was in here, adding to a hum of chat and clinking of glasses. The walls were a bare brick, covered in bottle shelves.

"Serious drink-up, sah."

They climbed onto a couple of seats and Stefan motioned a girl behind the bar with his fingers. There were two servers to a wall, each dressed in a standard white blouse.

"Yes, sir. How can I help?"

"Two of the best brandy and some Hawaiian."

She turned and fiddled with a bottle then leaned down to open a drawer. This allowed Curtis to examine the line between her breasts appreciatively.

"She does that on purpose, you know?"

"A ras. You fuck now."

"No really. Gets her away from the bar and she earns more money that way. You want her, you just ask."

"Man, I not really clear on the runnings here."

She was back with their glasses and a small porcelain plate with lipped edges. There was a mound of bush sitting in the centre of it. This was placed in front of them between their brandy glasses. Next she moved down the bar slightly and slid what looked like a doormat over to Stefan. It was a thin, black plastic square, covered in papers and other rolling equipment.

"Go ahead."

Curtis grinned and started to lick two papers together.

"You see, every woman in here works for us and will oblige, you get me? Just say the word. Also, any narcotic, you just ask for. The only thing we don't allow is basing. That can turn a man crazy. It's the same system as Holland with a board listing the draw. Oh, you get frisked on the way out too, so don't think about taking any with you."

Curtis nodded but the words were drifting over his head. He was staring at a notice in the centre of the wall. It was a list of blow from around the planet, some he had never even tried. He mixed the bush and some tobacco in his palm, spread it in a line on the papers then rolled the tube. "So guys just sit here getting trashed? One happy family." Although impressed by the layout he had kept his eye on the other guests. Some of them he had dealt with in the past and would not normally choose to be drinking with.

Stefan reached over with a lighter for the joint. "Ah. I see what you mean. You will discover the joys of neutrality though, Curtis, and it can be good for business. This room is a bit like an employment bureau. There is no fighting here though, don't forget it."

So Stefan had guessed he was not completely satisfied with Carl.

"Well, that hard to imagine. I take your word though."

"Just mellow into it, C. It'll grow on you. Why don't you try the girl?"

He had been giving her the occasional glance whilst they talked, peering through the haze produced from the joint he was pulling on. Stefan was perceptive indeed.

"Nah, man. I have a woman. Me a one-woman man."

"No such thing, boy. Anyway, it's you who's checking her."

"Well? Jes cause you on a diet don mean you can't look at the menu."

Stefan started laughing and sipped his drink to avoid a fit of coughing. "Yes. Been a while since I went steady. Almost envy you if someone means that much."

"Yeah, she sweet."

"That's good. But if you change your mind, remember, nothing gets talked about outside these walls."

Curtis sucked on the drug. It was a sweet, dry rush of air over his tongue and he felt a surge of heaviness spread down into his legs. "Man, this some criss draw, boy."

"Of course."

He reached out to Stefan, offering him the joint but with a flash of movement it was snatched from his fingers by another hand; a hand covered in gold rings. He pushed away from the bar, expecting trouble, his head clearing in preparation.

"You a calm youself, Curtis." It was Bunny, sucking hard on the joint so the lines of his face were amber in the glow from the tip. He was wearing sports gear but it was expensive. His muscles bulged under the shiny material.

Curtis thought he looked odd, built up out of proportion from too much gym-work. "I no a fear you, Bunny."

Bunny's eyes were a hard line but after a moment he turned to Stefan. "Your fren look fo you. Back at the door."

Stefan dipped his head as a goodbye, then slid off the stool and walked off. "Mind if I park myself wid you fo a spell? Never did get the chance to clear the air." He was already on the stool, sitting a head taller than Curtis.

"I ave a choice?"

"Wha ya drink?"

In the street the encounter would have been different. Curtis only remembered the man from a meet with Carl, long ago, but he knew what had happened at Maxine's after he had passed out. That had been back after the chase from the farm and his first experiences of gunplay all those months ago. Bunny would have carried him back to his paymaster Zack if it had been possible. He was a hired hand and had set his muscle man Alsash on to the team. People still talked about Carl's fighting from that night.

Curtis said nothing as he leaned forward and gestured for attention at the bar.

"So you freeze me out? You ave it wrong, boy. That time me earnin' a dollar, that all. Nothin' gainst you." The girl had answered Bunny's wave and he ordered a rum and the same again for Curtis.

"So where the big man?"

Bunny looked pleased that he had got some response from him. The reference was about Alsash and he smiled. "Him no afford the entrance charge. Which make me think you mus be doing sweet wid Carl. Times been hard fo me lately."

"Times is always hard."

"That true. Money gone."

"Well, you still ave all you jewellry there."

"Me a grown man, boy. This has to be bottom line."

She was back with two glasses and a bottle. "I can't remember what you had, sir." She sounded almost frightened, as though he would have her punished for the slip of memory. Her eyes were slightly red in the corners and he saw that her face was thick with foundation and make-up. Her looks were an exaggeration of normal feminine appeal and for the first time he was conscious of her as a prostitute. This time there was no come-on smile, she just looked tired.

"It was a brandy but . . ."

"T'alright. Leave the bottle there an' him can drink what I ave."

She looked relieved and hurried off. This was one girl who was happy to stay behind the bar for a while. Bunny tipped the bottle and filled both glasses.

"A toast to West Park, sah."

"You no live West Park."

"True, but when I reach West Park I know there is always a friendly face fo me."

Curtis had to laugh at the sarcasm directed at him. "Is true. One hour before now, I find you, I would a lick ya down, boy."

"Is easy talk. Besides, you in the den now an' we is all pasfists."

"Wha this 'pasfists'?"

"Mean we don fight, boy."

"You mean 'pacifist', Bunny. P . . . A . . ."

"So you is fuckin' spelling bee now, then. Anyway, yes man, them white boys set up a real nice club fo we. No fighting."

They were laughing from the grass and rum. As they talked they were still rolling and killing the bottle. Relaxed, they knew they could push each other a bit.

"Now ya talk fuckrie, man."

"Is who a talk fuckrie?"

"You, if you think is a black-white thing. Them boys just the same as we. Greedy and not too pure."

Bunny wailed with laughter and they were both quiet for a minute, amused.

"Ya may be right there. So anyway, I hear you friend Ben in trouble last night."

"You hear that? Me no hear nothin'." Curtis was concerned but the touch of alcohol coloured his mood. He was used to Ben being less of a conversation piece than he was becoming these days, and in this environment Ben's new status irritated him.

"Yes. Someone want a piece a all that money they make."

"They no make so much."

"That not the word I hear. Money fall out a the place."

They were talking in softer tones now, not the comic edge of before. Bunny cut in again. "Yeah. This time they come clear but I feel they have a bad ride soon."

"Wha you mean by that?" Curtis was sober now, his body tensed.

"Easy, man. Remember the house rule. No ras questions. What I tell you is volunteer."

"Safe. But Ben an' me close."

"Well, that being the case . . ." Bunny leaned forward, close to his ear. "I tell you as it no concern a me. But that club is special to someone, someone you no wanna fuck with. I give you tip, boy. You doing good now, making enough to get in here. Keep your face out a thing you not directly involve in and people may start to pick up on you. Let nature take it course, Curtis, leave Ben an' him fren to their own, cause they got big problem ahead."

"Wha you saying though. I mean . . ."

"Hush man. I here to relax an' you too. I jes tellin' you . . ."

"Tellin' me what?"

"Tellin' you I hear someone not happy, that all. Leave it a that."

Lucien was an hour late. When he strolled in at three, Ben was under the stage messing with the system wiring. Mike was still upstairs with Celia, and Ben knew it was unlikely he would rise, apart from to grab some food or a drink. The girl had many charms. Alfred was not answering his phone but Ben left a stream of desperate messages. For two hours he had been trying to come to terms with a circuit diagram and it lay on the stage covered in tools and cables. Lucien had brought some friends. One of them was an electrician and he had the PA working in a few minutes, which distressed Ben somewhat.

"Man, I been working on her for hours."

"I was told that your partner, he was the one who was good with this."

"He's . . . indisposed at the moment."

"Oh, I am sorry to hear so."

I

The other guy was Lucien's DJ and he was testing the decks as Alfred walked in, nonchalant as ever.

Ben called him over. "Mikey says these guys are known, is that right?"

"You kiddin'. They'll be charting soon. Not my style though really."

Ben was not so interested in the minor scene. There was a lot of talk but few of the artists hyped ever got anywhere. He liked the established music names in reggae and had only heard a few tracks of the jazz-rap style that Lucien represented. "I leave this stuff to you DJs I think."

"Nah, you'll probably love it. Stick around. Then again, you're pretty straight ragga so . . ."

Ben sighed and started backing to the stairs. "I hear it on the night, man."

A joint or two and then a phone-call, they were his present wants. Mike's conquest was making him feel a bit chaste. There was some catching up to be done.

Nine

Kimps stretched back on the sofa and shut his eyes, oblivious to the other people in the room. He had just showered and was enjoying the feeling of calm that enveloped him after washing.

"I really don't know how it happened. It was only intended as a simple warning."

He stirred at Harvey's muttering. "Well, I'm almost glad you screwed up. Means I get to meet up with some old friends."

The two men at the table opposite smiled. Harvey studied them for a second. They had the same big build as Kimps and wore plain T-shirts and jeans, tight to the body to show it off.

"You just underestimated these guys, that's all. We need to spook em properly."

Harvey felt his temper rise and had to suppress it. "You should remember my position here."

"Oh, and is that a threat? You've made your play."

The college boys beamed at him. Kimps was flexing his muscles but Harvey decided to make a stand. "Remember, I was ordered by your father to supervise you here and frankly, he worries me a lot more than you do. There is no way I can permit you to become involved in any violence."

"My father is on the other side of the planet. Anyway, he'd approve of me taking charge. He's been trying to stop those bastards stepping in for the last five years."

"Maybe over there. These people are not criminals though and it is for me to deal with them. I know your father wants the expansion but he would be angered should you participate in fighting."

There was silence for a moment. Kimps was aware that Harvey still carried some weight with his father. A call might be dangerous. He caught sight of himself in the wall mirror past Harvey's shoulder and gazed at the reflection, thinking.

Kimps was twenty years old but had the eyes of someone much older. He liked to think it was because he had killed a man and that brought maturity but in truth they had looked that way long before the act that had provoked his exile here. They were thin, jet-black and lined from years of life in the sun. His father had sent him here in an attempt to halt his exploits in America and appointed Harvey as his mentor. The man had worked for him as an accountant in the years before he moved and was trusted to keep him out of trouble. He would tolerate the constant abuse out of respect to his parentage but there was a limit to his patience. Kimps wanted to go home soon and a bad report was not in his interests.

"So what do you want, Harvey? You gonna have another go?"

Harvey wanted to smile. The spoilt brat could still be scared by the threat of a few words to his father. It was like a game of bluff between them sometimes, each measuring up the other. "Yes, I can take care of it." Now he was back in control. The clean-shaven giants at the table looked disappointed as he rose from the sofa to leave.

"Boys, you hear him. Guess we just go for a drink tonight, then. But Harvey . . ." Kimps did look a little like his father, the thick jaw, big limbs sticking out of the dressing gown. There was none of the power expressed in each simple movement though, the natural ease of command that comes from years of running a tough business. "You fuck up this time, then I come into the play. Deal?"

Harvey stared at him for an instant, wondering if there was a chance of him ever living up to his father's hopes. "Deal, mister Kimps."

Ben sipped his beer and contemplated life. Throughout the afternoon he had been trying to contact Sophie on the phone and had failed. The girl was on his thoughts and this worried him. Ben didn't enjoy dwelling on things too much. It made him think he was taking life too seriously. Coming down to Bliss was intended to take his mind off things but his brain still flicked back to the image of her honey thighs and he imagined her soft voice breaking through the murmur of the bar. *Oh Ben, yes, anything.*

It had been some time since he had visited the bar and he had thought it might seem different now he had money but this was not the case. Looking round at the other drinkers he realised that he was now in the same league, not a higher one. *Boy, you must a been broke, them day.*

All the usual players were here. The dealers were in the

back, making prolonged handshakes. Pretty girls sat at their tables. The office types ordered bottles of house wine and joked about other people in the department and public transport. Ben felt more separate than he had done before when he was here trying to make a drink last all night. The only difference now was that he was well dressed and could afford to get drunk. This he decided to do and started matching his beers with shorts.

"Boy, you look moody. Buy man a drink now you rich, will ya?" It was Adam. Slimy as ever with his movements he had climbed onto the stool next to Ben without a sound. Petie was behind him. He hadn't seen them for some time but Bliss was their regular haunt and it was no surprise to find them here. They were players in the Bliss black market after all.

"You know, I never see you boy apart."

"Well, we a team, innit."

Ben rarely talked with Adam but was glad of the company this evening. The alcohol was failing to satisfy him and at least he knew where he was with these two. They were all from the same patch.

"Well, is a big up fo Ben. You make that club popular, boy. I hear you an' Mike in the money."

Ben knew he was digging for information. Adam liked to know about people and their finances. "So you is still in the lending line, is you?"

"We do make loans, if that what you mean. The car business not too good."

He had heard they had abandoned the car-parts bit and knew all about Adam and his loan-sharking. There was more money in it for them obviously. Petie was the muscle, silent and imposing. Ben noticed the youth was still standing behind him, even though there was another stool. "Now, Petie. Sit yo self. Wan make me jumpy or summat?"

Petie looked embarrassed. Ben thought he saw a flush on his cheeks and heard Adam chuckle.

"Him have a little problem."

"Adam, man. Hush up!" Petie was shuffling from foot to foot, irritated but with a tiny smile on his lips.

"Well, you tell him the story, then."

"What story?"

"It nothin', B."

Petie was trying to look sincere and Ben had to laugh. For one thing both he and Adam were wearing style suits that made them look a little like a comedy duo; their respective sizes strengthened the image but also the sight of Petie trying to look so serious when Ben had known him since school was ridiculous. "Come now, Petie. Wha the problem? Me need cheering up."

Adam was curious for a second. "Thing not go well wid the club?"

"Nah, gal problem, man. Boy, Adam, you too pushy, man."

"Me jes wonder, that all. Anyways, Petie story make you laugh if some girl wind you up."

"So tell me then, Petie. Wha the story?"

The big man sighed in resignation. "You wan hear story, then you buy me a beer an' Adam can tell it. Me no in the mood."

Ben called for three bottles and turned to Adam, who was fiddling with a cigarette at his lips.

"Petie been seeing a gal. You know tha girl there, Lucy."

"No sah."

"Well, gal mampy anyway."

Ben smiled. He thought of Petie teaming up with Ruth. "Me ave jes the gal fo you, boy. She move in wid you."

Petie nodded sarcastically.

"Well, anyway. Him is round wid the gal evry night, you know."

"You making up fo lost time, boy."

At this Petie responded. "Is you say you in here wid gal problem."

"Easy. Me sorry. Gwan wid the story, man."

"So him deal wid the gal regular. Like I say. And she tell him she ave another man but him not there night-time, ya hear. That no problem, man can share a woman but most man, they would stop, say to them self . . . 'Hmm, funny that this guy is away every night'. But not Petie. No, sah."

He had mimicked his friend's deep voice for the line and Ben was already starting to laugh.

"But him jes enjoy himself. Him never tell me. No, is big secret till jes the other day when I meet him, we go bar and him say he 'prefer to stand' rasta. So me say, you know, wha go on, Petie? Well he say nothin' fo a minute an' then tell me. Him round this gal the other night an' after they finish, you know, he get a bit hungry. Boy is craven you know, he eat every ting in the house an' still him hungry. Gal mampy so she hungry too."

"Easy, Adam."

"So he think he surprise the gal an' order a pizza. Course by time pizza come they is in bed on the job you know. Petie say him hear nothin' till gal scream an' her man is in the room wid a knife. Petie get cut. See, her man, him . . ."

"The pizza boy, yeah. Bad luck there, Petie."

Adam cut in again. He could tell Ben was amused but not wildly so. "Story not finish there though. Me say Petie, how tis he prefer to stand. Petie get cut there, you know. Petie big man. Me work out, that when man see him, it have to be after the cut, yeah? Then him run."

"Make sense, I suppose."

"So I ask him and what him say?"

"You tell me."

"Him say it 'private'."

Ben was laughing loud now.

Adam was on the point of bursting out in hysterics as he talked. "Him say private. So me work it out. Him eating off two-foot table, sah. Man think him cut him top but him cut his botty, boy. Cause Petie working down-under. Ya dirty man, slack."

Ben roared with laughter. The drink was helping him along. Adam was almost in tears.

Petie spoke up very quietly but it only made things worse. "Is each man to him own man. You two is too moral."

"Aw, me sorry, man. But you pay fo you sin, you know."

Ben turned in his chair and slapped him on the shoulder. "Cha. Me buy you another, yeah?"

The remark had been addressed to Petie but Adam spoke up. "Yeah, another drink, then we dig up."

"Where you a go?" Ben had turned back to the bar to order the drinks. His spirits had lifted now and he wondered if they were doing anything of interest, thoughtful that the two were the only available company for the moment.

"Is a party. You wanna come?"

This was perfect. The only crowd and music he had seen for a while was round at the club. "Yeah man. Me come along. Who is it?"

"Some gal you don know. Owe me money."

"She owe 'we' money."

Adam glanced at his minder. Maybe he should take it easy on telling the story for a while. "Yes. Owe 'we' money, so she invite us down the party. It start soon though."

"So we get a cab?"

"As you wish, man. Then we ave time fo another." Adam sat back and smiled at him expectantly.

They pulled up outside a brightly lit terrace house and Ben

paid the fare. His accomplices hadn't opened a wallet yet but Ben was easy. They had come up with the party so he couldn't really complain. Ben didn't worry about money when he had it anyway. On the way over, Adam had warned him that it could be bad. He knew little about what kind of thing was planned but they had decided to give it an hour and see, their choice made partly by the fact it was a West Park address so they might know some of the people there.

Adam was walking up the path, Petie just behind him. The low pulse of music was humming in the air as he followed behind them. Ben started thinking about the party at Samantha's house, all those months before. It seemed longer. That had been a good night: rum, hash and body friction. Turning up without knowing the form was a bad move and he expected the worst. A few times before he had been trapped at dead parties, eager to escape conversations about the environment or surrounded by rugby-playing geeks. His pessimism mounted as a straight-looking white boy pulled back the door and stared at them like they were going to shoot him, the huge bulk of Petie being of particular concern. He was dressed in a scruffy linen outfit and pulling on a battered roll-up.

"Yeah?"

Petie bent down towards him, over Adam's head. "It's the police. This a raid so open up."

Ben started laughing again.

The party was in full swing. As he walked through the door into the front room he almost felt charged just from breathing the atmosphere. It was a smoker's paradise. In the centre there was a cluster of black girls swaying to the beat, a track only pressed on a reggae compilation LP he knew well. They were young, maybe just sixteen or so, and wore the street wear he liked to leer at. Round the edges of the room were the smokers, just rolling and lilting slightly to the music. It was loud. Not system standard but close and fine for a party. He thought of diving straight in with one of his lines but Adam tugged on his sleeve. "You wan meet the hostess?"

"Sweet man. Bes to be polite."

"Polite? Bitches owe me money."

The three of them pushed through the hall against a stream of people coming from the kitchen. As usual the hallway acted as a meeting place for all the transient souls that drifted about the house. Ben overheard the pick-up, the anecdote, the cynical rant and other snippets of conversation. It had been too long, he thought to himself. When they crashed through to the kitchen Petie went to work with his massive frame and cleared a space round a small table at the end. There were two girls seated there, deep in talk, and it took them a moment to notice Adam staring down at them. They were both pretty, round eighteen, and shared a similar tone to their features. Ben guessed they were sisters.

"Whappen, Adam? You bring a friend."

The girl to the right of the table was staring at him. She was trying to be brash but sounded a little nervous, he thought. Ben was amused by the way Petie and Adam were always addressed as one, as though the lumbering sidekick was just a personification of Adam's potential aggression should a payment be late.

"This ma friend Ben. B, meet the Smith sisters."

Ben reached down and took the girl who had spoken by the hand. "You have names a ya own?"

They both laughed and he was glad to calm them down a bit.

Adam looked unimpressed. "You have it then?"

"No, not now. If you can wait a day or two." The girl looked desperate, her eyes wide with fear.

Ben wondered what Adam had threatened them with,

knowing how sadistic he could be at times. Adam liked playing scare games with people.

"Well, then. You fuck now." Adam flicked a finger and Petie stepped forward. Ben couldn't believe he would use Petie but knew the big youth would do what he was told to do.

"Easy, Adam. They throw a party you know. That what I come for an' I see no need a get heavy."

A few months before Adam would not have taken it but Ben's status amongst the circles in the patch had grown considerably since then. In another six months, having links with Ben could be very useful and Adam was well aware of it. Nonetheless, he had an image of his own to maintain and word would spread if he was soft with Petie. He hesitated for an instant. Ben saw it and gave him an out.

"Just in the party spirit, you know. How much they down for?"

"I don't discuss this shit wid a friend."

"Nah, sah. Me pay it."

"Don be kwashi, B."

"I say me pay it."

The girls were staring up at him like he was wearing shining armour and sitting on a horse.

"Me pay it."

Adam was calculating the possible outcomes of the situation. He was cautious about a rift with Ben but wanted the money. "Is two hundred buy them off."

Ben pushed his hand deep into the lining of his jacket and pulled on it for a second, all the time staring blankly into Adam's eyes. He pulled out a roll. "That everything? No interest?"

"Total."

He peeled about half of the bundle away and stretched his arm out. Petie took the notes and counted them. Both girls jumped up from the table and started thanking him excitedly, kissing him on the cheeks.

"So now we can deal wid the party." One on each arm he pushed past Adam and broke for the front room. Ben felt like dancing.

The two sharks stared at his vanishing back, the big man reaching down for an open bottle of red wine that was still on the table and taking a heavy swig. "Me like him. But him think him fuckin' Robin Ood."

He hadn't danced this way for months. It was pure pleasure. The other guys were all hugging the wall smoking and he would stroll over for a blast now and again but in the centre of the room it was pure ladyland. The group of girls from earlier were still there and they moved in a tight ring around him, teasing him with the occasional brush of their bodies. As he got more trashed from the smoking the music took over and talking became impossible. The girls he had rescued from debt took it in turns to dance with him, stooping low against his body, leaning back in mock ecstasy. Ben had already forgotten about the money.

After an hour the party had filled to capacity. Petie was manning the door to keep people out. There was barely enough room to stand. He enjoyed being a bouncer. He and Adam were drunk, having drained a bottle of scotch pillaged from the kitchen and Ben was out in the hall with them. It was getting difficult to breathe in the front room and he was charged now, so a break appealed until he got his stamina revived. A few of the faces in the hall were familiar and he lifted his hand in acknowledgement but he made no attempt to engage anyone in conversation. He just leaned against the wall. The music flooded the space around him and Ben swayed to the beat, staring at the girls, a wide grin fixed to his face.

"So you happy, Ben?"

"Safe, man." It took him a moment to recognise Alfred as

his eyes seemed opposed to focusing. "Fuck man. You look well past your best."

"It a party, innit?"

The DJ was pushed up against him by the weight of people in the hall and Ben saw Mike's face trying to fight through the throng. "Mikey, man. Where the girl, then?"

Mike looked fresh although it was long past midnight. He didn't answer for a while but stared around the busy passageway as though looking for someone. Then he turned to Ben with a smile on his face. "Alright, B? I took her home. See her tomorrow, I think. Fuckin' rammed here."

He was checking the people around him and nodded whenever he caught sight of someone he knew.

"You jus reach? How you hear bout it?"

"Yeah, Petie let us in. As a favour, he said. It's Alfred who knew about it."

"You drive?"

"Yeah and yeah to the next question too."

"Safe, Mikey. Well, if I riding home in style, I might dive back into the pool again." Ben pushed away from the wall and staggered towards the dancing room.

"What this 'pool' you talking about?"

Ben span round and tried to adopt a fatherly look. "A pool of feminine temptation, my boy."

"Then we must drink it dry together, my son." Mike was by his side, dragging them both over to the doorway. They were met by a wall of bodies but pushed their way through to the middle.

Ben had only wanted to hang by the speakers as he was too relaxed to dance but a hand reached out to his as he stepped away from the dancers. It belonged to one of the Smith sisters. "Mike, these girls wan deal with you."

"Oh no. Come boy, dance up."

"I too tire, gal."

"Then we go lay down. You can rest up."

Ben woke up from the drugged torpor for a second. The girl pulled his hand down to her breasts and he watched as she moved up to press against him.

Mike was just behind her, beaming at him. "Before you vanish give me a float, will you?"

"I'm dry, boy."

"Just a bit, Ben."

What was Mike doing borrowing money? The girl was pulling him away but he managed to find two twenties and stuff them into Mike's hand. "Don't leave without me, ya hear."

"Yeah, right."

Mike drifted off into the crowd and Ben let the girl tug at his arm. As they quit the room and forced a way up the stairs he felt someone pushing behind him. He turned to shout abuse but saw the other sister grinning at him in hot pursuit.

"We do everything together, boy."

It was a dead-line ball and there was money on the game. He fixed his chin to the cue and let his arm swing, measuring the force required to secure victory. The wad of dirty pink linen on the bridge of his nose got in the way of his view slightly and he had to look at the shot from a different angle.

"Don't fuck up this time, Ralph."

He reared up from the table and stared at the figure opposite who had spoken. In the faint light from the overhead he saw a tall frame, wide shoulders and the hard face of a man pushing fifty. He had to squint to be sure it was him. "Ah, thought you might show up sometime. Didn't think you'd have the balls to come in here looking for me though."

"I grew up in places like this, boy. Only back then we

dealt with fuck-ups like yourself in a rather different way. Where's your friend?" The club was quiet for a moment and he scanned the dark walls for other shapes.

Ralph sneered at him, then went back to his shot. He was calm again now he knew the man was alone. "He's hardly gonna be playin' pool, is he? Not with his arm the way it is anyway. So, you come to tell me off?"

He was concentrating on the play again, leaning over the table. His opponent in the game laughed softly at his disrespect for the man. Ralph was a regular at this club and knew that if trouble started, the shadows from the other tables would help him out. He felt no threat from the older man dressed in his neat, office suit.

He had heard the stories about Harvey. Twenty years ago he was up there as a major player, dealing blows when it was needed, but now he was almost a figure of fun to the local youth, nursemaiding some arrogant Yank. From the line of the cue he could see him across the table, the has-been gangster. This time he spoke from his position at the table. "Look, we didn't get the money so we got fuck all out of it ourselves. An' we both got a beating, him worse than me but I still got a fucking nose bandage for my trouble. Why don't you piss off before you get on my nerves."

Harvey didn't move. His face was burning with rage but there was no tremble of his body to indicate it. He knew the power of concealing anger, focusing it into action. The way this boy spoke to him was almost a shock. It had been some time since he'd had to hire someone in and this arrogance from an underling surprised him. He took it from Kimps, only because he was supposed to be boss and Harvey knew what his father was. With one smooth movement he slipped the bottle from his jacket pocket, lifted it high above the table so it was in open view and tugged at the rubber stopper.

Ralph noticed it and paused, thinking it was perhaps

some medicine the man was taking, in a thick glass tube. "You're putting me off the game, git. Now, clear . . ."

"You don't even know what this is, do you?"

Ralph felt a tiny wash of fear overcome him and stared into the man's eyes. They were bright, like chips of ice. As he stared, Harvey twisted his arm so a thick liquid cascaded from the mouth of the bottle, staining the beige black.

"What the fuck you doing?"

The action had broken his inertia. The man must be senile, disrupting his game like this. But as he tensed the muscles in his legs to pace round the table he was still again, motionless from fear.

The first thing was the sound. It was a loud hiss like fat burning in a pan. The green cloth bubbled and split apart as though there was a flame underneath it, curling the torn edges. Then it was bare slate, black and smooth, exposed. Even this was starting to scar and he heard the crack as the layers began to peel off. There was smoke, thick, acrid and he could see nothing in front of him. Then there was a heavy ache in his neck, as though the muscles were cramping and the pain was so acute he fell to his knees and let out a cry of agony.

Harvey stood by his side, towering up above him, his fingers buried in the flesh of his shoulder. The grip was incredible. Ralph thought his skin would split under the pressure.

"Fluorosulphonic acid, boy. Very nasty."

He was paralysed by the pain. It spread from his shoulder across his neck and down into his back from the fingers buried in his flesh.

"On skin, of course . . . well, you can imagine."

The bottle was at his face, dancing before his eyes. He could see the fluid inside lapping at the edges of the rim as Harvey shook the glass base. Ralph started to sob. None of the others in the room had moved to help him. They watched the performance from a distance.

"A chance to redeem yourself, Ralph. I know you can forget who you are these days, speak out of turn, but you can make it up to me. It can't be easy for you growing up with all the changes we've had. Confuses you. I want to give you another crack at dealing with the same people. Fancy it?"

"Anything."

"This time I got a lot riding on it though. No fuck-ups."

"Anything."

"Then we can talk."

The hand left his shoulder and he saw Harvey walk back to where he had left the bottle's seal on the other side of the table. Ralph breathed heavily, trying to slow his heartbeat. He watched his attacker cork the bottle and slide it back into his jacket casually. One glance at his face and it was clear he needed no weapon to feel secure. Harvey was at ease, relaxed with his actions. He had regained the lost respect and knew it.

He was swimming in an ocean of flesh, the feminine pool. The drug still coursed through his blood, sapping his energy but giving the shifting banks of skin a glowing edge in his vision. Alcohol struggled for supremacy against the sleepy tide of hash, tempting him towards exertion but there was no need. The two flickering girls, a fantasy of duality, were bringing him to a height of pleasure as he remained nailed to the bed, motionless. Occasionally, he would lunge at a hovering breast or passing thigh as they journeyed the length of his body, kisses landing on every pore of his naked frame. But he would miss and they would titter at his clumsiness and soon he resigned himself to only passive pleasure. He cursed himself for being so trashed, as he had never been with two girls and just thinking of the diagrammatical possibilities was enough to excite him. He wished he had a camera. He was not sure where he was. All there was on the planet was the bed he lay on and the two threadless girls.

First they were separate and took it in turns to mount him roughly. The other would stroke his brow, patient for a turn, but after a few minutes of this they began to operate as a single, organic sex cell, as one ecstasy-provider. Their mouths would focus as one, teasing him with quadro-lipped expertise. Breasts became a valley of soft delight and he was marooned on a sexual isle of paradise. It was only his incapacitated state that kept him from release and they exploited this, knowing precisely when to let him rest for a few seconds and thus satisfying their own wants too. His absence from the sex circus for some time made their attentions doubly sweet. Not only did they sweep and caress him but also each other in a provocative display that aroused him even more than some of their more physical actions. They were entwined in a multi-limbed embrace and the positions that allowed only one access to his form provided the other with an opportunity to stroke or kiss her sister. Every sexual highway was explored until he finally cracked. He lay on his back with a sister on either side at his flank, their heads at his waist. Four hands were one shifting mass of soft flesh, sucking the fluid from his body in a gush. Then they lay still, panting at the sex-scented air.

He woke in the same position, the girls slumbering on each side of him. A ray of light was hitting his face, the bright-ness stunning him for an instant until he realised that it must have been the cause for his waking. He grunted, remembered where he was and crawled off the bed. Mike must have left hours ago, not wishing to disturb him.

Ben's head felt like someone had been trying to shrink it. He had to rub his eyes violently before he could trace his clothes. They were scattered about the room where the girls had thrown them those few hours ago. He dressed clumsily, putting the wrong arm into the sleeve of his shirt and losing his balance, falling against the bed. *Get a fuckin' grip, boy.*

Before staggering through the door he turned back and blew the sleeping girls a kiss, a happy memory forming in his mind.

The stairs were an adventure. A wild thirst was driving him towards the kitchen and he threw his battered frame off the top step, trying to engage his legs but almost falling. He clutched the banister to steady himself. With great difficulty he reached the bottom and lurched through the hall. The sound of conversation drifted along the passageway. Shaking his head to wake himself he pushed through the kitchen door.

Mike and Alfred were leaning on the worktop that ran the length of the room, both grinning like lunatics.

"Fuck, man. Me think you dig up. Wha time you have?"

Mike moved his arm jerkily round to his face and chortled. "Bout seven. A.m. that is."

Ben could see they were out of it and felt a surge of sobriety in response. Mike's skin was moist and blotchy and his eyes looked cataleptic they were so lifeless. "Wha the fuck you guys been doing?"

"Thought you were out of the show, Benny boy."

"Don't call me Benny. The name's Ben." He moved between them and looked down at an album sleeve resting on the side. It was covered in cocaine debris: see-through wraps, a blade and a rolled bank note. "Mikey. You do powder? A ras powderman now, is you?"

"What's it to you? Anyway, it's only a speed mix."

Ben stared at him. He was no puritan but seeing his

friend's condition he was angry. Mike looked sick. "When this start?"

"Who you with the high an' fucking mighty? Mister group sex . . ."

"That different."

"Bullshit."

"Na man, it natural."

Alfred grabbed a plastic wrap from the side and lifted it up to Ben's face. There was a thin line of white at the bottom. "This is natural too, comes from the earth."

"Ah, you a pickney if you think that. Amphetamine made in someone bathtub. Cha, it your thing man, you jus go on do it." He walked over to the sink and searched for a cup.

Mike was behind him, his movements still alert despite a night awake. "You're not really giving me a hard time about this, are you?"

"Don be silly. Each to his own, man."

Mike checked his face to see if he was being sincere. He looked anxious that Ben should not think badly of him.

"Relax, Mike. Evry man have to do his own thing." He filled a cup with tap water and moved back to one of the chairs in the room. The idea of Mike doing powder had surprised him but Ben knew he could make no moral judgement about his friend. There was nothing too bad about speed as far as he could see anyway, not that he was into it himself. It was the coke that could damage you. Even then it depended on the character of the user. Some people could deal with it as an infrequent luxury. Others got burned. You had to get past that stage before you had real problems; it wasn't like he was basing. But he had seen that path with others. Some people he knew had started casual, then tried the pipe and got stuck there. They were in a mess now. Ben disliked thinking of moderation in life and at the moment his head was pounding from the excesses of the night before. Alfred and Mike were still just staring at him like mutes. "So you gonna drive me home, Mikey? My head hurt."

Ten

He was playing errand boy again, picking up some money across the river, but today he didn't mind too much. Discovering the den had lifted his spirits and Curtis felt as though things were opening up for him once more. The only minor irritation lately had been the word from Bunny about the possible threat to the club. Worrying about protecting Ben and Mike's interests was not his chief concern so he had said nothing. He would leave it until they requested his help or he heard of something more serious going on. Besides, they were obviously handling things because they hadn't called for anything. Curtis decided to forget about it and concentrate on his own future ascent and how to turn it into a reality.

It was early afternoon so the traffic was still thin, rushing along the Embankment and up into an area of town full of bars, restaurants and envied apartments. At this time of year he could see the appeal. Trees broke the pavement's monotony with flashes of green and the buildings were well maintained, far removed from the ruin of West Park. The sun was everywhere. Crowds of smiling youth peered out from coffee bars, trying to look exotic. Some of them looked French or Italian, probably hanging out between lessons at the language schools that were hidden on every leafy corner. A year ago he would have hated the atmosphere here, venerating the bruised but genuine quality of the people in his patch. Now his values had changed and he thought of Amanda lounging on the steps of a townhouse. She was the right kind of girl for this area and he could imagine living with her in one of the tall blocks that lined the road. It appealed to him.

The realisation puzzled him a little. Ben had been ribbing him about his suits and the car for a long time but Curtis had always thought of himself as a West Park boy. Looking around he could see this area was full of the people he used to despise: the money class, vapid, spoilt, pretty, floating around looking for some meaning in their lives. They chose this area because they wanted the security of wealth and similar people around them but in an environment that was still a tiny bit 'arty'. Here they could pretend they were living on the edge, reckless. He smiled. They probably thought they were slumming it in this environment.

There was a small turning off the main road, not much wider than a driveway, and he slowed to steer the car through. Walls ran either side, with small doors leading into tree-blessed rear gardens. A ceiling of leaves made it quite dark, slices of light breaking through the gaps in the canopy, and he had to bring the car to a crawl. The street got even narrower until it turned at a sharp angle and he stopped, climbed out and paced over to an intercom-system set buried in the brick next to an iron gate.

"Is C."

There was no voice but he heard the scratching release of the lock and pushed through.

He was in a small garden that ran up to the rear of a huge house, covered in ivy. It was hot here; no breeze could enter the walled-in space and he loosened his collar. Bunny was sprawled in a sun chair, grinning at him.

"Why you always so formal, C?" He was wearing sports casuals as usual but today they were loose shorts and a light top to combat the heat.

Curtis answered him immediately to show no surprise although he had not been expecting to run into him here. "And is you always look like you about to do the marathon, Bunny."

"Na, these for the gym, man. Have some juice?" He waved at a small table with some glasses and drink cartons on it.

Curtis walked past it and sat in the chair opposite him. "You ave a ting fo me."

"Easy, boy." Bunny dipped his free hand and pulled a leather satchel from under his chair. He threw it over. "Pennies fo your boss, man."

Curtis ignored the jibe. He was still unsure of the man, even though they had been getting on at the den. This was on the outside. He opened it and saw some notes, then looked up at him again. "You get around, don' you? Who you workin' for here?"

"You can ask man question like that? I jes the agent fo someone, that all. Him ave to pay Carl reglar."

"Nice place you ave." Curtis was glancing up at the house, aware that it was out of Bunny's league.

"Is a friend of mine own it."

"Well, I dig up, ave a date. Later, Bunny." He stood to go,

feeling tense. The atmosphere was bothering him, like he was being examined somehow. It did not feel easy chatting with Bunny as it had in the den.

"Right, C. I buy you a drink."

He backed over to the gate, pulled it open and walked over to the car. Inside, he turned the scene over in his mind for a moment. His instinct told him there was something wrong with running into Bunny like that but he knew it was not so unlikely. Working as a fixer for people was his trade. Nonetheless, there was some tension in the encounter. He hit the ignition. *Cha. You get jumpy man.*

Bunny finished his drink and settled back into the chair, soaking up the heat like a cat. He didn't speak until he heard the engine start up. "Well, you see him. That what you wanted, though fuck knows why."

Kimps flopped down in the other chair and stretched his arms out in a yawn. It had been cool inside the house and the surge in temperature made him feel sleepy. "He's nothin'. I could take him with a broken back."

"All you did was look, sah. Im lick you down, I feel." Bunny relished the words, knowing they would infuriate the youth opposite him. One look at him was enough to know he saw himself as a fighter, a big man. Bunny needed his money too much to refuse but he could still show his dislike for the man. "See im know the vibe wrong. The boy have sense. You is weird just wanna watch him."

Kimps had seen the arrival check the garden and house like a cautious animal, then keep the conversation short and leave with no delay. It was clear he was no fool. "I just paid you for a look at what I'm dealing with. Keep your opinion in your fucking mouth."

"I gettin' soft, boy, taking that from you." He pulled himself out of the chair and stared down at the American. He knew who his father was but if there was another remark like that he would forget. It was better to leave. Kimps called to his back as he strode for the gate.

"Is he it? The only obstacle."

"Him no part a the club."

"Yeah, I know. It's two other guys but I hear this one is close."

"You may ave to front him if you hassle the others, yes."

"Well, it may not come to that but I like to check the opposition."

Bunny grunted and turned.

"Remember, not a word."

This time he didn't pause. The words were not worthy of a reply. Bunny was known for his neutrality and silence. This was his job, working for a dollar as a fixer, but even so he felt bad about this one. Curtis didn't warrant his betrayal and Bunny hoped nothing bad would come of it. He liked the youth.

Kimps went back into the house and fell onto a sofa. It was too hot to think out in the garden.

He didn't like dealing with Bunny but had wanted to spy his prey and knew the man could arrange it. If Harvey made another mistake, then he could step in without criticism and he wanted to know all the possible combatants before making a move. Curtis was the only potential fighter in the pack.

Kimps enjoyed formulating his battle plans, mulling over the risks. The takeover of the club was a trivial operation as far as he could see. He had been present at his father's meetings, times when they had planned raids with military firepower against the black gangs. The scene over here was a joke in comparison. The pick-up boy in the suit would break down and cry if he had a gun stuck in his face. He rolled off the sofa and punched the TV remote, staring blankly at the screen.

It was still early so Curtis took his time, gliding past the bars and boutiques of the highroad. The line to Bunny was just so he could exit, as the situation had put him on edge. The encounter had tainted his mood but was fading from his memory as he put some distance between himself and the tension of the garden. He had to get the money back to Carl, then pick up Amanda at her flat but there was no rush. They weren't going out for hours.

He found himself staring at the houses and shops again, with the same interest he had felt earlier. It was so different from West Park. The people looked happy, as though they were free from the dull anxieties of life. It was mainly youth, hanging out in the sun. Up ahead of him he saw a car pulling out from a parking space. For a second he deliberated, then swept into the gap and killed the engine. *Curtis, go buy yourself a drink.*

It was typical of the local bars, more like a coffee shop than anything else. Black stone and chrome lined the walls and the chairs were hard plastic. He dropped the satchel into the chair next to him at a small table and sat down. It was quiet inside. Most of the clientele were out on the pavement but Curtis didn't understand their desire to inhale car fumes just so they could pretend to be Parisians. Not all of his past animosity for this area had disappeared.

There were a few loners reading papers and some girls at the bar, talking loudly in the wide, horse-rider accent he despised. This didn't stop him from appraising their looks though and as he scanned their shapes, squeezed into the bar stools, his eyes lingered on the girl at the end. She looked slightly apart from the others, not an enthusiastic participant in the chat. If anything, she looked bored with the company and this intrigued him. The detachment was attractive. Her movements reminded him of someone but it was only when she half-turned her head to take a sip from her drink that he recognised her. It was the girl Ben was into. Sophie.

"Aright, Sophie." His voice broke through their noise and she turned, looking a bit alarmed.

"Oh, Curtis. How are you?" She slid off the stool and he could see the relief of escape light up her features.

"Sit yourself down. I buy you a drink."

"Can't really. I have to go along with my friends in a minute."

She was plainly dressed but he felt a strong attraction for her and it unsettled him. There had been a hint of it at the dinner but here there was no Amanda to distract him.

"How's your girlfriend? Said I'd give her a ring but I've been terribly busy." The remark made him feel as though he was handcuffed to Amanda but he said nothing.

"I might go down to Ben's club . . ." This was another blow to his ego. He was haunted by tales of the guy these days. It made him feel secondary and he considered telling her how he had put the money up for it initially, how he had a bank-vault pile of cash next to her, but he knew claims like that would paint him as an idiot. Best to keep those things hidden.

"Will you be there?" This surprised him. Her sentence had been almost whispered but not flirtatious, more like an earnest request.

"That last time I had a really good time."

"Yeah? Thought you were thinking bout Ben all the time."

She just smiled. He remembered she lived round here and for a split second thought of suggesting he took her home.

"I have to go. Maybe see you later."

Another smile and she was walking back to her friends. They stood at the bar waiting for her, eyeing him with a mixture of suspicion and interest. They filed out and vanished onto the street. For a long time he stared after them, deep in thought.

Eleven

The days when Ben was nervous calling a girl were long gone but there was a second of hesitation. He had already left messages and there had been no response. Maybe she had met some other guy during the week. No, that was ridiculous. Amanda had said she was interested. His fingers danced in the air above the buttons.

"Who you calling?"

The voice alarmed him. He had thought Mike was down on the decks and had crept up to the flat to make the call in private. They were only a few hours away from the show. Mike had come out into the lounge from his bedroom and was still buttoning a shirt.

"I slept in."

"Not now, Mike . . . slept in! It evening, you know?"

"Na, morning innit. Oh, I see. Calling her whilst you thought I wouldn't be around, are you?" He had woken up as he saw Ben's embarrassed look.

"It nothin' like that."

"What a traitor, man. Can't you take the competition anymore? Sneaking around on me."

"I gonna ask her down the club tonight, so you can 'compete' if it so important to you. Anyways, I feel you'll be blitzed with Alfred by the time she gets here."

"That'll just make me more . . . irresistible." He was checking himself in the wall mirror and they both started laughing. Mike was not looking his best.

"You ave a love potion, then? Cause you need it, boy. You look fuck." He hadn't seen much of his flatmate lately. It had taken a day or two to get over the excesses of the party, then there had been a few tasks he had to attend to before the weekend. Mike was keeping odd hours, so apart from one time they had met when Ben was getting up for breakfast and he was about to go to bed there had been little contact.

"Well, ring her, then. Don't let me stop you."

"I get round to it, man."

"What? You really worried about ringing? You a grown man an' all. Thought you said she was 'hot to trot', boy."

"Hey, Mikey boy. This girl special, man."

Ben looked hurt by his vulgarity but Mike continued. "It was you saying it. I mean, after your behaviour the other night . . ."

"That nothin'. I didn't really have anything to do wid dat."

Now Mike turned from his reflection to face him, incredulous. "Say that again. No, don't. Honest, things work just the way you think they do, don't they. You inhabit a separate reality, Ben, my friend."

"How you know? You wasn't there."

"Thank fuck for that. It was groan city from where I was in the kitchen."

"Well, haven't even kiss the girl yet. If we together, then I never go wid dem gal there."

"Sure."

"Is the truth."

"Ring her, then."

Ben made a determined lurch for the phone, checked the number he had on a scrap of paper and pushed the buttons. He stared defiantly at Mike as the ringing tone came on, knowing she never answered.

"Sophie Tarling." Her voice stunned him. Mike was beaming from by the mirror.

"Oh yeah, Sophie, it's Ben."

"Hi, Ben, how are you?" A sweet whisper at his ear.

"I been calling you a few times . . ."

Mike sank to his knees and clutched at his chest, adopting the pose of a theatrical lover. It was hard not to laugh.

"Just wondered if you wanted to come out . . ."

"I was thinking of turning up tonight, round ten. Would you put my name on the door?"

He had a vision of her honey legs and the wriggling mini. "Sweet. How's things with you anyway?"

"Can't talk now but I'll see you tonight. OK."

"Of course."

"See you tonight, then. Bye."

She sounded naïve and fresh to him, even though she was older. It was only a brief word but hearing her was a pleasure and he stared at the phone for a moment, thanking science.

Mike detected his euphoria. "I take it, from your sickening grin, that all is well with Sophie and she plans to attend."

"You take it right, Mikey boy." He rose from the sofa and made for his room.

Mike shouted after him. "Hey, we have a couple a things to get ready you know. Lucien's on tonight."

Ben shouted from his room, too busy to come back into the lounge. "I ave something to get ready too, boy, my beautiful body."

"Downstairs in twenty minutes . . . or else."

"That fuckrie. Or else what?"

"Then she gets a full life history on you."

"That no problem."

"Starting from the weekend."

Ben stormed back into the room but it was too late. Mike was running down the steps, sniggering.

Alfred grabbed his beer by the base, lifted it to his lips and took a gulp. The cold liquid stung the back of his throat. Conversation was making him thirsty. "I don't agree with you, Mikey. Now, Lucien is good, I grant you, but well there are plenty of people in this town doing things I'd rather be hearing."

"Alfred. Stop talking bollocks. Nothing decent's come out for months."

They were having their regular DJ argument. Alfred would keep up his slow drawl and defend the local scene whilst Mike was getting more into foreign acts. Lucien was one of his favourites.

"Now, you start showing your aggression again. You get too stressed that way, man."

Mike studied him for a second. Tonight he had gone for the beatnik hipster look more than usual. A tight fifties suit hugged his slim frame. The beard was getting quite long and he was fond of stroking it when he wanted to look pensive. His face was thin and dark-skinned, the only sign he was Asian, but with all the tie-dyed gear he wore Ben often joked it was just a suntan. He did look like he was straight off a beach sometimes.

"You got to mellow, man."

"Safe, Alfred."

The speech was what got to him most. Mike knew this was considered normal in some circles of the DJ fraternity but he could never relax with it. He was too used to the street talk of West Park and would sometimes slip into using the odd word more fitted to the soft accent of Ben and Curtis. Alfred sounded as though he thought he was in another decade.

"You check some of the vibes coming from Maxine's lately? I assume not. Well, they picking out some new soul ideas and it sound real . . ."

"Man, you talk bout this again." Ben had appeared beside them.

"I said twenty minutes." Mike was making a show of staring at his watch.

"You not fuckin' serious, are you? Only half-hour."

"Yeah, easy."

Alfred cut in. "See, you hassling him about time, man. You're getting too stressed out running this place, sapping your energy."

"Well, don see you gettin' stressed, Alfred. In fact, I only see you taking it easy and sippin' beer."

"That's because I know how to live, my friend."

"Oh, I see."

They were smiling. There was always a good atmosphere before the doors opened, up in the Basement. The bar was empty apart from themselves and some of the staff who were cleaning up. Alfred acted more like a partner than their employee but they liked his easy mood most of the time. He passed some cigarettes round.

"I enjoy the fruit of life."

"Mean you enjoy the drugs a life."

"I can take your abuse, Ben."

"Is good thing cause you gonna get a lot more. Think you should be on the decks pretty soon, boy."

"Relax, man. There's for ever to deal with."

Ben and Mike smiled at one another. They were slumped in stools, lining the bar, a haze of tobacco smoke rising above them.

"Ah, my friends. You work hard, yes?" Lucien was behind them and Ben noticed his suit in the mirror that lined the bar wall as he shook hands with Mike and Alfred. It was in the same class as a Curtis suit, cut impeccably, faultless. He span round to face the rapper. "Ben, ma friend. You well?"

"As ever Lucien, an' yourself. You ave a beer."

"Always a beer, thankyou." He joined them at the bar and they talked about his set for a while. Ben was less interested than Mike. Alfred gazed off into space. "I will only pay for a demi, thirty minutes, that way no person get sleepy, yes."

"Is something I have to confess, man." Ben had tapped Lucien on the shoulder. "I is not on this jazz-rap ting, you know. Me like reggae, some dance an' that about it. But I like you an' I look forward to your show."

"Well said, Ben. I'm sure he needs your encouragement."

"No, Mike. Ben must speak his mind. That what I do with my music. I hope you like it tonight and I think you will see it as from the same family as what you say."

"Hey, start over with that again, boy."

They had been there a while, time drifting, and Mike realised it was nearly time to open. The bar was lined with empty bottles.

"Gonna start taking all this beer out your wages, Alfred. Drinking all our profits."

"Now that's hardly fair, Mike."

"I'm only joking." He was off his stool and moving for

the stairs. Ben was chatting with Lucien and showed no awareness of the move. "Ben, remember what I say?"

"Wid you in a minute, sah."

"The Smith sisters, boy."

"Wha! Ah, the blackmail you mean. Lucien, chill man. I watch your set." He shook his hand and followed Mike. Already the beers were making his head feel light. He would have to watch his intake tonight if possible. There was Sophie to seduce and he would need a clear head for it. Thoughts of the girl were not only physical, though they formed a large part of the attraction. There was something in the way she had spoken to him, as though the levity of the conversation was full of promise. He was trying to figure it out as Mike grabbed him by the arm and pulled him towards the stairs.

"We have work to do, boy. You love-sick or summat?"

"Fuck you. That an illness me never gonna ave, boy." They walked down into the main room and over to the entrance, their trainers squealing on the polished wood. "An' what about Celia? She coming tonight, seeing as we talk about it."

"Nah, seen her loads lately. She might turn up, I spose."

"So you check the floor tonight?"

"Maybe."

"Nah, cause you ave a new love, innit."

Mike stopped in the middle of the hall and shot him a confused look. "Don't follow you."

Well, it white and it go up you nose. You powderman now."

Since the first night of the Chocolate Box they had been selling close to capacity. Tonight though, the lure of Lucien and his crew pulled in an extra crowd and the doors had to be locked at ten. It was a unique event in the clubbing history of West Park. Other clubs had broken the fire limits and had to lock up, they had been shut down by the police for safety reasons but no one had ever locked up at ten in the evening; it was unheard of. Most clubbers were still grooming in their bathrooms as the portals creaked shut. Cars were arriving at twelve, only to find a huge mass of people waiting outside the doors, still hoping to be let in after two hours standing in the street. Ben had to post a security team at the door with a description of Sophie and Curtis. He had to make sure his date could get in if she turned up and Curtis was a permanent guest. There was nearly a riot when she finally showed and was admitted under escort. They led her straight up to the Basement and got her through the crowd to Ben's table where he was holding court.

Nearly every face he knew from the patch had turned up that evening and the mood of the Basement had changed from the easy-jazz feel to a frantic buzz. The main hall was a solid block of people. Lucien had everyone talking. There were even some industry people there to check him out, sweating in cheap suits. Ben didn't let this detract from his status as a founder and runner of the club though. He was in fine form, ordering the drinks and shouting at the peak of his voice over the din.

The crowd was everywhere. On the other nights there had always been a bit of breathing space in the Basement if it was too crammed downstairs. There would be circles of friends talking and every now and again a table would change hands as someone left or went below to dance. This was not the case tonight. There was no free space to stand in at all. Every available inch of floor seemed to be occupied. The air was a grey sponge of tobacco smoke and drops of water fell from the ceiling it was so humid. They were way beyond their official capacity and these people were here to stay for the whole night, not concerned about moving from place to place during the evening. The club had finally gained the reputation of being the place to be on a Saturday and the crowd was more stylish than before, better dressed. They were coming from over the river now, the more affluent night owls. Some wore suits like the one Lucien sported, sharp, slightly jazz, but there was a lot of the hippy element too. Girls in flares and fluorescent tops swayed to the beat downstairs. Mike was on the system, playing more of the light jazz sounds he was getting into. When Sophie came up to their table, Ben was in dispute with Alfred about his choice of music.

"It no hum like reggae, man. Mike use to play criss tunes but im jus a jazz boy now. We ave to talk wid im, I tell you."

Sophie thought he looked a bit deranged at first as he was ranting but when he caught sight of her his eyes softened and she was reassured.

"You reach. Sorry there, me argue about the way things are going with the club. Wha you wanna drink?" He came round to her side of the table and pulled out a chair which they had saved.

"Looks to me like the club's going pretty well. In fact . . ."

"I know. I was only saying about the choice of music, you know I'm kinda set in my tastes."

"Can't you get used to something new?"

There was a suggestive glimmer in her eyes and he studied her face. The evening had been a crazed affair so far, everyone buzzing with the crowd and noise but he suddenly relaxed, staring at her. "I could try dance to it maybe."

Alfred pushed against him, trying to get out. "My set coming up, Ben. I've got a few vibes which are more your style."

Ben hadn't taken his eyes away from hers. "In that case we can dance for sure, if you in the mood, that is."

She smiled and dropped the jacket from her shoulders, lifting it onto the back of the chair he still held for her. Up until then he had really only noticed her face and the sweep of her hair but now he saw the exposed flesh of her arms and torso. The removal of the jacket allowed him to survey acres of her skin. Underneath it she was wearing a thin cotton T-shirt that stopped just at the line of her breasts, as though the bottom part had been cut off. It was so loose he could have lifted it with a breath. He swallowed in appreciation. The skin was the same rich honey colour as her legs and he focused on the tiny bulge of her belly as though there was a precious gem buried in her navel.

"You not get cold in that?"

"In this place. You kidding?"

"Sophie, ya dress naughty."

"I always wear stuff like this."

She sounded entirely unconcerned. How could she not be aware that he was leering at her, consumed with the desire to lift the flimsy top with his little finger?"

"Where's that drink you promised me, then?"

Below the waist she wore white hot pants, except the legs were shorter than normal, curtailed like the T-shirt. She could have got more flesh coverage from a bikini but that was obviously her aim. Sophie was used to guys who would admire politely and not comment.

"Don't you like it, then?"

"Uh."

Now she was staring at him, having noticed his examination of her clothes and body.

Ben decided to tread carefully. "No, I mean of course, yes. I think it's quite . . . let's get you that drink."

Once they got down to the floor below, it was obvious that dancing was close to impossible. The crowd was so tightly packed it was difficult enough to move an arm, let alone dance. The music was loud, drowning out the expectant murmur of the throng.

"Maybe we should go back up."

She was yelling at his ear and he could smell a sweet fragrance. He wanted to lick her bare shoulder and taste it. "I thought you wanted to dance."

He slipped his hands round to the small of her back and locked his fingers, pulling her into his chest. Her skin felt dry, not moist as he had expected. Tightening his grip he felt her breasts pressing against him.

"Give me a bit of air, Ben."

Her head was at his neck and the words were a light breeze on his skin. To accompany them there was a tremor of her body and he decided she was hassled by his move. Looking down he saw a flash of anger in her face and loosened his grip.

"Come Sophie, dance."

"We can dance but this is more like a hug. I don't like being mauled."

She was trying to back away into the crowd and he put a hand out to her but the space she was leaving was suddenly occupied, like sand filling a hole. Mike was in front of him, shouting.

"We got a fucking major problem, boy." His face was sweating, the skin rubbery.

"I got a major problem wid my date, man. She jus blow me out."

"This is for real, man. Look at me! There's a thousand police outside and they are seriously pissed off."

It wasn't sinking in. The deep pulse of reggae was booming in his ears and he could just see her starting up the stairs. "Wha? You deal wid it, Mikey."

"They want to see both of us now." Mike was forcing his way through the crowd, heading back towards the entrance. "Ben, don't fuck me about."

He broke his stare and joined him. "I ave time to speak wid her later. Policeman ave to take priority."

Curtis came over to her at the dressing table and softly bit into her neck. "We ave time before we go."

They were going round to a friend of hers for dinner and were already running late. His hands slipped inside the dress and pushed round to her chest. Amanda was checking her lips in the mirror, still applying the colour, and his caress caused her to fumble. Any other time she would have laughed and turned to kiss him, maybe even encouraged him in his actions but she had put up with his mood for the last hour and was getting irritated. Since his arrival he had paced the flat restlessly and only answered her enquiries with terse replies. She knew something was troubling him.

"So all of a sudden you want to make love? What's with you tonight?"

"Nothing. I jus want you, that all."

"Come on, Curtis." She pushed him away and went back to her make-up. "You can tell me you know. I want to know if you've got a problem."

"I told you. Nothing is wrong."

"So why are you shouting at me, then?"

How could he tell her that since meeting Sophie that afternoon he had thought of nothing but spending a few days in bed with her? He could still remember her every movement. If he made love with Amanda, then it might be forgotten but the thought of the girl was scaring him. He had been faithful for months, not even considered another.

"Jus leave it will you?" He approached her again, kissing the back of her head.

"That does no good in a row, Curtis."

"It's all I want right now."

"Well, thankyou." She dropped the lipstick and glared at him. "Just leave me alone if you don't want to talk. I'll go on my own."

"You do that."

He went over to the door, paused to look at her back and seeing her pick up the lipstick again went on down the stairs. At the bottom he waited again, to see if she called. He knew she was stubborn and would let him go. This was what he feared most. The thought that he might have staged the row subconsciously in order to have the evening free terrified him. What he had enjoyed with Amanda was rare and he knew it might be disastrous to turn up at the club. It was so tempting. There was Ben to think of as well, though he knew no woman was very special to him. There was only one other choice.

He walked over to the car and climbed in. After checking he had enough in his wallet he started the engine and thought for a second what the quickest route to the den was from here. That was a guiltless release for his desire.

The two partners sat there in silence. Hargreaves was doing all the talking.

"Now see reason, officer . . ."

"Detective."

"There's no point doing a check with all those people in the hall. It could be an awful mistake."

"You know I should do."

"Detective, there's never been any trouble at the club. If we sit it out . . ."

Hargreaves had only turned up because one of his staff had rung him a few hours ago to let him know they were past the club record. He had come over to count the attendance figures and was greedily thinking of doubling the rent when the police turned up. Now he thought he was handling the situation but the policeman spotted him as a fool and turned to where they were sitting at the desk.

"You see the problem we've got?"

Ben just stared at him. He was still thinking of Sophie and even if he had not had that as a distraction he wouldn't have paid much attention. When a policeman started to talk he turned off; it was the best way to deal with them he found. That way they were never part of the real world. This one didn't look too bad. He was middle-aged, big and fleshy, wearing a straight blue suit. His saving grace was that they could tell he was just as bored as they were, stuck in the dusty office. So he wasn't on some power drive at least.

"You're well over the numbers. I'd shut you but I understand there's some music act on, is that right?"

"Yeah, you're well informed. If you shut now you may have some real angry people to deal with." Mike tried his best to emphasise the risk. Shutting concerts down was never a good idea.

"Oh, relax. I'm going to wait now until he's finished. Then you can close. Just do it quick. To tell you the truth . . ." He went back to the side of the desk and sat down. "If I'd come across this on my own I would have squeezed you till the shit came out." He had moved his face close to theirs and almost hissed the words out. "As it is, I don't really care. Someone set you up tonight."

"You fucking wha?" Ben had spoken. He knew it was best to keep quiet but that only went so far. His temper was under strain tonight.

"You heard me, then? Thought you were deaf and dumb. Someone said you been taking the piss with the attendance and getting easy with smoking and the like. I was going to check you out in a week or two but had to follow this up. Don't like doing a club on a lead, usually helping out some other bastard with a grudge. Anyway, I don't need the grief tonight, so have the music, then get everyone out. Get me? We can do a tally as they leave."

"Sure."

They stood to go, Ben showing no sign of emotion but Mike obviously thankful the interview was over.

"Bit young to be running a club aren't you? Specially one doing this sort of trade."

"An' you not a bit old to be tackling the bad man every day?"

The policeman almost smiled as he ushered them out with a profane gesture of his hand.

There were only two or three people in the first room so he went straight through to the bar. The usual crew was missing, leaving only a few drinkers scattered round the room. Two girls were serving.

Curtis had a clear idea what he wanted but was confused by his feelings. It was not in his nature to question his actions but as he climbed onto a stool he felt his head spinning with questions. Did this mean it was over with Amanda just because he found another girl attractive? Maybe he had been kidding himself all along with her. And was Sophie such a temptation? He ordered a drink and rested his chin across his arm, wishing for clarity. Recent months had been so easy with Amanda.

"Something get to you, C?" It was Stefan, leaning at the bar next to him.

"Fuck, I never hear you."

"I have to be light on my feet. Comes with the job."

He let out a low chuckle and Curtis noticed he looked a mess compared to his usual sartorial perfection. "Look like something get to you, boy."

"Ah, I been up for a while, that's all. You sound well fucked-off."

"It nothing."

Stefan eyed him for a second, checking him over. "You fall out with the woman? The ideal woman."

"Maybe. What's it to you? I paid in, boy. You had your flesh from me already, so don't think you got to act concerned. An' don give me this 'ideal' shit."

"Easy. I know what it's like, that's all. You should take your mind off it. Sometimes you got to remember what you got."

"Yeah?"

The girl was over with his drink and as she laid it on the bar Stefan took hold of her wrist, so tightly Curtis could see the red imprint on her skin next to his fingers.

"You just come on?"

"Yes, sir."

"Then go up to your room. Number . . ."

"Number three one, sir."

"Go on, then."

She went back to the rear of the bar and spoke with the other girl serving before leaving through a small door. After a moment another figure emerged and started patrolling the bar.

"Now, Stefan . . ."

"That's what you wanted. Don't kid me, it's my occupation. Just go and let off some steam or whatever you do."

He was gone with the same quiet steps as before and Curtis turned back to his drink. When he had sipped the glass dry he walked through the gloom back to the lounge and took a few steps up to another door. There was a square of wire-meshed safety glass set into it and he could see a dim corridor running off into the dark. It reminded him of another time in his life. He pushed through.

It took him a few turns and lots more steps to find her number and he realised he must be on the third floor of the house, above ground though there were no windows. He felt as though he should have been taking the steps down; the symbolism was not lost on him. He hadn't really noticed what the girl looked like and this too struck him as fate. He was going on blind impulse.

When he reached her room the door was open and he hung at the entrance. She was on the bed, adjusting one of the straps that was part of the lingerie she wore. It was pearl white. The same colour as her skin in the faint light from the bedside lamp.

"You don need all that."

"Most people like it." Her voice saddened him. There was no element of excitement or eagerness in the flat tone.

"Take it off."

With a flick of her legs she snapped her body back and rolled the fabric from her body, then pulled at her bra, smiling at him all the time. She was pretty, with long dark hair.

Curtis went to a corner of the room and removed his jacket. Then he slipped off his shoes and stepped out of his trousers, draping them over a chair. He joined her kneeling on the bed. Her fingers were straight to his waist, searching. One hand held the plastic ring that she planned to dress him with. There was nothing there to indicate his excitement.

"You don't like me?"

The body was perfect, toned and full. If he had seen her in the street he would have happily imagined wasting an afternoon in bed with her but here in this service chamber his flesh was cold and he found her attempts to arouse him disgusting.

"This is a mistake. I shouldn't be here." He pushed her away and went back to his clothes.

"Will you say . . ."

"Nothing, don't worry. Here." From his wallet he took a

twenty and dropped it on the bed's yellowing sheet. "Have a drink on me."

The audience were starting to bellow over the music. Lucien was going on in a few minutes and they could scent it, like an animal smelling blood. Mike and Ben had retreated to the Basement for liquid fortification.

"We're fucked now, you know. When they all leave he'll have a few hundred over the limit."

"We can sort it out, Mikey. Keep drinking, you'll feel better." He was checking faces, looking out for Sophie.

Mike spotted him. "The girl can fucking wait. What we gonna do? Someone fucking stitched us."

"Let's jus make sure everything go smooth. We be alright. Is things we can do to find out about that. I'm more worried about what they're gonna make of his act."

"Oh. Don't worry about that. He'll blow the roof."

"Exactly." At last his gaze located her. She was pressed in a corner, drinking from a bottle and talking with a white guy he didn't recognise. "I see her, man. Take it easy."

"Ben! Ben, for fuck's sake." His friend was off into the crowd. Mike reflected that the only way he was going to be able to deal with the coming hour was to be in the company of Alfred and his expensive wares. He started pretending to sing, confident no one could hear over all the noise in the room. "Powderman come, come down again."

They were talking about some design company or something, the guy trying to impress her. Ben didn't like the way he looked.

"Hey, Sophie. I'm sorry about that. Just finished talking with the police and I couldn't find you anywhere."

"Forget it."

"Who's this?" He turned to the youth.

"My name's Stuart."

"Well, why don't you jus take a walk off to the boy's room or summat, Stuart?"

"Sorry?" He sounded full of feeble outrage, shocked that he could be insulted this way.

The girl sprang to his defence. "Stuart's an old friend of mine, Ben. I don't know what's got into you tonight but you're getting on my nerves."

This couldn't be true. He had thought the guy was hassling her or something. Ben tried to keep his cool but the strain of the evening was getting to him. "Oh, I apologise. Look. Sophie. I wanted a chance to speak with you an' . . ."

There was no time to finish the sentence and soften her appalled look. A weight of bodies pushed behind him and he was swept down the stairs as though by a tide of water. Lucien had taken the stage.

Ben was brought into the middle of the hall, carried by the flood from the Basement. Somewhere behind him, Sophie was being dragged by the flow and he tried to get back to her but it was too tight to move. At this point he stopped caring. There was a guy next to him smoking a draw and Ben had it stuck in his face. He took it and pulled deep, letting the drug raid his lungs and level the mood. Enough was enough. There had been too much hassle already this evening. He had promised to watch the act and Lucien was up there now, pacing to and fro, full of energy. The crowd roared for him to start.

"It get hot tonight."

The DJ cut in behind him. Ben could just make out Alfred and Mike up in the box but could hardly get an arm free to wave. The crowd had gone wild as the music came in, moving like one huge clumsy dancer. There was a crush at the front of the stage as they surged forward and he saw a few people getting pulled out, gasping for air. The lights were down and all he could hear was the rumble of bass from the boxes on the floor. Then with a blaze of reds, blues and greens the stage was flooded with light and Lucien started his rap. It was thick, melodic and indecipherable and the crowd loved it. They bayed like hounds. He saw some of the girls around him trying to drop low with the music but the press of bodies made it hard to crouch. At times he felt his feet lift off the floor for a few seconds as the crowd surged and it was so tight he thought he would pop out like a cork under the pressure. A person of a sensitive disposition would have fainted but Ben was loving it. After all the stress of the police threat, the breakdown with the girl and the informant coming to light he was glad to be able to relax in the lunacy of the crowd. Ben settled into the draw and the music.

Sophie was closer to the wall. It was not as bad here but she was still hemmed in by bodies and she shut her eyes to block it out. She felt alone and scared in the sway of the crowd.

"Sophie, you alright?"

Someone was shaking her, big hands on her bare skin.

"Say something to me!"

"I'm fine, really." She looked up to see Curtis standing over her, concern in his eyes.

"Come then. I been looking for you. Couldn't stay away."

Without saying a word she took his hand and followed his strides through the mass.

Lucien was active. His arms twirled and he ran about the stage, encouraging them to heights of mania in a language they didn't understand. It was of no importance, the energy was enough. The music was hard beats with samples and Ben spotted a few of the lifts from current tracks. After five minutes he was shouting praise himself.

"Go, Lucien. Big up fo the man, sah."

There was a flash from the back of the hall. It lit up the roof like an arc light. At first Ben thought it was some elaborate light trick Mike hadn't mentioned to him but then he heard the screaming. After that he smelt something. It was a strange sensation: not just like breathing a scent but feeling it reach up into your head and start burying into the brain. Then he felt dizzy and his eyes were burning. They were dry, like chalk cracking. It hurt. He knew what it was as he had come across it in a frenzied street fight one time. It was CS gas.

By this stage he knew they had a problem. With the hall this crowded, people were going to get hurt as they tried to escape. The gas was an effective weapon in a space like this and Ben cursed at the saboteur. Already there was a movement in the crowd. The odour was sweeping up towards the stage, where because of the added height from the floor Lucien's outfit had not become aware of it and were still playing. It only added to the mounting feeling of chaos as more people started screaming over the music. Ben struggled to get over to the steps for the Basement, thinking it would be an unlikely destination for the fleeing crowd and he might therefore stand a chance of getting out of the main room. That was when things got worse.

There was another flash of light, except this time it came from above stage left, where the top bar was. It had burst out of the Basement. This time there was noise, a powerful blast that made his ears scream. It was what he imagined a bomb would sound like when it detonated. Then after the sound, as time stretched with his fear, part of the wall mushroomed out and turned to dust. Pieces of wood and timber showered the crowd.

Now there was real panic. After hearing the blast, the police were rushing in as the crowd tried to escape and the glass door at the rear of the hall jammed. Someone smashed a pane of the glass with his heel and started to crawl through but got caught on the glass teeth still fixed in the door frame. The blood made people slip on the wooden floor. Ben couldn't move in the crush. The house lights came on and the music died, calming things a little, but all around him there was havoc.

Diving into the crowd he made it to the stage and followed the boards off to the right wall. The steps up to the Basement were intact but covered in glass and other debris. It was clear there was little point heading that way. He was just under the DJ booth and he called up for Mike or Alfred, his voice sounding tiny under the din.

"Mike, you still up there?"

His friend stuck a hand over the rim of the box and pulled his body up.

"Mike, lift me up now."

Despite the horror of the last few minutes, Ben wanted to laugh. Mike looked unhurt but dazed. He was staring about the hall with wide eyes, his hair snow-white from the dust of the explosion.

"Mike, you turn Santa Claus."

"What the fuck happened, boy?"

"Here, give me your hand."

He came round to the lip of the stage and crouched down so Ben could take his hand. It took a few attempts but he was soon hoisted up.

"Where the band, then?"

Mike still looked freaked and it took him a moment to formulate a sentence. "Think they ran backstage when they got the gas hit, just before the blow. There's no bodies lying about anyway."

"Alfred?"

"He's hiding in the box, getting charged."

Ben surveyed the hall. Most people were clustered at the rear, trickling through the door which had been freed now, but others were sitting by the walls or tending to injured friends. A feeling of quiet had come down after the mad noise of earlier. Police were strolling around looking over the damage and he could see the diminutive figure of Hargreaves, arms flapping in despair by the entrance.

"So Mike. What you say?"

Mike was clearly awe-struck by the situation and just looked at him open-mouthed. As he moved his head, little clouds of dust broke from his hair and the sweat on his face was leaving streaks in the grey make-up.

"Someone blow up the club, Ben. What a dis."

Twelve

There was silence between them all the way back to his flat. Curtis knew he was walking close to the edge but he felt carried along by some force, powerless to break the ride. When they were inside he collapsed on the sofa and tried to speak. "Sophie this is crazy. I'm happy with . . ."

Kneeling next to him she lifted a finger to his lips, then leaned forward. "Why are we here then? Just do what you feel is right."

Taking her hand away she moved her head closer. He could hear the rush of his breathing as though the room was airless. There was no thought now. He pushed towards her but she suddenly lay back on the leather, encouraging him. The cotton top she wore rolled up to her neck and he pressed his face into the soft warmth of her breasts, letting his hands drift to the shorts. He peeled them down to her knees and she shook her legs, trying to remove them, but he quickly lifted her legs as one, held together by the taut fabric. She saw his aim and obliged, resting them bound across his right shoulder. Seizing the top he tugged it over her head and around her arms so that they were stretched away from her by the action. By twisting it, they too were clamped together. Now he pushed against the bonded legs so her knees bent back and brushed at her breast. She panted at the constriction, felt his fingers play with her and fumble at his waist for a few seconds, then the shock of entry. A rush of air broke her lips in a cry as he pushed deep into her.

The discomfort of her position was replaced by a flood of pleasure but after a minute of him inside her she lifted her head to his ear and whispered. "You're forgetting something, I think. I know it's not very appealing and why it's me who has to say . . ."

"Relax."

"Can I?"

Her words had not broken his feeling for her. He found the soft enquiry attractive. She was sweetly concerned.

"I've had to get used to it. I'm old enough to dress myself, you know."

He could hear voices from the kitchen. It was Mike and the familiar bark of his own father. Sighing, he dragged some clothes on, wiped his face with the back of a hand and walked through.

"Lord, you get up. We gonna wake you soon if you no move." His father was excited. Ben had been away, enjoying his freedom but now he was back; the prodigal needed help. "You sleep all right?"

"Can believe mampy still rest up in ma bed?"

Mike sniggered, too embarrassed to laugh out loud.

"You talk like that in my house again an' you can go back to your burn-out place. Talk bout gal that way."

So Mike had told him about the flat being gutted.

"Have a drink fo me?" He was waking up now and remembered the details of the night before. "Need a coffee. What you say then, Mike? Thought we'd never get away from policeman last night."

"It was me who stuck around. You were only there for a while."

"So whappen anyway? They close us?"

"Me an' Mike been talking bout it all."

"Yeah? Should a guessed you'd have some advice for us."

Mike sat down at the table and took a tattered scrap of paper from his pocket. He peered at it before speaking. "If we can raise a bit of cash, put some time in, we might be able to go for next week."

"After the place blow up like that?"

"Nah. It's mainly our flat and the bar that were trashed. An' they're not even that bad. We can fix the bar easy. I made a list of the immediate costs."

"Police man, them. They no wanna close it, them?"

"They weren't happy but there's not much they can do. The 'bomb' was a gas tin left by a heater . . ."

"That fuckrie, it a sabotage, man."

"Boy, you watch your language or I clip you."

"I know that an' so do they but there was no foreign device so they can't prove intent. It'll go down as an accident. Insurance may cover most of it. The gear's all fine and Hargreaves thinks it might even be good publicity."

"Wha?"

"Only cause he's putting the bill up. He's just using it as an excuse. Anyway, I got another band. Alfred's with us, so we carry on."

"Course. You don't think we gonna rest up or summat."

Mike looked thoughtful for a second. "It was a clear message, you know. Someone saying pack it in. I think that fight you were in may have some part in it too."

"A ras. No threat stopping us, boy. We check with Curtis, he can sort it out."

"I've called him this morning but his phone's out. We need some money, Ben."

"You ave none?"

Mike shook his head.

"I'm nearly broke myself. You in the car?"

"Sure."

"Let's go round his yard there. Him probly jus sleeping anyway. I wanna ask him if he can find out anything bout all this. You see him last night?"

"Nah. Too much going on."

They both stood to leave and Ben lifted a foot onto the chair he had vacated to fiddle with his laces.

"Ben, boy, long as you here, you respect the furniture."

They walked out laughing.

Despite their enthusiasm for getting the club going, both Ben and Mike knew there were problems to overcome. Curtis was their first choice for help when things got tough.

"How much we need, then?"

Mike was driving fast, trying to cut round the highstreet traffic. "Bout a grand, I think."

"A grand?" When Ben first started taking the money from the club he found the quality of his life had soared but after a few weeks he was spending what he earned. With recent events a thousand seemed a lot. "Spose if we need it, we ave to get it."

"Think he'll lend it to us?"

"No problem. He's the bank manager, remember. We jus go in and make a withdrawal."

The car was noisy, the engine growling at Mike's request. "You know, Ben, we haven't sat down for a chat in ages. We should get out again, chill somewhere."

"Was the party."

"Yeah, but that was a rare event. What you say to a day out somewhere?"

"Day out where, rasta? You know me no country boy." Ben got nervous if he saw nothing but grass. Brick and stone was his familiar habitat and he was no fan of the great outdoors. "We should have a day out to Bliss or somewhere, that a good place to visit."

"Nah, we should get out of town."

"Mikey, the club almost fuckin' blew up last night. I was nearly crushed to death an' you talk about a ras picnic. We ave things to do, boy."

"Take it easy, it wasn't so bad. I'm thinking more about what'll happen next time if we don't find out who we're dealing with."

"Yeah, well settle down. C can sniff that out fo we."

"So, let's just head out for a day. I've got the car now, fancy taking her for a spin."

"Taking it for a roll you mean, boy. You drive reckless. I tellin' you."

Mike wasn't listening. "The open road, fresh air. Fuck, man, we could head for the sea or somewhere . . ."

"You fuck now, cold on the coast, man."

"Couple a girls maybe, bit a draw."

"Hmm. It get better."

"We could get C to come with Amanda in his car, make it a party. Sophie . . ."

"Fucking Sophie disappear last night, man, she not interested."

"Well, she might be interested in a day out though."

Ben thought it over for a second. The thought of the girl made him feel positive, even in connection with a trip out to the wilds. "Maybe. Me think it over." They were getting close to the apartment and Ben changed to thoughts of a tactic to secure the loan.

"Yeah, we could get out one day this week. Sweet . . ."

"Never mind that now. We need some notes first, so prepare yo flattery."

"But you will think about it?"

"Cha. I ring the gal an' see what she wanna do. If yes, then I come along."

"Right. I'll talk with Celia."

"Await. Me ave dealings with her, you know? I mean, me cool an' all bout you an' her but I don't know about her meeting Sophie furthering a man's cause, you follow me."

"Water under the bridge, boy."

"Nah, gal talk, boy."

"I sort it out. It won't trouble you, I promise you."

"Think it a joke, rasta?"

"It'll be fine. I'll organise it all." Mike found a space and pulled over, just a few houses from the apartment.

"Man I ave too much on my mind for this. You deal with it an' I stay here."

"His car's here an' he never walks, so he's in. Come on. Time to get down on our knees. The both of us."

Ben climbed out and followed him over to the doorway. They stared at one another, then Mike moved his hand to press the bell.

Curtis was staring at the mirror on the far side of his living room, thinking of all the other times he had studied it after sex. It was the same as ever: two figures stuck together, on the bed, framed by the arch. Though they were new to each other it had been smooth, fluid, and he stroked her hair with easy intimacy.

"You sleep well?" Her voice surprised him as he had thought she was still slumbering.

"Yeah, an' you?"

"A bit surprised when I woke up. Thought I was at home for a moment. I'm not sure if last night was very sensible . . . but I'm glad it happened so . . ."

"You sound indecisive."

"No, I'm just confused."

"Isn't that the same thing?"

"Curtis, I've just woken up." Already it was hot. The room had the musty tang of sex. "You got a bath?"

"Yeah, why?"

"We can have a bath together."

"Oh, I don't know . . ."

She was off the bed and tiptoeing across the carpet, covering her nudity with her hands. Half-way across the room she looked back at him with a smile. "Come on. I want you to scrub my back."

At this he sprang from the bed and chased after her but she doubled back on him and got the bathroom door shut before he could catch her.

She shouted to him though the thin wooden panel. "Make me some coffee and I'll let you in."

He heard the taps being turned and the trickle of water. "Deal. Don't forget to put some bubble in though."

He laughed and headed for the kitchen, flicking the radio on as he went by. Until her dash for the bathroom he had felt almost sombre, as though he had lost something in the night but his humour had returned after the chase and he started moving to the slow beat coming out of the speakers as he prepared the drink. He could keep Amanda as his partner and still enjoy Sophie's nimble charms occasionally. It occurred to him how perfect their respective bodies were. The mild buzz of conquest he always had from experiencing another woman was interrupted by the thought of the wet skin that awaited him and he hurried in the kitchen. Loading a jug of coffee, orange juice, milk and cups onto a tin tray he went over towards the bathroom, stopping at the stereo midway. The DJ had changed to playing a soft soul track he hated and there was a CD he had in mind that was more appropriate for the present situation. It was too heavy to hold the tray with one hand so he put it down on the carpet and threw the curtains open for some light. Ben was staring at him through the glass.

"Curtis, man. Park your dick there!"

He shut the curtains and heard the peels of laughter from his doorstep.

"Pussyclat!"

He had to let them in. If they had just rung the bell he would have ignored it but they'd seen him now and he cursed softly whilst dressing. It was not only that Ben was supposedly interested in the girl who was currently preparing herself for his sexual delectation in the bathroom but also the threat of a leak to Amanda if he found out. Curtis was well aware of the limitless power of gossip when it was spoken by a bitter tongue. However, there was something he could try. He could appeal to the male code. He opened the front door a crack.

"Boys, bad time to talk."

"You ave Amanda in there?"

"Well . . ."

"C, you play away? You greedy man."

Ben was smiling but Mike hadn't flinched. He still had their mission in mind. "We have to talk, C. There's been some real shit going on down the club and we need your help."

"Fuck, you laying it on a bit thick, Mike. I got a woman in here." Here was the 'code' attempt. How could anything take priority over his fleshly pursuits? He was whispering, to stress the inconvenience. "Give me a couple a hours, then I'll meet you. Down Bliss, yeah?"

"Well, I think we should talk now . . ."

"Oh, give him a break, Mike. You should know what it's like, though I am surprised at you, boy. Thought you were tight with the girl?"

At least it was working with Ben. "It jus a physical thing, man."

"Yeah, me know bout them ting."

Mike was huffing. "Right, so now you don't think it matters some fucker tries to blow us up an' gasses the place?"

"Wha? Down the club?" His body tensed but he showed no drastic reaction and he fought the feeling of blame that was flooding over him. Why hadn't he said anything when it might have been of use? These were his friends. Ben leapt in again with the code logic before he could speak.

"He's right though. We tell him all about it later. No hassle for we to wait two, three hours. Curtis we need some money, man."

"Safe."

"There you go, Mikey. We see you in two hour when you finish your duty here, boy. Alright?"

"Sweet, yeah."

"Let's go."

Mike looked unhappy about it but managed to grin. He was new to it after all. Curtis remembered.

"Two hours. Till then you ave fun."

They vanished into the street and when he heard their engine fire up he came back inside to where he had left the tray, throwing his clothes off along the way. The news about the club left him feeling hollow but it was too late for him to tell them about Bunny's warning now. *What the fuck is wrong with you lately*?

He put it to the back of his mind. They obviously weren't hurt and he would help out later to make up for it. It took him a second to forget, then Curtis thought of the irony that Ben had talked himself out of discovering Sophie in the bathtub. *Crazy planet, man.*

There was a splash from behind the door and he bent down to pick up the tray. He remembered her promise and all thoughts of the club vanished. *Boy, your mood up and down like a fuckin yo-yo these day.*

When he stood up, she was in the doorway, her skin pink from the heat of the water. She was still wet. A dollop of white foam covered her, gradually sliding down her body. He gazed at it, thinking how wonderful gravity was.

"Why you taking so long?" Then she started laughing, raising a hand to cover her mouth.

"What's so funny?"

"You look like a butler with that tray."

"Really."

"Yeah, a rather excitable butler actually."

He stepped towards her, thinking only of the infinite possibilities open to them in the next two hours.

They were in a booth when he came in, sipping at small glasses. He was on time but only because she had to get back herself for an afternoon party. Otherwise he would have found it difficult to make the right time, if at all. Sophie was a far more appealing concept than that of facing up to the vague feelings of guilt he was suffering from.

"Wha you drinking, C?"

"Oh, I'll have a white coffee." He sat down opposite them and pulled his jacket off.

"Have a man's drink, man. Buy you a brandy."

"Yeah, maybe I'm gonna need a drink, now I think of it. How much money you need?"

Mikey was straight in, gesturing the importance of their

predicament with wild motions of his hands. "It's a bit desperate, Curtis. In order to open this week, an' both of us have decided that no fucker is just gonna shut us down like this, then we can get going right off just with some notes up front. It's just expenses like the band and some of the staff. It cost us a bit last night as you can imagine . . ."

"Shut up for a minute, Mike. What happened last night, Ben?"

Ben explained the whole series of events and Curtis blew a tiny sigh of relief. There had been no sighting of himself mentioned and the bouncers would probably have forgotten letting him in after the chaos of the evening. He also noted that there was no gunplay. This made him feel a little better as at least there had been no direct attack on them individually.

"How much money you need? Await, before you tell me, better bring me that drink you a talk about."

Ben went over to the bar and Mike spoke up when he was out of earshot.

"Curtis."

"Yeah."

"Wanna ask you about something else."

There was a second of fear. Maybe Mike was in on it.

"You still seeing Amanda?"

A siren was screaming in his head. It must have been when they were leaving the club. It was best not to say anything and let him come out with what he knew.

"Only, we've been talking about a day out in the country or something. If you're seeing someone else, she can come along, I guess. I've been working on Ben but you know what a lazy bastard he is about things like that. What you think?"

"That'd be great, Mike. I am still with Amanda by the way and it sounds like a healthy idea, man. Count us in." Three cheers for secrecy.

"I didn't mean to say that, just you know . . ."

"Safe, Mike."

"One day this week, then. Another thing as well. I would prefer it if you didn't tell me to be quiet. Gets on my tits."

The note of pride in Mike's voice amused him. "Safe, Mike."

Ben was back with three glasses. He laid them down on the table. "We need a grand."

"And we need you to find out who fucked us about last night. You can ask around, can't you?"

"The money's cool. I don't know about the detective work though. You know it's not really my business."

"You must be able to ask though?"

"Well, I see. I get you the money soon though."

"Can make 'soon' today?"

"It a Sunday, man. Wha you wan me a do?"

"You ave money at the flat though. We need to get moving, man, an' it hard to track you down sometime."

He stared at them both.

"Why your fate always in my hands? Right, I ave money at the flat but me no sure how much, mind. We drop by now cause I ave things to do later." He had told Sophie he would be round at her house in the evening. Ostensibly it was to discuss their future relationship but he was in the mood for another bath. "Come now . . ."

Curtis was no slouch. They had to race to keep up with his car and were back at the flat in minutes. After finding a space they walked up his path and through the door, which he had left open for them. Their friend was by the far wall, hands dipping into a steel box he had pulled from under the bed. The air smelt of perfume.

"Gal smell strong, boy."

"That's freshener from an aerosol actually." He stood up and walked past them over to a chest of drawers. "You should check it before." Now he had picked up an envelope and was trying to open it with his damaged hand whilst holding a clump of notes.

"Me help you."

"Nah, it's alright." He stuffed the money inside and faced them. "A grand. Spend it as you will but I want it back. One month, that fair?"

"Couldn't be fairer."

The package was extended and Mike took it.

"Now, if you two can leave me, I have a girl to catch up with."

They all chuckled at the remark.

"She's here already, Curtis. You're spared the trouble of finding me." Amanda was at the door, nervously stepping into the room. "Hope I'm not disturbing you. The door was open. Thought you'd been burgled or something." She laughed but they were all silent, staring at her. "What's the matter?"

Ben broke the calm. "Nothing. You surprised us, that's all. How are you?"

"I'm well."

"Sadly we have to leave but you take it easy, yeah?"

They were making for the door and she stepped out of their way, over to the sofa where she sat down. Curtis thought how beautiful she looked just in a T-shirt and jeans and found the memory of his contorted mistress squealing on the same sofa a bit disturbing.

Mike suddenly changed course and approached her. "Sure Curtis'll tell you but we're planning a day out somewhere. Maybe down to the coast or somewhere out of town anyway. I can let you . . ."

"Sounds great, Mike. I'll come along. I'm off work for a while, so anytime."

"And Ben was gonna ask Sophie along."

No, it can't be true. He can't have said that.

"Oh, I'll give her a ring about it. We got on pretty well. Yeah, I'd really like that."

The tinkle of imaginary ringing haunted him like the sound of an executioner sharpening his axe. She had the number.

"We can sort it out tomorrow, better go."

Ben was through the door and Mike followed, nodding goodbye. Curtis went after them to lock it and take a gulp of air.

"Curtis, boy."

"Yes, Ben."

"Hope your strength up, boy."

They laughed and walked over to the car. He steeled himself for the confrontation and went back into the flat.

She was gone. He scanned the room, puzzled, then saw the mound of her clothes on the sofa.

"Oh, Curtis."

It was her sex voice, coming from behind him. He flicked his head round and her lips were cemented on his. Holding her he felt the brush of her bare skin and managed to break free from the embrace. "A minute, baby . . ."

"I turned you away last night for no reason except you wanted to make love to me and it was inconvenient, a hassle. I was wrong and know I should value our love-making more than I do. I put other things before it so . . ."

He had been thinking of telling her straight, coming clear. *Amanda, I fucked some other girl last night.* His mouth wasn't working though. The words were alien, he could never say them. It was like trying to speak Martian. Her soft form was dropping to his waist, expert fingers undressing him, and already she was stroking his flesh.

"Let me make it up to you."

Then she could speak no more but he had lost interest in conversation himself.

Thirteen

The doors to the garden were open and he lay on the sofa, letting the breeze rush across his face. It was stifling in the room so even though he was only wearing knee shorts and a loose T-shirt his body felt heavy and wet in the heat. "Harvey, the sweat must be running round your balls."

"You mean from the temperature?"

He twisted his head and stared at the man in the suit sitting in a chair opposite. His temple was bone dry. "I don't think I've ever heard you try and be funny before. You must be nervous. Considering your actions . . ."

"My boy . . ."

"Your boy . . ." Kimps sat up stiffly and glared at the youth standing in the corner of the room. He was reminded of a guilty schoolboy by his stance. "Is hardly the most subtle emissary. In a way though, that makes for a more interesting field. They'll be on guard for me now. I did think you might have had a bit more imagination though. A couple of gas canisters and some pathetic cracker . . ."

"They're not going to open. Not after last night."

"We'll see." He stretched his long frame, stood up, then paced over to the table in the garden to mix himself a drink. They had to sit in silence until his return. "Letting the police know was particularly stupid. Give it a couple of days and they'll be running again."

"I scared em good." Ralph had said nothing up until this. He found the American's manner arrogant and wondered why Harvey was so subservient to his outbursts. His voice was harsh, thin and aggressive, directly opposed to the slow, deep tones of Kimps.

"Shut up, dick." Kimps spoke with no hint of a threat in his voice. They were about the same age but Kimps had more respect for a piece of furniture. So used to commanding others, he found Ralph inconsequential and had only asked Harvey to bring him here to increase his mentor's embarrassment. The plan had clearly been adapted by Ralph. Harvey was no fool but he had to take the blame.

"You don't speak to me like that, you fuck."

Kimps flashed a look at Harvey, to see if he would speak, reprimand his hired help, but saw that the older man had drawn some amusement from the insult. There was a tiny smile curling on his lips.

"Big talk but do you really wanna play?" The attack from Ralph had surprised him but Kimps was not agitated. He stepped towards him, relaxed. It was the insult of silence from Harvey that had annoyed him. "If you're pissed, then do something." He stood with his face a few inches from Ralph, who was looking to Harvey for guidance.

"I can't touch you . . ."

"That's right." Harvey had whispered the words from his

chair without even looking at the two. There could be no actual conflict allowed.

"Oh, don't spoil the fun, Harvey. I give you . . . permission to allow your poodle a fair fight. If he wants it anyway."

Kimps was still amused, sipping at his drink. He had savoured the words, knowing how they would infuriate.

"I'm tempted by your offer I must say but . . ."

"Fuck you, Harvey. Go on, Ralph. Try it."

Ralph paused, still unsure how to act. Kimps was so close, holding a glass with one hand.

"Alright, Ralph."

Harvey had only muttered the words and Ralph lashed out. His fist went flying into empty space though, as Kimps had bent his tall frame to one side. He tried to grab him, keep it close but the American took three steps back and dropped his glass.

"Go, Harvey with the fighting talk."

Ralph was trying to corner him but Kimps kept to the open, his hands raised so one arm was out straight in front of him, the other locked to his stomach. His feet made light steps from side to side and his movements were sharp, almost delicate.

"Go on, Ralph. Do 'im."

The year of servitude, taking it from the youth, had made Harvey bitter. He tried to curb his mouth but the thought of Kimps getting battered was too appealing. Already he was thinking of explaining it to his father as some kind of accident and Kimps would probably be too ashamed to accuse him directly.

Ralph threw two light, tracer punches but Kimps dodged them. He was quick and confident, smiling at his attacker. "You heard the man, Ralph. Gotta keep him happy, haven't you?"

The reference to Harvey as his boss angered him and he

rushed forward, thinking he could finish it close. That was how Ralph had learnt to fight. From the playground to the street, then to the bar-rooms and clubs as he matured, the rule was to hold your man, hamper movement, hit him, choke him, bite him. There was no such thing as a clean fight for Ralph. He had only seen viciousness and brute strength triumph. Bring him down quick, hurt him. Most fights were won on the first blow.

His arms tried to sweep around him and he brought a knee up to connect if he could trap the upper body. At the same time Kimps seemed to freeze in terror, his eyes wide open and body tense as the arms locked around his chest. Ralph clenched his muscles and squeezed but felt his leg blocked by something. Kimps had turned his body. He was now shoulder-on to Ralph's chest.

Through the thin fabric of his shirt he felt the sweep of a hand up his back, light like the passage of an insect. It clamped onto the back of his head, fingers buried in his hair and then his neck braced against a downward pull. Kimps was laughing as he tugged at the hair, easily over-powering the other man. Ralph decided to break away but it was too late. He saw the cream carpet rushing towards him and then howled in pain as his face hit. Kimps had turned and fallen on to his back, using his body weight to increase the impact.

It was a soft surface but the bones in his nose cracked and he tasted blood. Before he could react to the pain, Kimps rolled off him and stood, not even panting from the exertion or heat. His hands dropped back to the same position, one in front, one to defend. It was at this point that Ralph knew he was doomed. The repeat of the fighting stance was a clear sign the American was a trained fighter. As he lifted his body, pushing away from the floor with his hands, Kimps stepped next to him neatly and kicked him in the side of the head. His leg was a blur and only extended for a second but when the victim's head snapped back into position Harvey could see the tread marks of the trainers Kimps wore on Ralph's cheek, such was the force. Ralph passed out without a sound. His heavy gulps of breath were the only sign he was still alive.

"Not your day, Ralph, I'm afraid. I did like your eagerness at my little act of being worried to death though. That always gets em, Harvey." Kimps maintained his stance until he was sure Ralph was out, then relaxed and sauntered back to the garden area.

As he left the room, Harvey cursed and rushed over to where Ralph was lying. He had to move him to clear the blood that was flooding his air passages. When he was sure he could breathe he stepped out to the garden himself, walked past Kimps, who was sprawled in one of the low chairs and fixed a drink. "He could be dead. You'd be out of the race then."

"Oh, Harvey. You, a sore loser?"

Harvey sat down opposite him. "Where you learn that, then?"

"Pretty good, wouldn't you say? My father paid for me to have a private tutor. Several actually."

"Should have known but, look, you do know it was only supposed . . ."

"I know, Harvey, it was an attempt at humbling and you fucked up. In fact, not only did I enjoy the experience of kicking the crap out of your assistant, this also means I can step in now with no worry about a call to Pops from you. Means I can finally do something round here that might impress him."

"Enough for him to take you back, you mean?"

"That's the idea, Harvey. So, let's wait an' see what happens down there and then react accordingly."

"Alright, Kimps." Harvey took a deep swig of his drink and stared back into the living room. The breathing was quite audible out in the garden. Then he noticed the American's face, full of dark fury. It was a frightening transformation from his relaxed smugness of an instant ago. His eyes were hard lines. "Yes?"

The words were a low snarl through his lips. "That's mister Kimps, Harvey. Don't forget the mister, Harvey." Then he broke the look, his features relaxed and he stared out into the afternoon sky.

Their flat and the Basement had taken the force of the explosion but even there the damage was not so great. Mike managed a joke that they could demand for their rooms to be decorated. Hargreaves and his staff had already tidied the Basement and it was ready to open for the weekend. The rest of the club bore the vague marks of a stampede of people and it had been left for them to clean up the hall. They were walking round with bags, picking up litter and sweeping piles of glass, dirt and cigarette butts.

Hargreaves had been hostile to opening the club up so soon, until they flashed some of the Curtis money under his nose and promised him a percentage of the door. The way the bar had been prepared for business made it obvious he was just holding out for more money. He had talked about installing security equipment at their expense and this had depressed Ben, who had seen how cameras and metal detectors killed a club night dead. There was some truth in the idea that a one-off incident might attract a crowd but when the dance room was protected like an airport lounge, there was no atmosphere. Now his mood was sombre. Because of the attack the police had assured them that they would be monitoring the club very closely. This made him feel more uneasy than the thought of another raid.

"Ben, you look vex."

"Yeah, well, me ave reason."

They paused in the middle of the hall.

"We've almost finished though."

"You is sleeping on a ras sofa, then?"

"Oh, is that it?" Mike had a concerned look on his face but the easy calm of his movements showed he was not irritated in the same way as his partner.

"No, Mike. That not all. I don't know how you so easy bout all this . . ."

"I'm just mellow, man."

"Six month ago you would a been bawling like a pickney. These day you jus walking with a grin on your face all the time."

"Gotta get it all into perspective. We are here to have fun and be . . ."

"Only thing you ave in perspective is your nose, boy." The way Mike had been drifting lately worried him. It was not so much the drug, more the fact it had separated them and he was spending more of his free time with Alfred. The expense was a factor too. "I mean. Why you ave no money? You always ave savings before."

"What you talking about? I don't see how my choice of relaxation is any of your concern. You're just pissed off, that's all. Leave me out of it. I don't want to row."

"I'm not baiting you. This club all we ave though, Mike. It been sweet but I feel it end soon, less we work on it."

"You saying you put a lot of work into it?"

"I know I been slack."

"That is the exact fucking word. You just been cruising."

"We gotta start making plans though, looking round."

"I don't follow."

"Maybe a new club. You know a good club can only last so long. An' this thing get real jazzy."

"Now you're just looking for an argument. Maybe I am getting more into that. So what? I am the DJ, you know."

"Alfred play the right tune."

"You siding with Alfred now? Usually you slag him."

Ben could feel his temper slipping. "Nah. I'm jus saying we should get serious now. We got to decide what we want and take it, you know."

"Drop it, Ben. You're a free agent any time you want." He picked up a bag and walked towards the stage. "Don't get the impression I'm not worried about all this. We only open this week by the skin of our teeth and there's pressure every side. I just don't want it to end because someone decides to fuck with us and we fall out, you know? That would be stupid. Just keep it easy and we can set it all up again."

Ben was going to answer him but there was a voice from the rear of the hall.

"You have a family fight, then I come back, yes." It was Lucien, striding across the hall with his usual ease. He looked smart as ever. "I come at a bad time?"

Ben shook his outstretched hand and Mike came over.

"No, this how we have a business meeting in West Park. Tell me, you sleep in that suit, man?"

Lucien immediately started to examine the material cut so elegantly on his body. "It is creased?"

Ben laughed. "Nah, just you wear it all the time, don't you? I never seen you in anything else."

"A suit is the sign of the man, my friend. Anyway, my last suit got a bit . . . charred is the word, I think."

"Shit, man, what can we say? Pressure come down like that, we sorry, real sorry."

"It's alright, Ben. I phoned Lucien and apologised. He's cool. Knows there was nothing we could do."

"Yes, I just joking. Cheer you two up." He reached into his jacket pocket and pulled out a silver cigarette case. It was clicked open and proffered. Ben and Mike each took one.

"So you enjoy the firework?"

"Oh, my God. I thought, Lucien you never hear a crowd so big noise before. Then I see my band they run from the stage and everyone screaming. Terrible for the nerves, yes?"

"You could say that."

"Anyway . . . time. Now I really cheer you up." He glanced at his watch and Ben noticed his body was doing about five things at the same time. He had the same energy as when he had seen him on stage. The cigarette was dancing at his lips, whilst the case was placed back in the pocket and his limbs were all moving in unison, feet tapping the floor, arms gesticulating.

"Man, you charge?"

"That is one of the few questions you cannot ask a man, my friend, but I am in a good mood though. You will be in a moment also."

"Really?"

Mike was smiling and for a second Ben suspected some drug empathy between them. He had a vision of Alfred supplying everyone he knew with powder and felt quite isolated by his purity. It was an unusual feeling.

"Yes, because I speak with the girl at your music company."

The thought of Sophie distracted him. Mike was looking excited.

"What you talking to her about?"

"She ave a name, Mike."

"Ooh, tetchy there, boy."

"Well, me still have to smooth things over with her. It not over . . ."

"You two must fight like sisters later if you must, yes. Now, I talk with her and arrange I play with you this week. The money for last time I will take for this performance."

"But you were in the right the last . . ."

"No. I like to finish what I start."

"We have another band though."

"That is no problem. They can warm the crowd for me, I think."

Mike was ecstatic. With the inclusion of Lucien they could bill it as a repeat show. "You're on, boy."

"Same as before, then. Now I must go." He turned and started for the back wall, then shouted back to them. "Ben, smile a little. Just for me."

"I see you on the night."

He disappeared through the doorway. "Yeeees."

Mike stared at him, his face glowing. "We're set, boy."

"It good news, yeah."

"So now we get back to the radio, do the posters, do the whole fucking lot and crash back in on Saturday. What you say?"

"It good, yeah." Ben was staring down at the floor, pensive.

"You're not still fucked off, are you?"

"I just feel that something wanna block us with the club now. I don't know, maybe I'm thinking of this gal an' it get me down."

"Not like you to worry."

"You think I don't see that."

"Well, you see her this week if we get out."

"Not this day-trip bullshit."

"Course." Mike was chirpy now. All concerns had vanished with Lucien's offer and he only thought of the positive. Celia and Alfred were both supplying him with happy diversions and his changing tastes in music were being implemented. Mike was in good spirits despite everything that had happened and saw nothing odd in plotting the excursion.

"So while we go paddling, we jus leave the club to run itself, do we? An' whoever fuck us over take it easy?"

"Relax. Curtis can deal with that. Anyway, you wanna see Sophie, don't you?"

"Yeah."

"That's good because I spoke to Amanda this morning."

"You call her?"

"She called me, really enthusiastic. She's sorting it with Sophie for you. I guess I have to let you have another stab at the contest seeing as Celia's coming along."

Ben smiled. Then his mood soured again. "Can't go to some ras beach, Mikey. This England, you know. Only fool go down the coast."

"We anticipated that. Just to make you happy there's been another suggestion."

"So what now?"

Mike paused, relishing the role of party organiser. "Tomorrow, provided we sort out the details here in time . . ."

"Easy." Sophie was a powerful urge to work.

"Then we're going out of town. It wasn't just that I knew you'd moan we can't afford to take the whole day off, but Amanda found something else. It's a new water centre, pool and slides."

"That alright, I suppose, but we ave that stuff in West Park, man."

"They don't have a laser dome though."

This was better but Ben still had reservations. "They ave one in town, man."

"One you can hire out for a party?"

"You mean we ave the whole ting?"

"That's what I mean."

"Then, Mikey, maybe you not so stupid after all. But who pay, man? Can't be cheap for something like that."

"That's the best part. Amanda seemed confident that Curtis would pick it up."

"You joking?"

"Nah, an' he don't even know about it yet."

"Well, boy, wanna be ready, so I better get sweeping then."

"Yeah, could be your big day tomorrow."

The air in Maxine's felt dusty so he ordered a beer from the bar and wet his throat. It could have been the light from the street, picking out the millions of tiny particles floating in the atmosphere but Curtis felt there was another reason for his thirst. The scene with Amanda was causing tension.

Curtis had been in some very stressful situations but had never experienced anything like this. The threat of a knife to his throat paled in comparison with his current dilemma and he finished the beer in another gulp.

"Give me a brandy, man."

There were a few of the team lolling round the bar, sipping drinks and smoking. Carl was back in his office, making him wait until he was called, enjoying the feel of the leash. His had been the first call of the day, only a few hours after Amanda had left him with a sweet kiss on his drowsy brow.

"Curtis, you come round by me in an hour, yeah? We ave words."

That was bad enough for one day. The pick-up with Bunny and a couple of other things he had done for the man should have seen him clear for the week, so it had to be one of Carl's little chats. It was getting more difficult to sit there and nod his head in obedience to the guy. After the last warning from the boss, Curtis hadn't been thinking too much about where he was heading exactly. Admission to the den gave him ample opportunity to connect with other players and he had decided to take his time making plans. But if Carl got heavy with him again, it might push things over the edge and he wasn't ready for that yet. His mood was bad by the time Carl had hung up. Then there was the next visitor to the telephone.

Sophie was not in a wonderful mood either. "So, you've started fucking me around already. That didn't take long."

"Wha you talk about?" It had been so good with Amanda the night before and he felt so close to her mentally. He had been planning to ring Sophie to tell her nothing could possibly happen between them but she was shouting in his ear.

"You were supposed to see me, remember?"

"Shit, yeah. Look, I've only open my eye a minute ago. I'm really sorry bout that."

Where was his speech, planned the night before as he lay next to Amanda, informing her he was in love with another girl? He sat up in bed and reached over to the bedside table for a smoke to fortify himself.

"I know you were busy. I just spoke to your girlfriend."

Time to clasp his forehead with the palm of a hand.

"And she tells me she saw you last night and there's some plan to go swimming or something."

"There was no chance to speak with her, Sophie. You didn't mention . . ."

"No, I was leaving that to you." Now her voice softened a bit, as though she understood his difficulty with Amanda. He found his resolve crumbling and started to imagine her lips, the conversations they had that night. "Look, I know you're seeing her, we have to meet. I'm not sure how I feel and . . . it's a mess, Curtis. Tomorrow sounds like a nightmare."

"I heard about it but I didn't think it was going to happen."

"Well, I'm being set up with Ben."

"Say you can't make it."

"She was really keen. I had no choice. Besides I want to see you."

"With Amanda there?"

"For all I know you don't care about what happened. I mean, do you?"

The same feeling took him over. There was some element to the girl which made it impossible to resist and he found his mouth moving. "No, of course it mattered."

"Then we should speak to her. I have no intention of being your convenient mistress."

The voice sounded a long way off on the telephone. He wanted to see her then, assure her. "Sophie. It would be madness to confront the girl. Let me handle it."

"I'm still coming. I couldn't get out of it anyway. I'll see you then and we can talk. I wanted to check you were genuine, that's all."

The line went dead and he flopped back on the bed with a moan, perplexed. The worst thing about the whole situation was his confusion. Curtis was used to seeing several woman at the same time. That had been standard until he met Amanda. With her he had decided it was worth being faithful. Indeed, until Sophie there had been no temptation. Now he actually felt torn between the two girls, not able to deny both fleshly and mental interest in Sophie. His brain felt like an electric light with both of them tugging at the switch. There were other considerations. Ben and Mike were expecting a degree of loyalty from him over the club and he knew he should push Bunny. The fact that Bunny was not exactly a casual victim of information harassment was not the only reason this was unattractive. Sophie's link with Ben, though tenuous, was enough to make him feel a cheat and he would rather stay out of their path in the meantime. The added guilt was a burden. He had lent them the money after all, that was enough. Seeing the boys doing well down there did not make him jealous exactly but he was fully aware that his position was starting to look more humble in comparison. Curtis had always been the one making the breaks. The imminent hassle from Carl was troubling him and he felt as though the den might not provide him with another option. Things round West Park were looking sewn-up and Curtis was feeling the strain. *Boy, you better out a the country fo a while.* The brandy stung his tongue as he finished it and brought him back to the reality of Maxine's. "Get me another there, man."

"Beg a drink, C."

Carl was next to him, his bulk settling on a stool.

"You not want a go through to the office?" These talks were getting more public and Curtis knew it was a sign to the other members of the team. If they saw him taking it from the boss, then they were more likely to tow the line themselves. He stared at his own reflection in Carl's shades.

"Rest up, man. You no look so good there, Curtis. Too much pussy go round fo you maybe." His boss let out a cough of a laugh and sipped his drink.

"Me sorry, Carl, but today a bit busy. I come down to talk with you."

The older man stared back at him, eyes invisible through the black glass. "Me hear about friend a you running a club. Doing good, yeah?"

He sighed. Could he not escape from mention of the place. "They doing fine till someone step in with explosives."

"That what I hear about. An' I have to remind you we ave no concern wid these people."

"You mean . . ."

"I don wanna hear their name even, C. Now I don't care whappen round there but I say you gone, you hear? These men I rather not fuck with an' that means you don't touch, boy."

The threat was frustrating him. He wanted to defy Carl and being told what to do was becoming insufferable, but somehow it was a relief to be given the command. This was another justification for not getting involved with the dealings at the club.

"I don't know what's happening down there . . ."

"That the way it gonna stay too."

"But I want no part in it anyway, so no, me not sticking my face out to get hit."

"That good, man. Then everyone happy."

They picked up their glasses and started talking of some deal Carl was toying with. Curtis didn't really listen but went back to nodding in agreement with his boss. He was thinking of Ben and Amanda, people he was letting down, trying to find a solution to the long list of problems he had at the moment. He had a bad feeling things were about to get worse.

Mike pulled up and parked. It was close to midnight but he had phoned her earlier about the expedition to the water park and she had told him to come round when he could. The problems with the club had taken up most of the afternoon but the thought of Celia on the drive over had been enough to excite him and the fact that the house lay in darkness did little to dampen his desire. He climbed out of the car, carefully shut the door, then walked lightly over to the low wall that fronted the terrace. After a moment's fumbling he found a few small stones and tossed them up to her window. There was no response but as he stooped to find more projectiles, he heard the window slide. She was staring down at him, wearing a T-shirt and rubbing her eyes.

"Admit me, my Juliet."

"Mike, it's so late. It too late." She was trying to whisper but her words were punctuated by giggles at his antics. He was on one knee now, an arm stretched out in anguish.

"For I shall die of a broken heart lest you do."

"Right, right but be quiet. My mother sleep light."

He went through to the front door and waited for her. As soon as she opened it he saw her rush back up the stairs and followed after her, pushing the door behind him.

"You can't stay, Mike. You know that?" She sat on the side of her bed, trying to look serious. They still spoke in whispers.

"Celia, can I stay tonight?"

"Cha, Mike, you too much sometimes. I . . ." He was kissing her, pushing her back onto the bed but she rolled free, letting him fall forward and lie down. "No, I mean it."

"It's been days."

"An' it can be a few more days."

"Cruel. You're just punishing me for not being around."

"An' wha make you think that bother me, then?"

He reached out to her but she got off the bed and walked over to the window. His eyes studied her form against the mottled wallpaper and film posters.

"Trust me to go with a virgin."

"How can you resist me, darling? You wearing anything apart from the shirt?" He was on the floor, crawling over to her like an ashamed hound and trying to look under the T-shirt.

"You a ras pickney, boy. What am I doing letting you in ma house?

"If you don't kiss me I'll scream an' your mother'll run in."

"Boy, you . . ."

Now he climbed up her and she surrendered to the embrace, letting him caress her.

"Alright. You bring anything with you?"

"Something like this?" He held a wrap in his palm, a thin blue envelope of powder. Even in the dark he could see her eyes light up.

"Mikey, you didn't forget me, then."

"You're only with me cause I can afford to stoke you with this stuff."

"That the truth, boy. Come now, I ave something to cut it with."

"Thought we might do something else with it."

"No, sah. That only a special treat. Don't be greedy."

They were almost struggling over the tiny package. His fist was wrapped around it but she was tugging at his fingers. It was in play but Mike knew she wanted it badly. Since the night they had first got together it was Celia, not himself, who had really taken to the drug. Now they never made love without her using some but this didn't bother him. With the club running he could afford it and Mike was still enjoying sex more that anything else. Celia was proving to be a competent instructress. Tonight though, her need for it was so clear to him that his lust saw the power he exerted over her. "Think I'm being greedy? Maybe I should clear out, then." He took a step for the door but as he had suspected her arm followed and pulled him back.

"You can have what you want, I guess. Afterwards, yeah?"

"No, right now."

It was still close to play. Their relationship was based around his silly voices and making dumb gestures and requests. Celia quite liked Mike, though she had not intended to be seeing so much of him. She did not associate him with the chemical she wanted.

He pushed down on her shoulders, in the same jaunty mood, expecting her to rebel as she usually did. This time she complied. For a second he felt guilty, he wanted it to be equal, but then he rationalised the act and saw no harm in it. In a moment he was inside her and the complications of the situation were replaced by pleasure. It was brief and he felt the spasm at his waist, heard her little coughs. She cleaned him with a tissue, then looked up at him expectantly. The look surprised him.

"Shit, this is for real. I mean, you really want it for that, yeah?"

"Just give it to me, Mike."

He passed her the wrap, which was still tight in his palm and she hurried off to a corner of the room. On a small table she had the tools to cut and blow it and he watched the preparations until she let out a long rush of air. Then she lay down on the bed, grinning.

"You got it bad, Celia. We have to talk about it." Now his body was satiated he felt bad about being so demanding. "I should have just given it to you."

"Forget it, Mike. It just take the edge off things, that all. Now we can take it easy, take our time." She was motioning him to join her on the bed but he hesitated for a second, thoughtful.

"I say don't worry. I ave no problem with it."

Mike felt so much younger than her. In her twenties, she must know the score. He put it to the back of his mind and joined her on the bed.

"Now relax, Mikey boy."

Only she and Ben called him that. It made him feel close to her. "Sure. I'm quite tired actually. We could just sleep."

"Well, I'm not. Touch me now."

He rolled round to her side and dropped his head slowly along her flank. Celia's tutorials were by no means one-sided. It occurred to him that by kissing her the same way he could absolve himself of his earlier actions. Mike didn't want to feel like her employer in any way but there was a lot going on in his thoughts. He had never felt power before. "Yes, Mike. Take your time. Then I be sweet to you again."

He started checking the sounds she was making, to be sure of her progress, and turned his thoughts to the prospect of the day ahead.

Fourteen

"**A** big up fo ya people but why you live so dull?"

"Me no know."

"You no know but I do. You work all week, yes?"

"Money ave to come from somewhere, man."

"That right. An' you get stress an' duress, me right?"

"Ya know I feel so."

"So wha calm you down?"

"Thought you was tellin' me?"

"Me is. Check the frock down the Box, man."

"Down where?"

"All the prettiest gal, sweetest sounds."

"You no mean . . ."

"Yes, sah. Check the Chocolate Box for a bit a relief from

you problem. You find it most satisfactory when it come a ease ya pain."

"You wha? Is gunplay an' war down there, sah. Tha no calm we."

"Where ya hear that? Hanyway, we cater for all section a the community. Gangsta man welcome."

"Ya can say that an' still think me pass by?"

"Rest up, man. You believe what you hear in radio hadvert?"

"Well, I . . ."

"An' on this station?"

"Could be . . ."

"Listen up. You wan hear the best ragga, reggae and a drop a new too? An' special time we ave Lucien and some local heroes if you make it down this weekend, so get there early. Gal free before ten and all usual drink price. What ya hear history, people. We is the only place to be on a Satday and it stay tha way."

"Me try it, man."

"No, ya can't come, rasta."

"Wha ya talk now?"

"Ya too moody, sah."

"Me brighten up."

"Bring the hatmosphere right down, I feel."

"I could tell a few joke."

"Oh, it get worse now."

"Me can be funny, I tellin' you."

"Put the people right off."

"Cha. Shows me bes no a listen them rumour there."

"Yeah, man. That a right."

The car was closing on him, getting larger in the side mirror. Through the windscreen he could see Mike howling with laughter in the driver's seat, begging the car to match his speed. The girl was next to him, smiling but looking scared, he thought. With only a small depression of the accelerator Curtis felt the car respond and lurch forward. Mike's image started to shrink.

"Curtis man, slow down. Think him have something for us."

Ben was winding the rear window down, waving for Mike to have another try. Next to him Sophie was rigid. Curtis caught sight of her eyes in the overhead mirror and saw them soften. There was a hand on his leg. "It's a beautiful day, don't you think?" He couldn't tell if Amanda knew. She had been pretty weird this morning so far but maybe she was just in a strange mood. Curtis kept repeating to himself that it would all be over in a few hours.

It was noon and they were heading south, out of town on a dual carriageway. Because it was mid-week there was no real traffic and Mike was trying to catch him on a straight. This was courageous. The dinky sports coupé was screaming at ninety whilst the refined beast Curtis drove was purring along, happy to go well into the one ands. He dropped the speed to ninety-five.

The day had already been chaotic. Mike had turned up at Ben's house with Celia (clearly buzzing on something), Alfred and his girlfriend, Medea. They were supposed to meet the others round by Curtis but Ben found it impossible to squeeze in the back of the car. The coupé was a crush with the two passengers it already had, not that Mike had mentioned to anyone he planned to invite Alfred. His girlfriend looked like some eccentric mystic, swathed in silk scarves and wearing a huge floppy hat. Ben was amazed that Alfred had a sexual partner and her vagueness reminded him of a hippy girl he met once. They had to make the trip in stages, so Celia got the chance to talk with Sophie and Amanda for twenty minutes and found the atmosphere rather odd. Ben couldn't understand why

Sophie wanted to meet over by Curtis but apparently he had picked her up earlier or something. Everybody apart from Curtis seemed excited by the prospect of a day out of town.

The two cars pulled level and the occupants stared at one another. Mike was struggling to keep the speed up but he got Celia to roll her window down and shouted over her to Curtis. Curtis hit the button for the window to drop and moved his head out into the airflow. At that speed it was hard to make out the words but there was a distinct yell. "Papers!"

Curtis turned back to the passengers in his car. "He's kidding, yeah? Is he serious?"

"Course, man. Here, get a bit closer, can't you?"

Despite the air blasting between the cars, Ben pushed his head out of the car, then his upper body, leaving his knees pushed against the door, holding him to the seat. Sophie looked on in disgust. These stunts were not impressing her, Curtis noted from his regular glances in the mirror.

From the other car, Medea was dispatched to make contact and Ben could see Albert holding her legs with a pained look on his face. "Sophie, take my leg."

She didn't know what to do. Amanda was laughing like a maniac in the front and all she really wanted was for Curtis to sweep round and tell her how he felt about her. She grabbed Ben by the legs and braced her body, feeling slightly ridiculous.

The cars tried to stay straight but it took a while to line up the first 'snatch'. It transpired that they needed tobacco and draw as well as the papers, so Ben and Medea were sent forth to link three times. She had left the hat in the car and Ben thought she looked pretty good in a wind. There were breaks for slow traffic now and again. Finally, Mike sent the car curving so perilously close that it almost scratched the paint. Curtis just stared at Celia, impassive as she lurched towards him in the passenger seat, and just as he was about to pull out to prevent a crash she snaked a hand out with the smouldering joint produced by their endeavours. She was so close he didn't even have to stretch. With a clip of his fingers he took it from her hand and then pushed the plate to the floor. Even at that speed there was a skid as the torque hit the wheels and Mike was left standing, flashing his lights and sounding his horn.

Amanda kissed Curtis on the cheek. "Darling, I haven't had so much fun for ages."

It was only twenty miles out so they were there in less than half an hour. Ben saw the massive pool building from the dual carriageway and started enthusing immediately. "Man, you see that tube? Big, sah."

After a few turns they pulled through to the main entrance and were delayed as Curtis fished in his wallet at the barrier.

A beefy man in a uniform walked off with his money and came back with a plastic card. "This grants your party over-all access and confirms your booking, sir."

Then they were in. It was a huge site, overshadowed by the bulk of the main building. This rose up into the sky and housed "The Water Arena". There were two other large buildings though and a collection of smaller, more fair-type rides. One of the concrete blocks was the laser game and the other a botanical collection with walkways through mock-ups of various climates. This must have been the concession to the council, a cultural bribe. The scale of the place was huge and they all rushed off in the direction of the main building.

At the front, like a nervous guide, Amanda turned to speak. "Before we all get in there, can you make sure you get to the laser dome in two hours time. That's our booking and we don't want to be late."

"Yes, miss."

"Alright, Celia, somebody has to know what's going on."

"Sorry, Manda. You jus sound a bit high and mighty, you know."

"Of course." Nobody, in her entire lifetime had called her "Manda". She just stared at her until Alfred piped up.

"We'll see you in there, then. I think Medea and I want to check out some of the plants."

" 'Medea' an' I, is it? Is royalty talking, boy."

"No, Ben. I always talk like that."

"Well, I want the water on me so let's go."

Curtis lagged behind, thinking how sweet Amanda sounded, trying to keep everyone happy. How could he hurt her so? One glimpse of Sophie provided the explanation. "Amanda, think I go for a walk."

"C'mon, C. We need numbers, man." Ben was cajoling them all towards the turnstiles at the entrance to the building. "Is everything alright, Curtis?"

"Yeah, sure. I come swim."

They were in a reception area and broke off to go into the respective changing rooms. Mike gave Celia a long kiss before she went through and Ben yanked at his arm. "You get your tongue back, boy."

When they got through to the locker room the conversation was unhindered by the presence of feminine ears as they changed.

"Last night was something else. Celia knows her stuff, I tell you."

"Yeah, me know, rasta. I ave ploughed that turf me self."

"That was just a one-off."

"So you in love, Mikey?"

"No, it's nothing like that. It's . . . just really good."

Curtis broke in from his corner. "Hear me now. You come

wid this 'real good' talk an' gal is your first time, man. You should look around a bit, Mike, an' don't get too sweet on the gal. Anyway, why she look so spaceman?"

"Just a quickie with Alfred."

"Curtis, you no hear? Mikey doing powder now. The old white nose, boy."

"You jokin'?"

Mike looked embarrassed under his stare.

"Hardly any, man."

"A rasclat. You really do that shit? Man, that where all my money come from, boy. Fool like you making my man rich."

"Oh, fuck off. Don't tell me you haven't tried it."

"Me no touch it. You, Ben?"

"Yeah. One time at a party but my head spin afore I do it so me no sure if it do anything."

"There you go. Nothing wrong with it."

"That not the point, Mikey boy." Curtis had finished changing and stepped over to him, adopting a serious tone. "You see, the drug itself dangerous because you think like that. Already you ave to say to me it nothin', though I bet you is spendin' big-time money on it by now. Soon as you start piping, you fuck, simple as that. But me no tell you how to live. Man free to choose how him live. I jus say take it easy, you know."

Mike stared up at him, thoughtful for a second, then Ben marched across the white tiled floor and interrupted. "Cha, you two need lighten up, man. Gal, a brew, bit a smoke, that see you clear, man. Need to take life easy."

"You're lucky you got the club now, B. Afore that it not so easy not a worry."

"Me always live like that."

"You no a lie there."

"So, me talk straight. Right now there are three, real sweet little gal out there just wait fo we. They no wan hear bout problem. So loosen up, man."

"Yeah, me chill, relax."

"An' Mike."

"Yeah?"

"Thought you'd be joining Alfred walking with the plants."

"Fuck off."

"Bet him think him a Brazil man. In the jungle there."

"Who this gal him wid?"

"She's really interesting, studying I think. You should have a chat with her."

"Yeah, well. Maybe I will. Now let's get to the pool, man. Me need a wash down as it is."

The mood with the girls was a bit more restrained. Celia had talked incessantly about what a good lover Mike was and how lucky any girl would be to have his attentions. This speech was mainly to combat the silence between Sophie and Amanda which was making her feel nervous. Both girls seemed to be evaluating each other. They changed into their swimwear, hardly saying a word, and went out into the hall.

It was a standard Olympic-sized pool, lit from above by spotlights hung in the ceiling, and they loitered at the edge for a moment, taking it in. At the far end there was a network of bright tube slides and stairways, coiled in a tight knot.

"Not busy, is it."

"No. I'm surprised by that. Thought it would be packed."

The words between them were polite, formal. Both girls still held their arms tight to their sides even though it was steaming by the pool, and Celia imagined they would look more relaxed in office clothes.

"You no test the water yet, then?" Ben was behind them, a wide grin on his face. Being at the pool made him feel mischievous. He had run up to Amanda and Sophie to shock them but as he tried to halt himself on the wet floor he stumbled and grabbed Sophie by the waist to steady himself.

"Ben, get off me, will you."

The momentum of his charge was too much and with a cartoon-character-type flourish of his arms he plunged into the water, carrying her with him.

"Well done, Ben."

"Stay away from me, you . . ."

Mike took hold of Celia and dragged her to the edge where they had a brief struggle, then joined the two shaking heads in the bright blue. Amanda stared at Curtis as if to ask for the same youthful treatment but he was already lowering himself in, leaving her to perform an elegant dive.

"Ben, that was really stupid."

"Ah, don't worry yourself. We here to ave a bit a fun."

"And what if I couldn't swim?"

"Well, me can always give you mouth-to-mouth in an emergency." In the water it was hard not to dwell on the hard tone of her body, set out by the wet fabric. He swam over to her at the side of the pool and tried to look earnest. The other swimmers were starting to spread out, laughing and heading over to the slides. "Not much of a joke, was it?"

"Really."

"You know, I'm sorry about the other night at the club an everything but I wasn't . . ."

"Forget it, Ben. We're not an item so you've no need to worry."

"An' what chance I have to change your mind?"

"Not too good whilst you act like an infant all the time." She was looking past him, not even paying him the courtesy of concentrating on his words.

"I thought you was thinking a it though, Sophie."

"Well, you thought wrong." She brushed the hair from

her face and swam past him, intent on catching up with the rest of the party.

Ben stared after her, confused. With any other girl he would have got over the rejection in a few seconds and examined the other targets in the pool but the pursuit of Sophie had already turned into something of a mammoth quest. *Girl, me no a finish yet.*

He followed after her bobbing rump, thinking about the chances he might have throughout the afternoon to persuade her of his charms.

They had to climb several flights of dripping steps to reach the top slide and then wait for a turn, bunched on a small platform. Out of the water it seemed cold but Ben decided against wrapping his arm around her bosom. He was last on the steps, just behind her. Mike went first, his feet vanishing round a bend in the giant orange tube and Celia whooped in approval. "Yes, man. Me go next."

Amanda and Curtis were standing together but saying little. He helped her into the pipe and she turned to kiss him but he twisted his head away at the last second. She slipped off down the tube and Curtis let out a sigh.

You blowing it, Curtis. Take it easy. It was too hard to deal with Sophie, lurking just behind him, her partially clad form a testimony to his infidelity. Amanda was getting curious, he could tell. "Ben man, you next."

"Wha, I was last up here, boy."

"Come man, I need you go first, make sure it safe."

Ben laughed, stepped forward and climbed into the chute. "You no scared by this, boy."

Curtis dropped his head, feigning confidentiality. "I know. Just wanna check see if Amanda say any thing to Sophie bout me an that ting I deal wid the other day, you know. She acting funny, man."

"Yeah, me know. They that close, then?"

"You know how gal talk, B."

"Aright, I see you down there, sah." He was gone, carried into the tube by the torrent of water under his back.

"Look, there only a second, Sophie."

"Kiss me, Curtis." Already her arms were around him, her skin pressing his.

"Wha? You lose yo mind?"

"We're too high up for anyone to see."

It was tempting. Drops of water were sliding down the line between her breasts and the costume she wore was screaming at him to be whisked away with the brush of a hand. Somehow, restraint triumphed. "You crazy. I still don't know how I feel."

"Alright, neither do I. But I can make it through today. Then we can talk on our own somewhere."

"You shouldn't a come."

"There was no way out. It was Amanda who called me, don't forget."

He looked into her eyes, his instinct telling him there was some deceit there. Curtis could see her turning up today to force her position, put Amanda on edge and then step in. The fact he didn't know her well enough to be sure she was telling the truth alarmed him. "You ave to go with Ben."

"What?"

"You heard me. Look, there no time for this. You here now but you got to show her you with Ben. She think you like him."

"I just told Ben there was no way."

"He won't argue if you change you mind."

"I can't believe you're saying this. We should get out now, go somewhere and talk."

"No . . . fucking . . . way. If you want the chance to talk with me at all, then you gonna have to do this fo me. An' you ave to wait. I can't deal wid the atmosphere between you. She gonna find out."

"So what do I have to do, O master?"

The sarcasm was harsh but he could see sadness in her eyes. Maybe she really was as confused by it all as he was. 'Jus kiss him or something. Don't ave to give him anything else. Go for a walk with him."

She said nothing but walked past him and climbed into the chute. Then she was gone. Curtis hesitated for a second in torment, then threw himself into the mouth of the tube.

Amanda was off to one side of the group waiting for him to arrive. They were all floating a few yards away from the touch-down area of the slide and Curtis saw their legs swaying underwater for a few seconds when he crashed through. Amanda was next to him instantly. "Great ride."

"Yeah, really good."

She was about to say something but saw his eyes drift over to where Sophie was treading water. Her heart sank. It was clear the girl interested him. They had been exchanging looks all day.

"See Ben an' her get it together."

Ben was still wiping the water from his eyes when Sophie arrived at his side. As he stared at her approaching face in bewilderment, she leaned forward and planted a kiss on his cheek, then pushed herself away.

"Catch me and you can have another."

Ben didn't spend much time deliberating but took it philosophically and tore off after her. *Woman is capable a infinite change a mind, boy.*

Amanda stared after them and then hugged Curtis, her mouth at his ear. "Knew they'd hit it off." Her hand dropped to his submerged waist and shaped itself to him. "You a bit turned on, Curtis."

"Uh, yeah, the water always get me like that."

The time went quickly, with the couples splitting up round the pool. Curtis kept taking the slide. He found it took his mind off the sight of Sophie being swamped by

Ben at the other end. Soon Amanda called to everybody that they had to move off to the laser game. In the changing room Ben was full of bravado.

"Gal all over me."

"S'funny. Look the other way to me. Like you ave to pin her to the side a get kiss."

"Can't see too well, boy. Me squeeze up her titty an everything."

"Please, Ben. We're both happy about you an' Sophie but . . ."

"Don't see you being polite. Celia look like she gonna start scream at one time. Is only Curtis stay away from him girl."

"Oh, so she your 'girl' now, then?"

"Well, look good, innit? See how it go in the dark, boy."

They filed up to the other building and met Alfred and Medea waiting in the reception area. The room was done out like some kind of spaceship, with banks of dials and coloured metals lining the walls.

Ben was gripping Sophie's hand, taking in the architecture. "Room criss, boy. It like this inside, we sweet."

Alfred had noticed the locked hands. "So love is in the air?"

"Easy, Alfred. What you and Esmerelda make a the wildlife?"

"The name is 'Medea', Ben. From the Greek."

"You in shipping business then, gal? Alfred, you strike lucky."

"I'm a student, Ben, studying classics."

"Wha, like the sport car, then?"

"No, books."

"Come on, everyone; we have to establish two teams and then get into the equipment, so . . ."

"I'm afraid Medea and I have to miss out. She has a headache and I think a swim might be good for her."

"Sorry bout that, Alfred. We no see much a you as it is."

"Well, we'll be waiting for you when you come out. Maybe we can all have a drink later. When we hit town again."

It was not treated with utter dismay that the couple were stepping down and they retreated towards the exit as the others started talking.

"Gotta be gal against the men. Sisters, you know."

"Yes, that is one option, Celia."

"Sound good to me. Should be easy."

Amanda stood in the middle, happy to free herself of the responsibility and Curtis had agreed. She missed his stare at Sophie and Sophie's relief as Ben's grip was relaxed. The sexes shuffled to opposite sides of the room. "Fine, let's do that, then."

The parties were led off to the changing rooms and given a brief lesson on how to play. The team objective was to capture the enemy flag. This could be hidden anywhere in the three levels of battle area so it was best to be tactical in the search. After the lecture they had to strip down and put on some nylon jumpsuits. Then they each donned a backpack which the gun was wired to by a short cable. The other armour registered the hits and consisted of a wrap-around chest and back plate and a helmet. With the visor down it was impossible to see the face as the glass was tinted to protect the eyes. There was a radio system in the helmets which allowed them to talk with one another. Once the guide had explained the rules he left them to go through to the battlefield in their own time.

"Curtis, man. Can skin up?"

"In all this shit me a wear. You fuck now."

In addition to the backpack there were gloves and knee-pads to put on.

"I hardly move, boy, an' me sweat like a pig already."

"Here. I'll do it." Mike was still dressing. He dropped the helmet, searched in his coat and drew out a thin, white tube. "A jazz cigarette, boys."

"Light it up, then. We ave to go through in a minute."

"So whappen here? We just go out and start shooting."

"No, ya kwashi. There no limit on the bullets . . ."

"Bullets! Is laser beam, man."

"Aright, anyway no limit what you a fire but they can see it, man. Gonna be dark out there so if they see ya fire they can track you."

"So what you say we do, then?"

"Jus take it slow, stalk em, yeah? One shot to the head is a life an' you ave to come back an' sit in here for ten minute. Chest and back, you get three chance."

"Can always say they never lick we."

"Nah. The man him ave it all on computer. He tell you when to leave an' turn yo gun off."

Mike had been nodding and toking as Curtis spoke. He was still out of it from the drive and a smile was fixed on his face. Now he passed Curtis the joint.

"A fuck, Mikey. You look stone, boy."

"I am a bit."

"Well, straighten up cause this get serious, ya hear. This a question a respect now." Curtis had thrown a glove off and was pulling deeply on the smoke. He held his visor up with his other hand.

"Curtis man, you look like the general, sah. Pass it here, man." Ben was laughing at the sight of him in the military costume, pulling on the joint, clouds of heavy white smoke rising above him to the ceiling. He took the offered article.

"I serious rasta. Them gal is crafty. Know for sure they ave a plan work out. Check your radio."

They snapped down the visors and the room went dark.

"Mike, you there, man?"

It was a metallic click in his ear but quite clear. "Yes, boss. All present and correct."

"Safe. Hey, we all speak at the same time, then it gonna get confused, so keep it down, yeah?"

"Got you, C."

"Are you lads about ready to go in?"

"Shit, tis the control man a speak to us?

A new voice was booming round the speakers. "I can speak to you throughout the game. The girls are ready to go out so I'm gonna open the door in ten seconds, alright?"

"So you can see us, then?"

"No. There's a few cameras out in the field for spectators but I can only talk to you. Get ready and best of luck."

"Cha, man. Me need a minute." Ben clicked his visor open to ditch the burning ember of the joint. A cloud of smoke wafted from the helmet. "Man, me canned already."

"Me an' all, boy." Mike was starting to gurgle, suffering from the advanced stages of the chemical's effect.

"Straighten out, ya fuck. Me wanna win this."

The exit at the end of the room was shaped like a water-tight door, round and with huge hinges. It started to creak open. Curtis stepped forward purposefully. The day had been too bizarre already and the surreality of the game took it over the edge for him. He was almost starting to enjoy himself. They stepped forward into the dark.

It took a moment for their eyes to adjust, then they could see a system of walkways, stairs and partition walls. This was immediately in front of them and stretched off into the gloom. There were tiny red and blue lights hidden in the floor and walls and these gave the shapes and shadows a sinister tone. Thick smoke hung in the air.

"Fuck, man, how we gonna find em in this?"

"Keep it down. We only talk when must, Mikey!"

Mike was carrying the flag. It was a thin metal rod and a circular base, topped with a yellow bulb that was shining bright.

"We ave to stash the flag, man."

"It's a bit heavy, you know."

They could only see the outline of each other in the dark, so gathered in a tight group.

"They bound to check one level at a time, so it make sense to go to the top, yeah? One man guard and the other go off to hunt."

"Guess that's me then, innit."

"Well, seeing as you stone anyway . . . come on."

They clambered up to a flight of stairs and started up. At the top was the next level but Curtis marched up to the highest level, number three and cautiously paced out into the middle. He could hear Mike breathing hard. "By this wall, sah."

Mike came over and dumped the flag behind the partition. The glow from the bulb shone through the material.

"A ras. It show, man."

"Fuck it. Mikey, you go an' hide and shoot anyone that turn up. We keep talking on the radio, yeah?"

"Happy hunting, boys."

They started back to the stairs and went down.

"Ben, you start on the bottom, I take the middle."

"So you is giving the order?"

"You wan the middle, my fren?"

"Cha, just don't take it so serious, man."

Curtis turned onto the middle level. It was hard to see clearly with all the smoke and hardly any light, so he decided to work around the wall.

"Curtis man, come in, do you read me?"

"Mike, take it easy. You sound scared fo real, man."

"Well, it's fucking eerie up here on my own."

"We all on our own, boy."

"Never mind the bullshit head talk. There's someone up here. I can hear them moving."

"Jus sit tight, man, I be up."

Ben cut in with a crackle. "Me on it, man. There nothing down here anyway."

Curtis glanced behind him and saw Ben racing up the stairs. As he passed the level exit there was a bright flash and he froze. Thin red beams were surrounding him in a web of lines, bouncing off his chest and pounding the visor. Curtis saw two shapes kneeling only a few yards away from him, the origin of the red wash. They were so close but he had missed them. The smoke made it hard to see more than a few inches in places. "Ben man, it an ambush. They waiting for you a come up the stair. Get back down, man."

"Contestant A three is out of the game for ten minutes. His radio and gun are disconnected and he must return to the air lock."

Curtis raised his gun to blast them but paused. They were standing and moving forward. Ben was tramping down the stairs, so they had a numerical advantage now and knew where the flag was. He decided to shadow them, wait for a better moment. When they were out of sight he started up behind them and saw them hesitate at the top. "Mike, their flag must be on the top near you. Listen, when I say the word I want you to start firing at the top of the stairs."

"There's no one there though."

"They is, two a them who jus do Ben. It just you can't see them. Now start shooting."

He saw the line of Mike's laser trace the top of the stairs and the two figures turned to escape. He was only a few feet away and took them by surprise. He only pulled the trigger twice, one shot landing in the centre of each helmet.

"Contestants B two and three are out. Please find your way back to the . . ."

"Mikey, you see anything?"

"Good shooting, C. I tell you. Someone been creeping around, man. I can't see them but I can hear them. Something . . ."

"I come up."

"Contestant A one is out of the game for ten minutes. Follow previous instructions."

"Mikey, what go on? She get you?"

"Your team member is out and has no radio contact."

"Shit. She by the flag, then?"

"I am not able to answer that."

He raced up the stairs and dived through to the level wall, thinking a direct assault might scare the prowler from the flag if it was still theirs. A line of red connected with his chest as he steadied himself.

"One life deducted from contestant A two."

He pushed along the wall trying to spot the source of the red lines reaching out to him but she was moving around in the gloom and the shots had no fixed point.

"A two has one life remaining."

His breathing was rushed and he fired blindly, throwing himself to the ground. Then there was silence. He could hear the rush of his own lungs in the speaker at his ear.

There was a clearing just to his left and he crawled round a wall to get a better view. Realising his mobility was limited on the floor he dragged himself up and took light steps into the space. She had to be close.

Something flashed by his visor, a movement and he charged the far wall, letting loose with the laser. When he reached it he saw there was nothing there and he looked around desperately. On the floor by his own foot was a solitary boot. There was a click at the side of his visor and he was looking down a barrel. *Me fall for that? Gal just throw her crepes cross the room.* Instead of seeing a red blur the gun was withdrawn and the figure stepped back a pace.

Sophie slipped the helmet off her head to let him see who it was, then dropped it to the floor. She moved up to him again and pulled his hand under the chest plate.

Curtis clenched her bare breast until the pain showed on her face. "So you knew I'd be the last to go."

She broke free, sank to her knees and pressed her head to his waist, parting the velcro ties that held his suit.

"Contestant A three is rejoining the game."

"Shit, there no time for this."

The warmth of her mouth enclosed him and he pushed into her. All the denial of attraction he had maintained throughout the day vanished. Soon she had the rhythm and he felt the muscles in the back of his legs tighten.

A red beam cascaded off his shoulder and she pulled away, hurriedly reaching for the disguise of the helmet. Once it was tight on her shoulders she heard the laughter.

"Sophie. Shit you don't waste no time, gal."

"I take it you didn't hear of our release."

"Yeah, I was . . ."

"We see all that gal, the whole thing."

"There seems to be some collaboration going on, Celia. I have a feeling Ben might be coming over to our side."

Curtis vanished into the smoke and left them huddled in a tight group.

"Ben no wan a finish what he start, then?"

"It wasn't . . . what it looked like."

"Sure. We no pickney, well used to them thing at our age. How we gonna war when the troops get down to it though?"

"I thought you were out of the game."

"We were. Told you we got released. Been fighting our way up here."

Their chat was broken by a burst of light from the rear.

"Don't know that I can take this serious now, feel I should find Mike for some a the same."

"There's time for that later, Celia. We're in the lead so we should play it out. Come on, I know where their flag is."

The girls had won. They took the flag soon after finding Sophie and the male team quickly lost enthusiasm after the first defeat. Mike was too out of it. Curtis had lost heart and Ben kept getting killed. He was quite reckless on the battlefield.

Amanda and Celia were laughing as they loaded up the cars but everyone else seemed tired out by the day. Ben was by the sports car, arranging to meet Mike later. "Maybe round ten, then."

"Cool, Ben. We should be set for Saturday."

"Hmmm. Hey, me get nervy or there some funny look a go on?"

"I don't get you."

"Since we come out the place. Celia an' Amanda been leering, man."

"She's said nothing to me. Must be your nerves there."

Ben slapped him on the shoulder as a goodbye and walked over to Curtis. The girls were chatting at the boot. "You notice these look I catch, rasta?"

"No, sah. Ya get pa'noid or something, Ben?"

"I'm gonna have to deal wid it, talk wid them there."

Ben made to go, a determined look on his face, but Curtis had him by the arm. "Rest yourself there. It nothing. Leave em be, man."

Ben thought for a second and then relaxed. "So you coming Satday? We ave two band playing and I stand you the brandy a usual."

"Maybe, B. Bit busy myself at the moment, you know."

"So you find anything out, Curtis?" Mike was next to them. He had walked over from his car where Alfred and Medea were crammed in the back.

"You guys, you know it not easy."

"What does that mean, then?"

"Well, it mean no. But I turn to it soon, real soon."

"We open again Saturday. What if something goes down then?"

"Shit, man, well me so sorry. Me no fuckin' detective in the dirty overcoat, you know. You boy can handle it, I think, whatever."

"Asking for your help, Curtis."

"An' me tellin' you I already lend you a grand, not to talk a the first loan and today simply a real bad time to ask for anything."

"I thought we all had a good day."

"Yeah, it sweet. Cha, I see you later, Mike. Can't wait for you on the road this time." He moved to the driver's door.

"Hold on, there. Alfred and his girl invited us all back to their place for drinks if you fancy it."

Curtis made a tiny groan. Would this twenty-four-hour period never come to an end? When he turned back to Mike, Amanda was blocking the view.

"We can take the address but I think Curtis is a bit tired."

"You speak for me now, then?"

"Just trying to help."

The rear passenger door clunked open and he caught sight of Sophie climbing in, looking fatigued. Despite everything, she smiled when she saw his eyes in the mirror. He thought of her kiss. "Come, we dig up. Amanda, we all had a great time, get in the car."

"No need to sound like that."

Ben pushed back in the leather next to Sophie and put his arm round her. He started whispering in her ear. "So we go by your place, then?"

Curtis saw her trying to wriggle but Amanda was still keeping him under watch and he said nothing. He gunned the car so the needles on the dash jumped over to the right.

Sophie answered Ben's enquiry with a loud and confident tone. "I think I fancy a nice, long bath." Her eyes were in the mirror.

"That sound good to me."

"You two certainly conduct things out in the open, don't you?"

"Come again, Amanda. I don't understand you mood lately."

"Your display earlier."

"But I'm afraid it will have to be on my own, Ben. I have things to do tonight."

Ben couldn't decide how to react. Amanda's image of him was less important than a night with Sophie though, so ignoring the confusing remarks from the front he turned to the girl next to him and whispered again. "But you been coming on to me all day. Why you go cold on me like this?"

"Don't hassle me, Ben. I make up my own mind about what I want to do."

Now he sighed and looked out at the darkening landscape flashing by. He found the mood in the car very strange. Curtis was never a comedian but his temper was usually fair. At the moment his hands were glued to the wheel and he was driving fast, deep in what looked like some involved, painful thinking. Neither of the girls made any sense. He tried not to get depressed and started thinking of other things to keep his mind off it. Maybe he should call the Smith sisters when he got home.

They were soon flying through West Park and Ben was dropped first. He moaned at the sight of his house and jumped out. "Ruth gonna be sitting there watching a show, for sure."

Curtis left the engine running and came round to the back to let him get his bag from the boot. The girls were silent in the car.

"Tha gal strange, man. All day she act eager, then nothin. Man ave to keep trying I suppose. Anyway C, come down the club, my fren."

"Maybe I see you down there."

Ben went up to his door and waved the car off before going in.

With the traffic light they were crossing a bridge in minutes and he drove straight to her street.

"You've got a good memory, Curtis."

"It not so long ago we here."

"Well, thanks for the afternoon. I might see you again."

"If you're seeing a bit of Ben we'll probably run into each other."

"Oh, I don't think that'll come to much. Anyway, so long."

She was anxious to get out of the car, to avoid Amanda's scrutiny. He watched her run up the steps and go through the door without looking back.

"Strange girl, she is."

"Really."

He pulled away and pointed the car south. The same chic houses and bursts of green lined the streets until they crossed the river. Then the dull greys and rust reds of the buildings signalled their return to West Park.

"Yeah, you know when we were in the laser thing, well Celia an' I found her an' Ben in a rather delicate position . . ."

Her words floated past him and out of his lowered window, mingling with the gush of sounds from the high-street. Curtis was far away in thought. The dilemma of his situation was still acute and he felt all the confusion of before, but as Amanda reeled out the story he thought of his siren, reclining in her bathtub. Sophie had left her bag in the boot. Amanda was going home in a short while and he would drift back to the arms of the girl on the other side of the river. The trip out had been one long ordeal for him and he reflected on the stress of the day. He had paid his dues. There was always tomorrow for his worrying.

Fifteen

There was no ten o'clock shut out tonight but it was still reasonably full. People were milling around in the lower hall and the Basement was starting to get busy. Ben and Mike were drinking beers at one of the tables.

"It look alright."

"Considering, yeah. Can't really expect the same amount to show after the fireworks."

"Don't worry, Mikey. As soon as we get through tonight, we gone clear. The club start tick over again."

"Maybe. Why's Curtis so eager to get involved, then? I don't fuckin' think."

"I think him a bit jealous. Sound to me like he has problem with his girl."

"Tell me about it." Mike was concerned about the

evening ahead and his face showed the strain that Ben had expected but he looked troubled by other things as well. He was slumped over the table, tilting the bottle back periodically.

"What with everybody, at the moment? Y'all look so misry. I never see you look so."

"Oh, it's lots of things, man. Having grief from Celia."

"It look sweet the other day."

"It was. Until the evening anyway. You missed out on Alfred's party."

Ben had not seen much of Mike that week. He had been fighting the Sophie sulk with visits to the sisters.

"It was a nightmare, man. We piled around there soon as we got back and you know Celia was out of it anyway, well Alfred pulls out some fuck-off bag a pure and her eyes light up. She starts smarming, it was horrible."

"You all doing it?"

"Yeah, but in moderation 'cept for her. The girl's craven. I mean it, she has something wrong she must sort out, boy. Then her and Medea got in some row. Alfred was trashed and wouldn't shut up about free love an' me an' him fell out. We left and argued all the way back and I ended up dropping her and tearing off. She's coming tonight and I can't be fucked, you know."

"Think you have problem with women? I been fucked round by Sophie bad, man."

"What? Thought it was going fine when I left you. You an' her were getting it on, I thought."

"Was sweet till we leave in the car. Then she wan be alone. It really get to me, you know. Think the girl something special."

"Ben. You falling for her, then. Old stony heart in love?"

"Don't be kwashi, boy. I have sensitive feeling like the next man, that all I'm saying."

"Aright there." It was Adam, dropping into a chair next to them.

"Safe, Adam. Decide to come look, after the fun last week, then?"

"Me ave Petie as a shield."

His colleague was at the bar ordering some drinks.

"How him botty, boy?"

"Settle down, I feel. So whappen? I hear you open an account with the sister there."

"Oh, that your sensitive side, is it, Ben?" Mike had perked up, hearing of Ben's indulgence.

"A ras. I just let off steam there, that all."

"Boy get him ration in full with them two. Hope your heart up to it, B."

"Me don't do nothing. They all over me while I is taking it cool."

"So you haven't seen much of Sophie, then, if you been busy? Try to talk with her if you're really interested."

"Cha. Who this Sophie? Two not enough fo you, boy?"

"Ave to travel sometime, Adam. Gal like nation a the world, you know."

"If you had a bit more respect, maybe Sophie would come round to seeing you. She's not really the type of girl who's gonna mess around, is she?"

"Wha? You saying she no fuck around? Listen, man. You is still in your first innings. Them gal just as bad as we."

"Not her. She's dead straight."

"You fuck now. Nobody straight, I tell you. She up to all sort, I bet."

Mike thought of the story Celia had told him on the way back to town. "Guess you're right. People can surprise you. I heard about the laser bit, caught in the act an' all."

"Me jus kiss her a bit, that all."

"Thought it was the other way round, boy."

"Me no follow your meaning, Mike."

Petie was over with a drink for Adam and himself, prompting Ben to lurch forward, grinning. 'So, Petie. You drink alone tonight?"

"Money tight, boy."

"Yeah, tight in yo pocket, sah. When I see you last, I buy the drink all night."

"Sweet, when we in heaven, the beers on me."

Petie spoke slowly in his low growl and everyone at the table laughed. "Me stay thirsty fo a while yet, then."

"You live in hope, boy."

"And you die . . .'"

"Yeah, me know, me know. Here's to what await us. Mus be simlar to here anyway."

They nodded to the toast.

"Hear yo advert, boy. Made me laugh."

"Oh, you liked it, yeah?"

"Was funny, man. You doing both voices, good idea."

"Wha time the show start, then?"

"No till midnight. An' we on bes behaviour tonight. Policeman have him eye on we."

"I see any youth get facety, then they out, man."

"No, Petie. Don't mean you should go round beat up the people there."

"Ben, you lose your humour these day. Turn business man on we."

"Could be right there. Spose that how I buy you all them drink the other night."

"Settle down, man. I get you a beer before the night done."

Kimps straightened his tie and adjusted the cuffs. The suit was loose but still showed the power of his physique. That was the touch of expense. The others were out in the street waiting for him. They had sounded the horn only a moment ago. He flicked the curtain back and saw the low curves of a powerful car, this year's registration. It was a new sports model and he was well aware there were few cars on the road that could come near it. Kimps smiled and finished checking his look, then went out to join them, slamming the door behind him. The passenger seat was free for him and he climbed in. Wayne woke the engine and they pulled away with a soft whine from under the bonnet.

They were old friends, from college days when his father's money had bought him a place in a renowned institute. These days though, many of the pupils had a similar background and they had met and become a unit. It was accepted that he was the casual leader.

That had been a few years before but Ryan and Wayne had been over here for the last few months and chased him up. His difficulties had interested them and they were only too happy to help out.

"We'll have more than a drink tonight if you think you're up to it."

Ryan's lanky frame was in the back and he leaned between the front seats to speak. Kimps could smell his aftershave through the smoke of his cigarette. 'We getting dirty?" It was a thin, nasal-whine enquiry.

"Depends if you're in the mood, as I said. These people are soft as shit."

"Maybe we should stop by my place, pick something up?" This was Wayne, softer-spoken but Kimps knew how his mood could twist to savagery. Wayne had been with him on the shooting that had exiled him here.

"You carry something with you? Over here?"

"No, think I'm a fucking moron? I mean a hard weapon."

"It's all under control, boys, no need to pick up a fucking monkey wrench or whatever you had in mind . . ."

"They can help sometimes. We're only three."

"I have the answer stuffed in my jacket here, stop

worrying." Kimps pulled a parcel from under his arm. It was a soft leather square and he gently unwrapped it.

"Fuck. That's a Browning. You got the full clip on it?"

"Absolutely. All thirteen. Who's the moron for getting this through? Harvey would love to know about my little pet."

"That fairy'd shit bricks, boy. You gotta show him you're boss."

"I did already. Beat the crap out of some trusty sidekick figure he's been using."

They were both laughing. He fingered the long barrel, a dull, chrome rectangle.

"Those fuckers go through steel. Bit of a hammer for an egg, Kimps. I thought this was a soft job."

"Well, it's only a scare. Brown-pants time all around."

"How'd you get it in?"

Ryan was reaching over to hold the gun but Kimps clutched it to his chest. "Had a plastic coat made for it and used the post. They can't see through some types less they go and open it."

"You took a risk there."

"No fun in life without them, Wayne."

Already the adrenaline was pumping round his body but he kept it in check. Nearly a year had passed since he'd ventured out like this.

"So, they over the water?"

"Yeah, take a bridge. We'll head down there but have a drink first. I'll talk you through it. No sense in rushing things, is there?"

Ryan retreated to the cramped rear seat and started telling Wayne some joke. They started laughing as Kimps packed the gun away and gazed out at the river.

The flat had been badly damaged the week before, so they

were marooned in the Basement. Neither of them liked prowling the dance room until it got later and the crowd was lively but as it got closer to his shift on the desk, Mike felt a rush of nerves and got up from the table.

"Where you go, then? You not on till eleven."

"Just taking a wander downstairs, aren't I."

Ben motioned for him to drop his head to where he sat and whispered in his ear. "You not planning a powder your nose, are you?"

"Fuck off. That's my concern anyway."

Ben watched him walk away, then broke into chat with Adam again. Mike was right. It was his deal what he wanted to take.

Mike took the steps in a few bounds and circled round the stage. The stairs for the DJ box were on the other side and it cheered him slightly that he had to push through the crowd. The hall was filling up. Pulling back a curtain he went up to the stage and squeezed in next to Albert.

From here you could see the whole dance space and he stared out at the audience. It always fascinated him to check the crowd. For a DJ it was like a doctor taking a patient's temperature, making sure all was well. Alfred was doing fine. There were people gathered at the edges who were waiting for the live music but there was a central body of dancers swaying to his beats. Although Alfred had a clear hippy image with his slow drawl and period dress, his taste in music was moving to strong ragga and it was he who was holding the club in this style. Mike had been getting into a lot of hybrid stuff lately and was feeling more experimental than his partner on the decks. He had to admit the crowd was into it tonight though, and his eyes fixed on the girls grinding low. Then he was reminded of Celia by the forest of lycra and remembered his present aim. He prodded Alfred in the ribs and the DJ came back from music-land, placing his cans on the stationary record.

"You fuck it like that, boy. Gonna scratch."

"Not if you believe in the great vinyl god, Mike." Alfred's eyes were tiny dots and his smile a long line from ear to ear across his face.

"Man, you look trashed already."

"I have . . . indulged. It frees my spirit. And you can hardly defend yourself as far as visits to that activity."

"Point taken. Which brings me round to the question . . ."

"I can't front it but I do have some. Has to be paid for though, Mike."

"You can see the people out there, can't you? That means a thou for me, easy. Patience for an hour or two, that's all I ask."

"Lucien's generosity funding your drug habit, I see. But in this club anything can happen, as I know only too well. Should be paying me danger money, build an iron cage around the box even, no that would be negative . . ."

Mike pulled some notes out of his jeans. It was the advance ticket sales and he hadn't split it with Ben yet. He had forgotten the debt to Curtis in his eagerness as well. "Nough of the rambling, guru. Take this."

"And for that . . ." He was counting the money, feverishly adding up the random collection. Mike wasn't sure how much was there himself. "You get this." He fished into the jumper he wore, then dropped three wraps into Mike's hand, covering them with a five-pound note. 'Your change, sir."

"Sweet. I didn't think there was so much there."

"Excuse me." Alfred nudged him to one side and triggered the dormant deck into life. The crowd switched up to a faster beat and he selected a new record for the previous deck, packing the old one away. "How like life is our trade, Mike. A process of birth and decay."

"Cool. Check you in a while. I'm gonna do a bit before the first band."

"Yeah. Have fun in the toilets, won't you."

Mike smiled and rushed off down the stairs, heading towards the back of the hall.

Ben was guzzling. As the club filled up, he let his tension roll on a tide of beer and the chat with Adam and Petie got progressively drunken. All around their table familiar faces floated by and the atmosphere of the bar lifted with his mood. Ben was in good temper. The attack of the week before was forgotten. He had no problem putting it to the back of his mind and thinking of more pleasing things. Everyone walking in was a few pounds in his hungry pocket.

"Place cork, sah."

"A yes. Look like you get ya bit a bad publicity."

"This club still the only place to come on a Sunday, an' me gonna branch out soon."

This caused Adam to lean forward, interested in his words. "You try a little ting on ya own?"

"Maybe. Mike seem happy wid the runnings here but I have plans, spread my wings maybe."

"Like, what you thinking of, then?"

"Can't go giving my ideas out like that, can I? Adam, you too foxy, man, me know you long time, remember. It enough to say I might try a little thing."

"What's this you're talking about, Ben?" Mike was back at the table, eyes shining.

"Nothing."

"Him talk bout him expansion plan there, Mike."

"Well, anytime you feel like quitting, you let me know."

Mike's confidence irritated him. Ben only wanted the chance to be able to talk big to Adam. He knew how it bothered him and it was only an idle conversation but Mike had come straight in with the ego response. Ben knew what fuelled this boldness but said nothing.

Amanda had just appeared at the other side of the table. "Evening, everybody. Thought I'd come down and have a look at all your hard work."

She was dressed in a tight. French-style black dress and only deference to Curtis restrained him from gawping. Adam and Petie didn't hide their interest. The soft light of the bar made her features look delicate and Ben detected a hint of nervousness. "You alright? Look a bit off colour there, Amanda."

Petie lumbered up from his chair, prompted by a stare from Adam, and pulled it back for her to sit.

"When I see you at a party before, you were the life a it."

"Oh, I'm a bit tired, that's all. I seem to be more exhausted on holiday than I am at work."

"I know the feeling."

"How that, Ben? You only try the holiday so far."

"I pacing myself, Mikey, that all. Get some drink in my fren."

"Sounds like you've had a few already. Amanda, what can I get you?"

"I'll have a gin please, bitter lemon."

"May I say how attractive you look?" Adam had adopted his media accent with an educated tone and intended to be charming. Ben could almost see the tongue licking his lips.

"You may indeed. I'm most flattered."

"My name is Adam and this is my work colleague, Peter."

This was too much. He had never heard anyone refer to the mountain of quiet violence standing behind her as "Peter". A manicured hand was being offered and Adam had that sly look on his face that Ben had seen so many times before. She was smiling politely but he could tell she would rather kiss an iguana. "So, Amanda, you look for Curtis."

He saw the apple race up Adam's throat and heard him

emit a loud gulp, even over the blues break playing low in the background.

"Yes, thought I might surprise him."

"I didn't know Curtis see anyone at the moment." The accent was slipping in, now it was no longer worth maintaining.

"Yes, he's my partner."

Ben was amused by the word she chose to describe the relationship. He had never quite understood Amanda or what kept her and his friend so close.

"This 'partner', you no wan call him 'boyfriend' sometimes."

"I think it's a bit childish, don't you? It can get confusing as well."

"You mean, if him say he ave a few 'galfren', yeah?"

"That sort of thing. So do you say you have a 'girlfriend'?"

"That depend if it the first time we get down to the job in hand. Don wanna put the gal off."

Ben and Adam started laughing but Amanda only managed a thin smile. "A bumba, Ben. You too much, sah."

Mike was back with a tray of glasses. "Ben giving a lecture, is he?"

"Don't get so iree there. Me no ave a drink-up fo a time. A dear." Ben was wiping a tear of laughter from his eye.

"We talk bout the complication a modern-day affair, that all."

"Ben doesn't think 'partner' is such a good word."

"Well, it have no passion in it, you understand. Better say 'lover' or something if you have to designate it sexual."

She was impressed by his use of language and her estimation of him lifted. Amanda held the same reservations about him that he had for her. The times she had met him before he had never bothered to put effort into communicating.

Now Petie cut in with his low boom from behind her ear.

"It hard to talk bout them in numbers, you know. I mean, what you call them two gal Ben fucking at the same time, then? They 'galfren' or 'partner'?"

There were silent and repressed chokes of laughter around the table as Petie looked on in all seriousness.

"Maybe you would have to call them partners of a kind too, Peter."

There was a coy smile on her lips and she turned to face Ben. He was silent for a second then burst out laughing. "Gal draw a card there. Amanda one of the team, I feel, sah. Me know it all along."

"Yes, well, maybe we should get away from Ben's love life."

Ben started chatting with Adam again and Mike shot a friendly smile at the girl.

"Are you playing records tonight, Mike?"

"Yeah, the first band comes on soon. I play round their off time."

"Are you expecting Curtis to arrive? Feel a bit foolish if he doesn't. I thought he was down here every weekend."

Mike wondered if she was probing him. "Oh, I couldn't say. He usually turns up at some point in the evening." He wasn't going to commit himself to the truth, that Curtis hadn't been seen at the club recently. Mike knew nothing of his night-time activities. "Why don't you give him a ring, to make sure?"

"He's not exactly going to be in at this time of night, is he?"

"Who knows? Maybe he's reading a good book." Mike could tell from the way her eyes moved back to Ben that she was not impressed by his sarcasm. Her being here tonight made him suspicious. There was something else though. Mike was riding high, the chemical boosting his self-esteem and making him feel hyper-aware but he couldn't trace whatever was lurking in his memory that added to this feeling of doubt. He noticed her movements lighting a cigarette were quick, jumpy almost. Some words from Celia maybe. "Time for the band, I think."

The heavy bass drone from downstairs had cut out and been replaced by the sound of a voice.

"You come watch em? They supposed to be good."

She got up from the table and Ben came round to go down with her. He watched her take the stairs and fade from sight in the mass of people. Like trying to recall a well known title or name, he knew it would make sense later.

He could only relax cocooned in the flat with her. On his own, out in the car or in the street she filled his mind; the problems were too impossible to solve.

"I can feel the tension in your back, Curtis, like rocks."

The last three nights had passed like this. They had stayed in bed, not caring about the world outside, not talking about the situation. His concerns about ignoring Ben and Mike, betraying Amanda, all were obscured by her naked presence. He hardly spoke.

"Let me rub them out for you. I'll be your antidote."

But Sophie was the poison in his blood. Since meeting her his perceptions were clouded, ambitions forgotten. Nothing had mattered but to hold her. Spread on the bed, the nimble girl pounding his back, Curtis stared at the wall and felt the darkness closing. "This no good, Sophie."

She ignored him and continued with the massage.

"I feel bottle up by all this. It not right by Amanda."

"Are you going to speak with her, then, tell her it's over?"

"No. I've made a mistake, that all. Should never a start this. Tis we who have to stop."

She was silent for a moment, then her hands were slipping further down his back. "As you wish. One last time, then, for me to think back on." Her head bowed and she kissed at his flesh, lifting her weight with her arms so he could turn and face her on the bed. The smile on her face surprised him.

"I serious, you know. Amanda . . ."

"I'm serious too, so stop talking."

Again they drifted off, skin blending as one. As he entered her, Sophie stared off over his shoulder, her eyes alive with thought. His speech was nothing; each time between lovemaking she saw the agony in his gaze. Each time she won him back with her body. Curtis was hers. As the feeling within took her over she dug long nails into his neck, marking him and forcing a cry.

Mine.

There was space to move and this gave him mixed feelings. In terms of financial gain it was a blow. They had hoped for the same maximum capacity of the previous weekend but Lucien was not pulling the same crowd. A lot of them had just wanted to be able to say they had seen him and were not really interested in the music. Lucien was a style act, Mike realised. The "darling" crew from across the river were a bit thinner on the ground also. Maybe they had been scared off. However, it was still busy enough to be deemed a success. The audience was mainly West Park youth and the band playing at the moment had a lot of friends here to see them.

The slight decrease in numbers did mean more space and in this way he was happy. He was in a mood for dancing. Mike was rushing and wanted to be able to move to the music in the crowd. Just in front of him were Ben and Amanda, staring up at the stage occasionally and in movement. Mike had a perfect view of her dress wriggling as she pulsed. She could dance. Ben was almost trying to move in on her in his drunken state. He pulled on a white stick, boxed in his fist, hunched his shoulders low and circled her, looking for chances to rub up close to her, push a knee between her swaying limbs.

"Ben, you have face, you know."

He spoke to the air, drowned in the thick, bass rumble from the band, a grin cemented to his face. They were almost a revival band, playing straight, slow reggae but breaking into a quicker drum pattern for some songs.

"Mike, me look everywhere for you." Celia was yanking on his arm.

"How you doing? Thought you'd be here later."

"No, I got bored at home. Listen, why don't we go off somewhere?"

"I'm dancing."

"Ya call that dance? I've got a better idea for what we should be doing." Straight, she talked in a clear, soft voice and Mike realised it had been some time since he'd heard her speak in this way.

"I've already had a shot baby."

There was a flash of anguish, then she recovered. "But you have some more, don't you? Come on, Mike."

"Take a break, Celia. It's been every day lately."

"An' what about you? You ave snow nose too."

"Yeah, but I'm chill with it. You change when you get trashed." The drug did affect her profoundly. She was relying on it more for confidence and esteem than a hit.

"It make me feel good, that all. Come, I be real nice to you." Her body was pressed against him and she still had the power to rouse him. Something about her pleading was of special appeal and he relished the control he had. It was getting to be a straight swap, providing the drug for her attentions. His lust blocked out the questions.

"You have anything in mind?"

"Anything you want. I sure I come up with something you like."

"There's nowhere for us to go. The flat's still a wreck."

"You ever make it in a car?"

"Dumb question. You know I haven't."

"Let's try that, then. Fire me up first an' I see you out there."

There was no way he could think clearly with her offer open to him. His hand rummaged for the wrap. "Ten minutes, then, and anything."

"Deal."

The car got looks from the doormen as it pulled in and parked, finding a space in a line of vehicles around the building's perimeter. Kimps noticed the stares and thought about the risk but decided it was slight. Wayne probably didn't have it registered in his own name anyway. They paused before climbing out.

"How do we know them? Walk in and ask?"

He ignored the sarcasm and caressed the metal lump at his chest. "We can have a drink and sit it out for a while. You worry too much."

They climbed out and strolled up to the entrance.

"It's not full, I hope. We need some tickets."

"Just go through to the box office. See the girl."

Tonight Hargreaves had two men on the front door. They were the best "security improvements" Ben and Mike had been able to persuade him to adopt, under promise they would consider installing the systems he wanted. They were big, more agile than the usual staff, but the Americans still dwarfed them. Ryan slouched past, smiling at them. "Take it easy, boys. Don't work too hard."

The front hall was empty so they paid and pushed through the glass door. On the other side was a wall of noise from the band.

"Man, they have another bar? This isn't exactly my kind a thing."

"You don't go for roots, Wayne? Thought you'd been out there."

"Wasn't for the music. I had other things on my mind." He modelled the shape of a woman in the air and they started laughing.

"I see some stairs. Maybe a bar up there."

Pushing through the crowd Kimps started examining faces, wondering if his prey could be staring up at him. Apart from their height their clothes set them out as conspicuous. The shape at his chest gave him a feeling of security. His companions seemed unconcerned. Wayne particularly was at ease, even smiling at some of the swaying girls as they squeezed by.

"Yeah, it serves drinks."

They were up in the Basement and took a table against the wall. It was quite empty, most of the throng having moved down to watch the band.

"It's on me. Beer or what?"

"They sell pitchers?"

"Ryan. This is the wrong side of the river for that."

"I'll take a couple of bottles, then, and make sure they're cold."

Kimps ordered the drinks and checked his suit in the mirror at the bar. He was looking forward to the next hour.

Ben was gradually cornering Amanda against the other dancers. He moved in sweeps up to her and she responded by backing away, nudging the people behind her to escape. But each time, her retreat was less determined. She wasn't sure if she liked it or not. It felt as though they were flirting, although neither of them had spoken or even looked up at each other.

The band was going down well and had been picking up the pace, leaning more towards a slack style to keep the crowd's attention. As they kicked in with a new tune Ben took it as a cue to take her hand. There was a tremor of reluctance but he tugged her close and dropped his arm round to her waist, pulling her onto him.

For a moment Amanda went with it, then broke away from him. She was motionless in the forest of swaying bodies, then moved off for the stairs. "Me no coming on, you know."

He strode after her, the confidence of alcohol fuelling his pace. "Hey, cool yourself."

She walked on up to the bar and took a seat. "Gin and lemon, please."

"On my tab there." He dropped onto the stool next to her, shouting to the barman.

"I can get my own drinks, Ben."

"Think you got the wrong impression back there. I dance that way, that all."

"Really, it's alright. I'm not in the mood for it right now but I do know how to dance."

"Is this boy troubling you in any way?" Off to her other side Kimps was bringing himself up to his full height, gazing at her. He smiled courteously, a note wedged in his hand waiting to pay.

"Oh. I thank you but you got the wrong idea."

"Who this 'boy' you talk about to, ras? Me lick you down tally."

Kimps was a head taller than Ben and the cut of his suit emphasised his height. Ben wore his usual loose sports gear. "If that was directed at me and I understand you correctly, then, yes, I am talking to you. Can't you see the lady is unhappy?"

"None a your concern, ya fuck. Drink you drink and drift, man." Ben was still feeling quite drunk and regarded the Basement as his patch. He was undaunted by Kimps.

"I've no truck with you, I suppose." Kimps turned to

Amanda again with his concerned tone. "Only if you're sure you're not being bothered."

This was too much for Ben. He jumped off his stool, stepped round Amanda and stared up at the arrival.

"You pissing me off, ya hear? Me an' the gal here, we is fren, not that it any a you mind. You fuck wid the boss man, Yankee. This my club you is in. You on my deal here."

The smile broadened and Kimps raised an arm. "Now that really is good news."

This was not the reaction Ben had been hoping for. As he pondered his next move, anxious not to lose face with Amanda, he felt the presence of someone behind him. Though fairly drunk his instincts were still awake and he stepped away from the bar, looking over his shoulder. He walked straight into Ryan's chest.

"You going somewhere? Just when we came over to say hello as well. Not much of a host tonight, are you?"

His mind was racing. There was another behind him, another giant pinning him in. Ben couldn't see an out, so resorted to a word play. "You fuckers back off. Before you mess wid me you ave to deal wid the whole team."

Kimps idly glanced over at the barman who was calling down to the front hall, then turned back to Ben. "Ry, take the stairs."

He walked over to the top of the steps and Wayne shuffled round so Ben was facing him.

"Where's your partner, kid?"

"You boy fuck now. Best you try run afore we dash you away."

The few people in the bar were silent, spellbound by the confrontation, so he could hear the sound of heavy steps over the music. The two men from the door, dressed in their cheap suits, had come up into the bar. They were sizing up the man who blocked them. After checking Ryan to see if he had a weapon the front man barged into him, landing a fist to the side of his chest. Ryan doubled up, pulling his hands to his chest. The other doormen tried to get to his other side, reaching out to grab an arm but the American stepped back. He hung low, his head down and legs braced, urging them on. Wayne and Kimps looked on with disinterest.

As they rushed him again, the big man twisted and leaned back, keeping his fists high, bunched at his neck. Arching away from them his left leg came up at the opposite angle and he kicked out. The foot was a blur, almost head height. It crashed into the front man's chest, then snapped back. He was shuffling forward with tiny hops and lashed out again at the other man who tried to defend himself with a boxing position. It was a feeble attempt to halt the deluge of blows. Ryan was all over him, leaning in with punches, then stepping back and kicking out again. The doorman was crushed towards the stairs. His colleague was absent, kneeling on the floor trying to breathe over the pain in his chest. Ben watched as his saviours were annihilated. The one on his feet made a last desperate attack and got in close, reaching out with his spread hands. Ryan could have kicked him down but chose to accept his challenge. He stood tall, chest-on with the man, their hands high above, locked together. For a few seconds it was even, both men taking the strain but the doorman soon started to fade. His neck thickened and his breathing became a dry pant. Ryan had a twisted smile on his lips. Weakened by the earlier force, the man began to sink, his will slipping. Then he collapsed and fell to the floor, gulping for air. Ryan rolled him over with his foot like a sick dog.

"Let's go and talk, bossman. Want to go out with you for a while."

Ben was no coward but he realised this was not the time for a valiant stand. He crashed through Kimps and Wayne but Ryan seized him by his jacket and locked an arm round his throat.

"Come on, we've wasted enough time."

"What about the other? You said there were two."

"Well, I think he'll get the general idea, don't you?"

"An' this one?"

"I wanna show him the piece."

Wayne chuckled and went over to help Ryan.

The car was not designed for two bodies on the same seat. After a few curtailed exercises in gaining entry Mike found he could kneel on the floor with her legs grazing the low roof. She was giggling at his antics and he had to lift her off the seat.

"Mikey, this no gonna work."

"I disagree. It has to work. Press your feet on the screen."

"What if they a go through?"

"Then I'll call for the breakdown people."

She shrieked with laughter and switched her feet so they were planted on the windscreen. They slid about with all the condensation.

"That's it. I think it's gonna be all right."

"Mike! Mike, are you out here?"

"Fuck, that's Amanda."

"Hush an' she go away."

They could hear her shouting his name around the car park.

"Mike, Ben's in trouble!"

"Ya hear that?"

"Ben's always in trouble."

"I think you bes have a look anyways."

"Celia, if you hadn't noticed, I'm occupied."

She wriggled underneath him, pushing him away. "Gal sound desperate."

"She can join the club then." He was opening the door and peering out, pulling his jeans up to his waist. The girl was with three men and Ben. In the darkness it took Mike a few seconds to see that they were almost carrying his friend, his feet dragging on the asphalt of the car park. "Fuck, they got Ben."

"Who got Ben?"

"Three huge, dangerous-looking guys, that's who. Pass me that fuckin' crook lock."

It was hard for him to believe. His mind was still awash with the sweet confusion of the drug but he knew he had to respond. He could see that they were pushing him into a sports car but Ben was gripping the door frame and resisting. It was like watching television.

Celia stuck the iron rod of the wheel lock in his lap. "Do something, Mike."

Amanda had seen him staring blankly from the half-open door and was yelling over.

Mike made it onto his feet. His brain felt like mince. "Fuck." He was running, stumbling towards them, picking up speed. One hand was at his waist, holding the flapping jeans, and his shirt blew round to his back. The ground felt cold through his socks.

"Kimps, weapon behind."

He twisted, flicking a hand to his chest, rolling the gun out as his body curled in one movement. The glimmer of metal caught his eye and the barrel swung up, his right arm straight supported by his other hand at the elbow. The long square of steel bolted twice in his fist and he turned, climbing into the car. "Get him in the fucking car."

Ryan slapped Ben in the neck, stunning him, and pushed the folded body through the door. "Go."

Mike felt his stomach open up like a suitcase. His feet left the ground in a jump and he was pushed back through the air. When he hit the floor his hands were warm. He lifted his head and watched the black circle spread round his frame.

"Mike, ya bleed, man. Hold ya belly."

He felt nothing. The powder blocked the pain, filled the hole in his stomach. He was conscious of the girl next to him weeping and voices a few yards off. "It's OK. I'm fine really."

She just cried, slapping his hand and wiping the blood away from her knees.

"Oh, Mike. Dear God help you."

Wayne was driving fast, shooting lights.

"Take it easy on the gas."

"You just shot someone."

"All the more reason to relax. I don't want a speeding ticket right now, do you?"

Ben was struggling wildly in the back, pressed against Ryan. His mouth was covered by the leather but they all heard his muted cries.

"I think this one's pissed off, Kimps. Could be you . . ."

"Yeah, I know. Head for the house."

"Where you live?"

"It's cool. No one knows I live there. Anyway, it was a stomach hit. He'll live."

"Oh, well, that's just dandy, then."

"Listen, Wayne. You have to show these fuckers we mean it."

"The gun was supposed to be for show, that's all. I saw you. You just went fuckin' automatic again. I was there last time you . . ."

"Get me back, then you can dust if you want."

"Fuck that. This guy saw it all."

Ben was in agony. The position Ryan held him in made it impossible to move, hard to breathe, but he screamed vengeance. He had heard the shot, seen Mike's body lift from the ground and crumple on impact. He had never seen a shooting. The noise was still a pounding hum in his ears.

"This guy's too much to hold all the way back there, Kimps."

"Neck him again, then."

Ryan chopped at the rear of his head with a cupped palm. After the third blow Ben lay still. "All quiet now, boys."

They lay motionless, drained from the night's embrace. Curtis could hear her breathing it was so quiet.

"You can't deny there's something."

He said nothing but rolled his legs off the side of the bed and sat upright. His fingers played with the stub of a joint on the side table and he lifted it to his mouth.

"You're just going to sit there and smoke? I'm talking to you."

Amanda would never have reprimanded him like this. He thought of her ease, the differences between her and the one he lay with now.

"Well, say something. We did that to show there was something there, didn't we?"

"We did that because it something we do, that all."

"Don't put it down to some bullshit man-and-woman debate, Curtis."

He lit the stick in his mouth with a wave of a match and stepped away from the bed. "I've done something I may regret that's for sure."

This time with Sophie had made it clearer. The first base sex sessions between them had been an escape. It had felt novel, a change of style, and now he saw it for that. "Man, me still ave some growing up to do."

She followed him across the room and slapped his back, leaving a pale stain between his shoulder blades.

The violence irritated him. He ignored the stinging pain and didn't react. Curtis wanted her to feel insignificant.

"How dare you say that?"

"Thought you wanted words from my mouth? It don't feel right with you now, that all. Something's happened."

"So, what's changed?" Her tone was softer now. She saw the seriousness of his mood. "Talk to me."

"There nothing I can say." It was as though he had stripped away the confusion of his feelings of late. Sophie looked plain, her naked body was of no interest. He felt sad for her if she believed she was in love with him. "Nothing to say. Let go, that all."

There was a sound from the gate and he heard someone rushing up the path. He looked to his wrist but remembered his watch was lost in the pile of clothes by the bed. The bell for his flat rang.

"It late. That Ben, I kill him."

He would not have answered but it was a release from the strain of Sophie. His head was clearing. Throwing a long shirt across his back, he walked over to the entrance. Amanda pushed through as he opened the door. She said nothing. Her eyes were lost in Sophie.

"It over, finish. It nothing."

He tried to hold her but she backed away from him, her face ashen. "Mike and Ben need you. Someone shot him . . ."

"Gun, you say gun?"

"Round at the club they run, three men. Americans. I was down there looking for you."

"Who shot?"

"You'd better go and help."

She made to go but he caught her arm and shook her. "Whappen here? You say there a shooting but who? Tree Yankee man, was all of them with gun? Where is he now, which hospital?" Curtis was thinking fast. He could see she was disturbed but needed the information from her before the shock of what she had witnessed this evening hit her.

Already the issue of the two girls had been swept from his mind. Sophie was back at the bed, slowly pulling on her clothes.

"It's Mike. Shot in the stomach and they took Ben off in a car. I only saw one gun, Curtis."

The way she said his name surprised him; not cold or detached but a soft whisper. She was only inches from him and he wanted to hold her, wait for the other girl to slip away so he could talk, explain to her. But he had another priority. "Mike alright? You know where they take him?"

"Yeah. Celia's gone with him. What about Ben though?"

The crisis was uniting them. Neither of them wanted to face the other problem.

"I deal with that right now."

"We don't know where they took him though. He could be anywhere in town."

Curtis was dressing, dashing round the flat. When he had covered his nudity he went into the thin kitchen and bent to open a cupboard under the sink. His hand searched the rim of the bowl until it found a wad of oilcloth. His fingers tightened and he pulled it out delicately, then parted the folds of cloth until it lay flat in his hand. It had been some time since he had felt the weight of the revolver and he flipped it over in admiration before sticking it under his jacket. "Feel me know someone that might be able to tell though. Might take some persuasion but Ben, ya chill. Curtis be with you soon."

The first thing he was aware of were dim circles of light bouncing on his eyelids. It was possible to play games with them, like some elaborate colouring set, and he was reluctant to leave. Then the pain cut in and his neck muscles throbbed, causing him to moan. It reminded him of waking from a short but deep sleep and feeling bemused for a moment, before recalling the events prior to sleeping. The recollection of tonight sent a shudder of rage through his body and he swore. It was muted though, as his mouth was dry, like paper.

He was stiff and tried to stand, opening his eyes to check his whereabouts but his legs were bound, clamped together by something, and he crashed back into the sofa's cushions. Now he felt the pressure at his wrists and knew it was a rough rope biting into his skin. It was futile to wrestle against the cord. Ben knew the cowboy-film rope tricks were ridiculous. If someone ties you tight when you're out, then you stay put. Thus immobilised, he decided to study the room, looking for another option.

A thin mantelpiece topped the fireplace directly opposite him. That was the only shelf. The walls had an unbroken cover of dull cream paper. The carpet was a similar shade, thick and expensive. With great pain he twisted his head slightly and saw that off to his right were some open glass doors. These he assumed led into a garden or backyard as there was a slight movement in the air. Voices echoed from the area beyond the doors, indistinct to his ears. Turning his head back the other way he saw the armchair a few yards off. Ryan was sitting in it, beaming at him.

"You wanna take the place, then? Got a deposit?"

It took a long moment for Ben to understand this was intended as a joke. The casual remark had surprised him. "Boy, for one in deep as you, you mighty easy?"

"Oh, I'm not too worried. They're out there now trying to figure out what to do with you. Sure they'll come up with something suitably 'reassuring'."

He had not thought of this, of himself as the witness to a shooting. Mike's battered frame leapt to his mind as he dwelled on it. "I shoot you down, ya fuck. You an' the two out there, y'all dead men to ras." Fear was rising in his heart. They had already shown the ability to commit violence. He remembered the noise, the flash of fire. There was still a tiny ringing in his ears. "How long me out, man?"

"Only a few minutes, just lying there groaning. I didn't hit you too hard, did I?" Ryan's inane grin was set on his face. Ben decided he must be mildly psychopathic to act so cool. He had only seen it with crazy guys, holding face in a stand-off.

"You a ras maddy boy. Think you gwan bury me or summat? Will be me at your funeral, fucker." Keeping up the defiance with his speech was the only way to stay calm. He was shouting, putting menace in the words.

"Enough racket." Kimps strolled through the doors from the garden and stared down at him. "You want me to do it now or you want a bit longer?"

"Kimps, you got to call in your man." Wayne was behind him. There was anger in his voice and Ben guessed they had been arguing about his fate in the garden conference. Ryan obviously didn't warrant inclusion in the debate and Ben memorised this observation. Any rifts or tensions between them noted now might provide him with an out later. His brain was trying vainly to make sense of the situation, find an escape or some way to reason with them.

"I think we can handle it on our own."

"Come on, will you? This guy knows the details better than us and this is what he's for, isn't it? Looking after you."

"I wouldn't bank on the 'looking after' thing too much, Wayne. He's not going to be popping corks to celebrate this, an' it just fucks everything up."

"You know we need him. An' what about the fucking girl, man?"

They had been talking about Ben as though he was an inconvenience, some trivial problem to be cleared up. Now Amanda was the issue.

"Did she get a good look?"

"Course she fucking did, man. They know our names as

well. It's a fucking mess. It wasn't supposed to be bloody, so we've set ourselves up with all that crap but you go blasting. We've got to get moving. Kimps, get the cleaner in, man."

"Only cause you're backing out. I still think . . ."

"It's sensible, that's all. Then we can wipe our hands, you know."

"Alright."

He moved off to behind the sofa Ben was sitting on, out of his field of vision but he heard the sound of him punching buttons. Wayne stared over his head at the telephone operation, looking expectant.

"Put it on the monitor. I want to hear this guy."

"Harvey, got a problem here."

"Yes, Kimps, I heard. I had a call a few minutes ago with the news and I'm surprised you're calling. Thought you'd have fucked off on the run by now."

"Should we talk so openly on the phone, Harvey?" He was trying to be diplomatic as the omission of the "mister" was a clear indication of Harvey's temper.

"This is England. Anyway, I've nothing to worry about."

"Need your cleaning friends, Harvey. Got an unwanted body here."

"Another body?"

"A person, Harvey. Got picked up en route, you know."

There was silence. The speaker crackled as though impatient.

The breeze from the open doors made the room cool but Ben felt a lone, icy bead of sweat dribble round his eye to the bridge of his nose. "A ras. They talk bout me like I a bag, a fucking shopping they find."

"Shut up." Wayne stepped towards him and Ben glowered at him but kept quiet.

Harvey broke the hush. "I'll have to come round. Talk it over. Fifty minutes."

The phone clicked and started to drone until Kimps dropped the handle back into position. "Happy now?"

"That would be stretching it but it's a start. So yes."

"Guess we just wait for him to show, then." Kimps wandered back and flopped down next to Ben on the sofa. He was thinking of his father, what he would have done in this position. Like a chess player he tried to see the moves open to him but it all came down to Harvey. Wayne was right, in that they needed a local player to tidy up. It had gone too far for them just to scare the trussed youth sweating next to him and dump him somewhere. He was a risk and they needed to pass it on. He couldn't see any way to stop this getting back to his father's ears though. Harvey would demand that pleasure as payment, if he was able to help. Kimps sighed. It was a waiting game now.

He examined Ben's strained features, the look of panic in his eyes. Kimps felt no sympathy for him, he was just interested in the mark of fear. To Kimps Ben was an obstacle that would be surmounted, then become extinct, an inconvenience that might cost him dearly in his father's view. "If only your friend hadn't wanted to be a hero. If that had been the case you'd probably be at home now, licking your wounds. Not in your present hole anyway."

At first Ben said nothing. He was dreaming of release from the ropes and a weapon with which to cripple his gaoler. He wondered how Mike was: tubes and needles sticking out of his belly sprang to mind and he almost smiled. He would be eating ice-cream in a few days. Ben could think of a thousand places he would rather be than this sofa right now and thoughts and images flooded his thinking. At the front of them all, growing clearer in the wash of his brain was the picture of a man, dressed in a suit and struggling forward, searching for him. It was his last and only hope. He knew Curtis would be on his trail but would he find him in time? "Me can wait, man. Me ave time. Soon you no look so relax, that I promise you."

With the window down, there was a fierce rush of air across his face. It felt as though it was cleansing him. He gripped the wheel, taking turns fast and keeping the speed up, flying through the deserted streets of West Park. There was no time to waste with careful driving. Curtis saw the night's events for what they were. It was clear the gun had been brought along to scare his two friends and it was part of a hit. They must have panicked and shot off a few. The gunman was probably cursing himself for it by now. Whilst this meant a kill had not been their initial purpose, the rules of the game would have warped out of normal reason by now. Ben would be rather unpopular, a bad card to hold.

His only chance was Bunny. Carl had heard something about it too and issued the warning but this information would have to be extracted. The choice was clear for him. The idea of pushing Carl didn't seem realistic, though Bunny was not much more appealing. He hoped to find him at the den and he was only a few minutes away. The accelerator sank lower.

It had been a strange situation with the girls. Amanda was staying in the flat at his insistence and Sophie had slunk out with a scathing look. She knew it was a hopeless battle and the problems at the club seemed to dwarf their dispute so she had left without a word. He thought only of Amanda, hoping she would be there waiting for him when he returned. Then he flashed back to his task and let the adrenaline send a tingle into his fingers, lifting the heart-beat in his chest and heightening all other senses. Curtis could feel the gunplay approaching. Merely having the handgun next to his body excited him, sent him racing back to the farm and the shooting those long months ago. Apart from two or three occasions, used as a threat, the gun had remained dormant and had not been fired since that battle out of town. The knot at the base of his finger was a powerful reminder of the loss and change produced last time and he had to breathe deep to calm himself. He was getting close.

He found a space in the darkness of the street and parked. The trees were blocking out the stars and it was hard to see, but he found the right house and took the path round to the rear door, pausing before going down the steps.

He knew they were probably looking at him on a closed-circuit camera system, as each time he had been down to the den the door had opened before he knocked. To keep them happy he fumbled in a pocket, as though looking for a wallet. There was a problem. At the entrance to the first room they would frisk him. That meant no gun. Curtis knew the quickest, maybe even the only, way to get Bunny to surrender his knowledge was to ram the barrel of the revolver into his mouth and stare him out. A fist fight could go either way for him. It didn't trouble him to be honest about his fighting ability. His mind was trained on the fastest method of achieving his aim and he wanted the gun. That necessitated ignoring the frisk. He took the first step down.

The door swung open and he stepped through. One of the two doormen nodded hello and turned to get his paying-in draw, the other approached him with his hands out for the frisk. For a second, Curtis was amused by the possibility that Bunny would not be there, then he dipped his hand to his side and drew the weapon. "Keep it quiet, boys. I'm only after a chat with a man a mine, that all. I follow you."

"You can't do this here. You're finished the second they hear."

"You finish sooner than that less you do as I say, boys."
He motioned them to step back over to the door and they
walked towards the rear bar as a tight group. Though some
of the seated couples in the first room saw the gun tucked
in his fist there was no disruption of the march and they
strolled up to the bar without a word being said. Here
they turned to look at him with tired faces.

"Who you after, then?"

"Get up on dem stool there. It Bunny, where him dare?"

"Well, he's not here, is he. See for yourself."

It was gloomy in the bar so most of the drinkers had not
noticed the gun in his hand. Even if they were aware of the
scene, to them it was none of their concern anyhow. The
den was a very private place. It was the board and Stefan
who would be unhappy. He scanned the seats, checking
faces and keeping a watch on the two men before him at
the bar. Bunny wasn't there. "You sayin' he no come in
tonight, then?"

"That's right. You should leave now, my son."

Curtis was focused on his mission. The years of experience dealing with the street had taught him well and his
learning came to the surface at times of stress like this.
"You a lie, boy. I see it in your eye."

The doorman was on edge, his pulse quickening.

"Where the fuck Bunny?" He lifted the barrel in a slow arc
so it grazed the man's face. Then he moved it forward so it
pressed against him. "You hear me, man. You wan live, you
tell me."

"He's upstairs with a girl. I don't know which room
though. I just saw him going up, that's all. I promise."

Curtis lowered the barrel and marched off to the front
room and the door for upstairs. The memory of how he
knew the route depressed him but there was no time to
ponder his moods of late and he increased his pace, almost
running. There was shouting behind him but he thought

only of finding Bunny. There was no way he could have searched upstairs and minded the two men under guard.

He was on the next floor up and started checking the rooms. They were all of roughly the same design, boxy and plain. The first three were empty but twisting the handle of the fourth room he heard a muted objection and crashed in.

Bunny was flat out on the bed, naked. A young girl in all the gear was riding on top. "A ras, Curtis. This room taken, sah."

Curtis was relieved to catch him like this and stepped next to the bed before he could move, letting him see the gun. "Don move. Just rest up tha way, ya here me. Gal, don't move a muscle there."

"Wha you dealin in, sah. We fren, I thought."

"That right. Me need something from you though."

Bunny looked perplexed and his face was flush from his exertions. The girl looked on with a blank expression of worry, hiding her breasts with an arm.

"You is telling me bout someone the other day. Someone not happy with my friend there."

"A fuck, Curtis, I . . ."

"Well, one my friend lick down an' in hospital. Other fren a mine been taken and me need know who and where, from wha you heard."

Bunny could at least understand the situation now and he regained some composure, despite the girl mounting him. "Change nothin', as you know. All it show is I should never tell you an' you is still a fool pickney. I told you to stay away from it, C."

The gun was lifting, tilting to his head. Curtis let it hovver by his ear. "You hear me seen a bit . . ."

"Me know you ave pull a trigger, boy, it no big thing. Many a tried afore you, I tell you."

Curtis pushed the barrel into the soft skin of Bunny's ear

lobe. "We been gettin' on lately so I be easy wid you. First I gonna shoot the pillow by you head. That mean you lose the use of the ear."

Bunny was searching his face for a clue to see if he was serious about the threat. He didn't miss the steel in the youth's gaze.

"Then I do the other ear. Then I blow yo jaw, man, down from the inside a you mouth. Tha way you no talk or hear, so you don't ave to worry about secrets getting out. I need to know, Bunny."

"This guy fuck you up though, Curtis. Him is related with a man in the States. Can't go fucking with him, I tell ya. If you do, then you finish."

"Bunny. Me no ave time fo this . . ."

"I mean it, man, me no joke. This guy big, ras big. Asking fo a contract go fuck wid him son." The gun was nuzzling his ear, playing at the entry. Bunny sighed and relaxed his frame. "Kimps, sah. That him name. Guy a bit crazy, I think, so go easy, yeah? You find him a the house where you do the ting for Carl wid me, remember."

"I remember." He withdrew the gun from the ear but kept it close to the man's head.

"So wha? You ave it now, man, so go."

"Ave to make sure though."

"Oh no, man. Me no gonna do anything."

"Have to, man."

"Well, before you do, let me tell you. Kimps may fuck ya. If not him, then him father will. But if by some trick a fate you get away from them . . . then you ave me to deal with."

"Good night, Bunny." The gun came down in a rapid sweep, thudding into Bunny's temple and he passed out. Curtis stuffed it back into his pocket, then walked to the door. "When him come round, you be nice to him, yeah?"

He stepped out into the hall, thinking of the man's warning but suddenly froze. The corner of the door frame a foot or two in front of him had turned to dust in a little cloud. Then the sound of the blast hit him, a split second after the visual sign. He sagged his knees to lose height and ran over to the head of the staircase. Bullets were pounding into the woodwork around him and he twisted the gun out and fired two shots blindly behind him, not even looking to aim. Then he was on the stairs, taking them in great bounds, sprinting along the corridor, checking his body for injuries and finding none. The door to the front room was open but instead of charging through he stopped and kicked it with his toe. The sway of the door caused a nervous aim to fire from the other side. Two circles opened in the wood, big enough to put his head through. It was a shotgun and Curtis gambled it was the only firepower in the room and dove through immediately, hoping to catch them reloading. He knew there was someone coming behind him and had discovered a long time ago that it was sometimes better to act than to think in situations like this. Then you had no choice but to face the challenge and come out either way.

His bet paid off. One of the doormen from earlier was in the middle of the room, fussing with the red tubes of shotgun spray. He was out in the open, not having bothered to find cover and Curtis grinned at him. Why did people with shotguns consider themselves indestructible? There was a certain arrogance associated with the gun, he thought. This all flashed through his mind in the second it took for the man to drop the shells to the carpet and look up at him. It was probably the other doorman who would be emerging any instant behind him.

"You better run, boy. While I in a good mood."

The man dropped the long stem of the gun and ran for the other room. Curtis paced through to the entrance room and climbed the steps to the garden. He could hear shouts behind him as he reached the car, jumped in and fired the engine. Then the street was flying past as he floored the pedal. It would only take ten minutes for him to reach his destination at this time of night. He thought only of getting to Ben, making up for his earlier betrayal by silence, but Bunny's words were coming back to him. It seemed he was making himself a few powerful enemies this evening.

Harvey pulled up outside and studied the outside of the house. All appeared calm. Carefully locking the car door he walked up to the front porch and the door opened for him.

"Good evening, Harvey. You made good time."

"You're relaxed, considering you just shot someone." He was following Kimps into the living room and scanning the occupants. "This him?"

"No other. He's the problem."

Harvey came round to the front of the sofa and looked at Ben for a moment before speaking to Kimps. "It's no good. I can't wipe this up for you, boy. There's already rumours flying around. It's a turn-in, I think, your only choice."

"You mean we let him go and then walk into a police station?" Wayne was agitated, shaking his arms to punctuate the words. "I'm not taking an accessory charge for this, no way. Kimps can carry it."

"You're all implicated. Nothing I can do about it now." Harvey went over to one of the chairs and sat down. His mood was placid compared to the others.

"You hear the man, wha him say. Turn me loose, then." Ben was ignored in the discussion.

Even Kimps was looking edgy now. "I must admit I'm disappointed here. Wasn't the whole point of your coming out here to sort this thing out for me. That is part of your job. If it's a financial concern, then . . ."

"It's nothing to do with money. He's come here to fucking gloat, can't you see that? We need to lean on him."

Harvey stared up at Wayne with a whimsical grin. "That your solution to everything, is it? Well, it won't help, you hear. I've dealt with your kind . . ."

"Enough history. What exactly are you saying here?"

Harvey took a moment to compose himself before replying, adjusting the line of his trousers and leaning back in his chair. "I'm not taking the boy there. It'd be madness. Kimps, you've been on a short fuse since I met you and this is too much. If he was a crook it might be different. Less of a fuss, you see. But he's only a kid an' it's different with the other shooting on top of it. You've already done one boy, this would dig your grave. Let him go an' maybe I can help you run but even that I don't recommend. They're heavy on guns these days an' they'll want you bad. Everyone'll have your face from the club an' all. Probably getting a description out now. You have to see it's useless."

They were thoughtful for a few seconds, restless in the confines of the room.

Ben felt his stomach about to cramp with the tension. "You ave to listen to the man. Everything he say is right."

"I think you should go. You're obviously going to be of no help. We'll deal with it as we should have done an hour ago. You've wasted our time."

Harvey rose from the chair.

"He can't walk out now, he's in on it as much as me an' Ry."

The man on the far side of the room had said nothing for minutes but as though responding to his name he lifted his bulk from the chair and ambled over towards Harvey. "Wayne's right. This guy talks shit." With no warning he flashed a fist to Harvey's cheek. It connected with a dry crack and instantly Ryan swung with the other arm, slapping the back of his broad fist into the stunned man's face. Casually Ryan turned back to his friends. "Maybe that'll make the old bastard more amenable, like. We've been talking an' talking, getting us nowhere, man."

"Watch him, Ry. Reaching."

Harvey was on his knees in pain, rooting in his pocket for something and Ryan slowly lifted a leg to deliver another of his kicks. He was enjoying the hesitation of the blow, thinking Harvey was almost disabled by the pain in his face and allowing him the time to hope. But the older man was far from finished. Launching himself from the floor, using the strength in his lower abdomen, he crashed into the youth, winding him. He was as fast as Ryan despite his years and still tough. His hand found the bottle as Ryan steadied himself and prepared to fight. The rubber cork was prised off by his thumbnail and he waved it through the air, showering his opponent with the liquid.

Ben had never heard a scream so wild, a desperate animal wail. Harvey was still, watching the result of his throw and the others were shocked by Ryan's pain, trying to see what had happened. His arms covered his face and they were partly hidden by a misty smoke, rising from the crown of his head. At first he was motionless, legs braced wide apart but he suddenly raced out towards the garden, knocking Harvey out of his way and careering off the walls until he reached the outside.

Wayne ran after him and tried to prise his arms away to look at the wound but Ryan was leaning against the back wall sobbing. He could feel the liquid burning deep into his face.

"Kimps, come on, we should go. Leave the kid." Harvey walked over to Ben and stopped. He felt cold metal at the base of his neck.

"That was my friend, Harvey."

Kimps was behind Harvey, drawn up to his full height. Ben could see the expression of rage on his face, barely restrained fury.

Harvey didn't move. "I had to. We've not got much time."

"Dead time, Harvey."

The gun exploded in his hand, a thin lick of flame at the barrel. Ben's eyes closed automatically but he felt a spray on his face and screamed. Blood peppered his head and chest and his body tensed under a weight falling across his lap, forcing him to spasm in the seat. As he yelled he had opened his eyes and seen the older man slumping over him, his head turned at an unnatural angle, staring up at him. There was a gaping wound at his neck, big enough to put a hand through and a gush of blood was streaming out, soaking his clothes. Ben could feel the pool form at his waist, a hot dampness running round to the back of his legs. Kimps was pointing the gun, watching the sight as Ben thrashed desperately to shake the man off him. He was too heavy.

"Fuck, man. Ryan's out. He needs help." Wayne had come back into the room but seemed unaware of the dead man and Ben's writhing. He was trying to focus on Ryan's need, block out the chaos, but felt his control slipping away from him. Kimps was still caught in the death stare and he had to shake him violently to get his attention. "Kimps, get a grip, man. Come back to me, Kimps."

Kimps stumbled as if waking and finding himself here. His eyes were blurred for a second, then he turned to Wayne, remembering where he was.

"Ryan. I got the fucker for Ryan."

"Yeah, we got another corpse to deal with. You fucking collect em. Well, I'm out now. I'll take Ry, drop him at a hospital. You can clean up the shit."

"Kimps, I can't see you man, where are you."

The wounded man was taking tiny steps back into the room, still clutching at his face. Kimps could smell something bitter, like a sickly perfume drifting in the air.

"I'm blind, man, fucking blind." His voice was a low

croak, his normal tone forgotten. Walking into a chair he had to steady himself and then by impulse moved his hands out to check the space in front. Kimps studied his face. It didn't shake him at first and he was almost surprised. He was pleased he could look on the sight without turning away, as he was reverting to the fantasy aspects of his personality now, his reason gone. He couldn't deal with the situation any other way and would not admit to himself he had lost his authority of earlier or made mistakes. Ryan's mutilation was a test for him.

Strips of translucent skin hung from his cheeks, exposing the raw pink of flesh. Most of the tissue was exposed in this way. The eyes were revealed as their lids had curled open and bonded with the upper bone of the socket. One was a black stain, the other pitted with burns as though drops of wax had been poured into it. His mouth was burnt away; here the acid had been plentiful and his teeth were exposed in a demented, lipless grin. The burn spread round the scalp, stripping away the hair to leave yellow and red tissue scars. It went up to the ears which were misshapen, gnarled like some twisted elf.

"Think he's gonna live?"

"Fuck knows, man. If he'll want to, even. But we're moving anyhow."

"I can't deal with this on my own, Wayne."

"Don't see you have any choice. I'm freaked, man, running. Pin it on the black guy if you can."

"I'm in fucking charge here. You have a duty to . . ."

"You never were in charge, Kimps. Now, get out of the fucking way."

Ben was lost in the nightmare. His attempts to free himself of the dead man and the crimson sea at his waist were useless. The guy with the burn was a walking zombie, his twisted features were enough to scare him witless on their own but the other two were discussing his fate, deciding whether he lived or died. "Don't leave me wid this ras madman. See im shoot the man fo nothing." It was as though his voice was tiny, like that of some insect caught in a web. The giants in front of him were raging now and ignored his plea.

"We can still pull through if we stick it, Wayne."

"You're out of your fucking mind. Look at Ryan."

The wounded man had found a chair and was making wretched sobs, trying to speak but not producing anything coherent. His moans articulated the agony he felt.

"And that's some kind of acid, man. It could get worse. That shit'll touch your hand, you look fine apart from a rash, you know, an' the next day your whole fucking arm drops off, man."

"I wouldn't say he looks so good now."

"I despair for you, boy. Your fucking head's gone."

They faced each other. Kimps felt desperate. He could see no escape but for some reason it seemed imperative to keep everyone here. If they all just sat it out, then they could solve it, he was sure. Wayne moved over to Ryan. He threw a lap blanket over his friend's shoulders, then lifted him like a dying leper and led him off with an arm protected by the blanket.

"You can't go, man. Wha me do to you, sah?"

Wayne didn't pause in his exit. "There's millions of you an' I don't know one. Best of luck."

"Wayne, you can't do this. We need to talk."

"Talk's done, Kimps." He was close to the front door, moving slowly, hampered by the weight of the blind man.

Kimps planted his feet wide apart and raised his arm in a straight line. "I'll put a bullet in your head, boy."

Their eyes locked and Wayne could see Kimps was a long way from joking. They stood like that for a long time. Then a buzzer whined from the corner of the room and Kimps flashed round to face the garden. Someone was at the rear gate.

He had worked out the quickest route and pushed the car as much as he could. It carried him there smoothly though, the soft rush of the tyres urging him to reflect on the events so far, like a concerned friend, but he buried the thoughts. There was no halting now.

The thin drive up to the garden was dark and he had to take it carefully. There were no lights from the houses and gardens backing onto it and a couple of times he nearly grazed the car on the frames of the doorways. Before he reached the end he pumped the accelerator a little, then killed the engine, steering up to the gateway in silence. He left the door open and paced up to the wall on light feet. The gun was bonded to his hand and he felt the handle slip on the sweat of his palm. Better not to think about the decision, best to act. He knew the wall was too high to climb and the door solid, so he took a breath and rammed a fist to the button set in the brick. Far off he heard the responding click and movement in the house. He stepped back a pace into the dark.

"Must be the police."

"They don't know about this place."

"Then who? Some of their friends?"

Ben felt a shudder of relief and came back to life. He had a vision of an army storming the house.

"No one would touch me, Wayne."

"Well, some fucker pushed the bell. Who else knows?"

"Only one other guy's been here apart from you an' Harvey. Can't be him though. Fuck." Kimps saw the connection, cursed himself for his curiosity. "Could be the spade."

"What? You mean it could be his friend? Let's move."

Wayne's hand drifted to the handle but Kimps rushed

next to him and put the barrel of the gun on his out-stretched wrist. "Don't you think a call on the back door might encourage us to go through the front?"

"Mean he could be out there?"

"Maybe. I can take him anyway."

"Kimps, this is no fucking party game. If it is this guy . . ."

"He's probably unarmed, Wayne. He's a nobody, just a message boy. I'll deal with him."

"Curtis come to lick you down, sah. Him gonna shoot you, boy, put a ras hole on yo head." Ben felt a flood of excitement run through his body, like a wash of alcohol. The strain of the last hour and all he had seen was telling and there was a crazed grin cemented on his lips.

"Wayne, leave Ryan and go get a blade from the kitchen."

"I don't know . . ."

"We have to deal with this before you can leave."

Kimps accepting that he was going was a relief to Wayne and he put Ryan down on the carpet by the sofa and headed over to the door. "Where is it? I'll tow the line till we take this guy, then I'm out."

"Upstairs, hurry."

There was a thin flight of stairs opposite the doorway and he ran up them. Flicking a light on in the top room he checked the drawers until he found a weapon, then killed the light and jogged back down to the living room. In his fist he held a six-inch cook's knife.

The buzzer sounded again.

"Do the lights."

"We're two though. Best to keep the advantage."

"Maybe he's not alone."

Kimps threw a switch and the room was dark. It added to the sense of bewilderment Ben felt. Now he only heard their quiet words and light steps around the room.

"You go out and get the door."

"Like fuck. You've got the piece. I'll hold the fort, boy."

Kimps cursed softly and walked through the open doors to the garden. It was lighter out here despite the canopy of trees that shaded him. He hugged the wall, not making a sound, working his way round to the door. When he was next to it he paused for a second, listening out for a sound from the other side. There was nothing. Hesitating for a moment before acting, he counted to ten to calm himself, then lifted the latch with one finger and lashed out at the door with his shoe. It swung open in a great curve. Empty darkness faced him.

"Kimps, man. In the house."

After giving them a few seconds to respond and hearing the mumbled voices from inside, he changed his plan. To confuse them he decided to go round the front and after ringing the buzzer a second time, squeezed through a gap between the houses and onto the front street. Kimps had given him time with his count.

The house was dark and he knew that was good for him. Against unknown numbers he preferred the cloak of night. Moving quickly but silently up the path he leaned on the front door, testing the strength of the wood. He hoped it would give. He backed up a few steps and rushed it with his shoulder but was alarmed when he bounced off it and was thrown to the floor. It was solid. With no delay he stood up and calmly aimed at the lock. That was when he heard the shout from inside. He drowned it with the crash of the bullet into the metal and kicked through into the room, sticking to the nearest wall and crouching.

The first thing he sensed was the smell. It confused him as it reminded him of the labs at school, long ago, and he wondered if they had gas or some other danger. There was a man at his feet. He was out of the play though, that was clear. He looked as though he was holding his face in position. The room was small, with a wide couch or something in the middle and his eyes made out a head raised above the outline. The revolver lifted, found the mark and his finger was tight on the metal strip of the trigger.

"C man. You come at last, boy."

He let out a sigh and lowered the gun, for an instant thinking of charging over but then realising he had opponents in the room. There was movement in the back yard and he began to work the wall, heading for the rear of the house. As he flanked the wall he heard breathing, on top of Ben's murmurs.

Wayne was terrified and his lungs were begging for air. It was impossible to control his racing pants. He had thought the intruder would be unarmed and the kitchen knife sagged in his hand. From his hiding place he could see Kimps moving up from the garden, creeping towards the doors but the man was getting closer. His patience was exhausted and he knew the only hope was to surprise him before he got round to his position.

With a yell he jumped out from his corner, a blur of speed heading for Curtis. If he had been challenging another, one with less nerve, then his tactic may have worked but there was no fear in the man's movements, he didn't flinch. Curtis saw the approaching figure and the sparkle of the blade, high in the air. He aimed for the centre.

The gun came up and howled, firing twice. Kimps saw the flash of light from where he hid and shot. His finger pumped three times and then he crashed back for the darkness of the garden. The bullets pounded into the wall, screeching over Curtis's head as he ducked and fell by the sofa. All was silent for a second, then there was a huge crash as Wayne fell back against the mantelpiece, dragging the wall for support but collapsing. His head was spinning, life flowing from his form and he gulped for air as the blood frothed up from his lungs.

Kimps kept backing into the garden, calling out to his partner. "Wayne, you hit? Fucker hit you?"

There was a tremor in his legs and he ran for the open door to escape the battle. This was different from the times before. Then he had been the executioner, protected and confident. Against Curtis his courage was ebbing. It was equal numbers with Wayne gone and he wandered over to the car, half in a daze. The driver's side was open and he jumped in, checking for the keys. There was nothing in the ignition.

Curtis had reached Ben's side of the sofa by crawling round and now he was trying to shift Harvey's stiff bulk from his friend's lap.

"Me tie, man. Go after the other."

"He's going nowhere, man, settle."

Harvey was dragged off and dumped on the carpet, rolling to Wayne's shaking legs. The other man was dying, feeling the slow fatigue of rest wipe over him.

Curtis turned to Ben and felt for the rope. "Too thick to snap, Ben. Man have a blade somewhere." He faced the American and found his hand, still holding the knife. With a wrench he had it free and dropped the limp arm back to the ground. "Him done too. Just one other?"

"Yes, man. Fuckin maddy sah, you go for him, C."

"Easy."

Curtis sawed at the rope around Ben's legs, then concentrated on the hands.

Where Ben was free he fell forward and shook his arms, trying to bring the blood back to them. They were stiff and he felt the tingle of pain start in his fingers. "Go, man. I wan you to find him."

Curtis paused. He had Ben and could retreat but there

was still the threat from the man outside. Slapping Ben on the shoulder he stood up and crept out to the garden.

Kimps was still in the car, inert with fear. His ears detected a sound from the gate and he flung himself from the seat, sinking into the dark. If he could get to the end of the drive he would be safe. There at the end was light and space for him to slip away and he started walking away from the house.

"Yankee man. Why you running? Thought you was big man." In the thin avenue Curtis was pacing after him. Calling him out would be easier than stalking him.

"Back off. You don't know who you're facing here. Go back to the house and take your friend. Then it stops."

"An' the man you shot back a the club there?" Both of them were trying to trace the voice of the other as they worked their way down the drive, ducking in and out of the shallow doorways. Curtis was only twenty feet behind him but Kimps was hidden in the black air.

"He's alive, isn't he? Doing better than you if you keep following me." Kimps lifted the barrel of his gun and fired into the air, then dashed across to the other side. If Curtis fired back at the light of the shot, then he could locate him but his adversary was cunning.

Curtis knew he was being drawn out and was retreating towards the house. He was cursing himself for not thinking and pulling the keys from his pocket.

The engine fired and Kimps let out a pitiful sob. He was only about half-way down the drive, waiting for the shot to answer his when he heard it. The gun landed on the stone at his feet and he turned and ran, breaking the pink glow of the streetlights at the far end. Then he was bathed in light, the car sending a high beam down the centre of the drive. In a state of panic now, tears streaming down his face, he kept running but he could hear the surge of the motor behind him. Curtis had the pedal to the floor, closing on the sprinting figure and Kimps had to throw himself to one side, scratching the wall for a doorway to avoid the metal body of the car crushing him. As he went past Curtis hit the breaks and the wheels stopped, then he was out of the car in one leap.

The red of the rear lights was illuminating his cowering victim and Curtis stepped over to him. "You bawl like a baby, man."

Kimps was weeping, his words broken by childish sobs. "Please, I, I know we can come to some arrangement. My father is a very important man. You must listen to me. I . . ."

"Hush now, man. I come here to gun you, ya fuck."

His face was swollen in the red glow, streaks of tears on his cheeks. Curtis stepped closer, raised the gun. All the confusion and tensions of the last few week welled up in his mind. How could he have ignored the warning all that time ago? His finger tensed.

"No, I didn't want this. You'll never get away from him if . . ."

The top of his head was pushed back by the shot, thudding into the woodwork behind him. Curtis saw the dark spot of entry in the middle of his brow as the man crumpled and fell. The death needed no confirming. Kimps was wooden at his feet, the suit he wore creased and oily with blood. For a moment he paused and thought back on the last time he'd used the gun, the frenzy of the shooting, the fever that had gripped him. This time was different, a cold kill, and he gazed at the dead man.

"Curtis, you get him? He gone?" Ben was stumbling up next to him, rubbing his arms and staring at Kimps on the ground.

"All over, Ben. Come man, we dig up."

Sixteen

It stank of chemicals in the ward. She had to open the window next to him to let some night air in, then sat down by his bed.

"Oh, Mike. How we gonna get round this one?"

There was no reply. His face was pale, bloodless, and she seized his hand to let him know she was there, hoping her presence would be registered in his drugged sleep. He had been sedated after the operation and though she knew he would be out for hours she had decided to stay at his side.

The ambulance ride had been a voyage into hell for her. Still on the high, she had watched as one of the crew held his stomach together, trying to stop the blood flow. Inside the back box of the vehicle they were tossed about by the driver's frantic rush and she had to hold his legs to keep him on the stretcher. A minute after being hit he was unconscious and that was one of the reasons he was still alive. His body relaxed the moment he passed out and the gush of liquid slowed. Her top was a deep red from when she had hugged him in the car park. The stain felt cold against her skin.

At the hospital they had dragged him away from here and she had sat waiting for news. It had taken two hours in the surgery to bring him back from the edge of death. Now he lay flat on the bed, wired in to various monitors and machines. She knew it had been close but he would live. In her heart she swore vengeance on the man who had hurt him so.

"Mikey pull through." Ben was next to her. His face was lined with fatigue.

"Oh Ben, yes, yes him alright. An' you? What happened to you? We had the police here looking for you. They was saying you probably been shot somewhere an' had to find you. Asking everything." She was crying with happiness, not just to see him safe but because it broke the hold of the hospital as a place of dying. To see a face she knew reminded her of the outside, that Mike would be better soon.

"Me know, they downstairs now but I just walk past. Someone else find me first, don't worry. Mike can relax about the man who shot him too."

"What happened?"

"I can't say but relax. You should go get some rest."

"No, I'm staying. I want to be here when he open his eyes. Can't leave him to wake up in this place."

"Well, I have to go. We came to check that he doing alright. What the doctor say?"

"They had to give him a lot of blood but he's fine. Off the critical. Ben, he was bleeding so much, I never . . ."

"But he's in no danger now. Old Mikey had a go for me."

Ben dropped a hand to his friend's face and tapped him on the cheek. "Him up in no time. Guy's a bull, I tell ya." He stepped away from the bed and came back close to her. "You sure you want a stay with him?"

"I am, yes. I couldn't sleep anyway."

"Call him parent?"

"No, I think the police have done though. I haven't seen anyone come in cept me, Ben."

"I get in touch with them. Then come back first thing in the day."

As Ben moved away she reached out to him and caught him in a hug. "Ben, what happened? Why they shoot him?"

"They play big shot, that all. Wanted the club, I guess, but I tell you it over, finish with. They done." Kissing her on the cheek he motioned her back to the chair. "You watch over him. Him in a lonely place here."

Then he was gone, making for the stairs and down to Curtis and the car.

The lights were on in his flat. All the way back from the hospital he had thought of her, wondered if she had waited. There was a flurry at the curtain as he killed the engine, and he rushed up the path. Only when he reached the door did he stop and think. He pulled the gun out of his jacket and was reaching for the bell in a crouch when she pulled the door open.

"Curtis, you're safe."

They were kissing, the gun draped behind her waist as he tasted her. She pulled him back into the room and over to the bed but he stopped her and broke away. "We ave to dig up right now. Think I may need to stay with you for a time."

"Of course. But . . ."

"There no time, Amanda. We have to go." He went over to his wardrobe and picked up a light sports bag. It had a few clothes in it that he kept ready for trips away. Then he went over to the bed and emptied the notes he had left from his stash into it. There wasn't much cash. The loan to them had bitten into his savings.

Amanda was following him, tugging on his arm. "Did you get Ben?"

"Yeah. I drop him at home a minute ago. Mike getting by alright." He had anticipated her next question, his mind rushing.

"Are you in trouble?"

"Maybe. I have to check with someone about it. Look, we have to go. Amanda . . ." Now he was still. His eyes examined her face and saw only concern. "You forgive me, then?"

"For what?"

"Then you still want to be with me?"

"I do. I think I understand what happened but let's go. We can talk when we get to my flat." Now it was her who encouraged him to hurry. Seeing him again had dispelled the doubts she had.

"Then I can say it to you?"

"Say what?" She looked up at him, close enough to see the colour of his eyes.

"Say that I in love with you?"

"I've waited so long for you to say that and you pick a time when I can't enjoy it. Don't waste it now, Curtis. Save it till we get away."

"I in love with you."

She smiled and kissed him. Then they went out to the car.

Seventeen

Ben flicked his eyes open. His head was throbbing and his whole body ached but he climbed out of the bed and reached for his clothes. They were not on the back of the chair. Looking around he saw that the chair itself was missing and then he realised he was back in his own room. The mirror opposite woke him up. It showed him rubbing his eyes, trying to believe that the tired, battered youth in boxing shorts it displayed was himself.

"A ras, me look fuck."

"Watch your language there, boy." His father was behind him, leaning against the wall.

"Oh, I no see you there, Pops. This my room, innit? Wha go on?"

"The way you come home last night I can't make you bed

down on the sofa so I take it. Ruth in my room. I bring you some tea. By you bed."

"Oh, thanks." He sat down again on the mattress and took a sip. The events of the night before were coming back to him. "So you . . ."

"I hear all about it, boy, the shooting. Then them boy who take you all turn on themselves like dat. I only thank the Lord you not around fo that. Is gunplay, Ben. Gettin like J, these day. It on the radio an' everything. How ya feel?"

"It's been better, you know. I don't recall all a it. Bit of a dream, you know. Mike alright?"

"Him parent ring me to see if you safe, that first I hear. Say him not too bad. Then you come in and fall a the couch. Me bring you up here."

"But the radio?"

"Oh it jus say there was a shooting at the club an' then they found them body round this American house. Say there was a well-known gangster there dead and it look like they all kill one and each. But it sketchy, you know. Police been round a talk with you this morning an' they come back later. I tell em what you say about jumping from the car at that traffic light."

Ben remembered some of the questions and answers he had rehearsed with Curtis driving back. "I was talking then?"

"Yeah, but more asleep than awake. Can tell me later but now you ave a visitor."

"Wha? Fo me? You say policeman been and come back."

"That what I say. This no police. Wait downstairs fo you."

'Who wait for me, then? Is gal?'

"Ben, you don't stop, son, do you? No, it a grown man wan talk wid you. Him name Carl."

They had never really spoken before. A while back at

Maxine's he would sometimes get to say hello if he was with Curtis and after the last shooting Carl had given him money to look after his friend. This was one to one though and in his own living room.

Carl looked quite at home, seated in the armchair Ben's father usually occupied. He was sipping from a teacup and put it down on the coffee table when Ben came in. "Must thank you father for his hospitality. Sit down, boy." Carl was in charge no matter which roof he was under. His leather coat rustled as he fished for his flask and added some of the brown spirit to his drink. "Stronger this way."

Ben looked on in a respectful silence.

"I know you live here cause you a face. Him galfren not an' that why I here. No way to find her an' I feel that where him is."

"I can't help you, C. I've never been round her yard with him."

"Name is Carl, boy, not 'C'. Can call your pickney fren that but me a grown man. An' I didn't hear you say where she live."

"Cause me no know."

"Think him is gone clear? Him have big problem, you know. Probly wan talk with me. Know me straight with him even though I did warn him off."

"I haven't spoken to him."

"That fair but you will, an' then I come in to the deal, you understand. He need my help bad."

"But on the news . . ."

"Maybe they is saying it nothin' but I know why. That boy have big man father, you understand, me know all about it. Is a clean-up. Is a word for it, Ben. Word is 'internecine play.' Call it that, you know why?" He pronounced the word with a clinical tone, like a scientist.

"Wha the word mean?"

"Mean everyone kill off, no problem then. Him no wan

police on our fren. Deal with it in his own way. An' he will, I tellin you, so's you tell Curtis. We have to meet today. Me in the park at two. Him be there."

"I can't . . ."

"Me gone, man. You carry the word." Carl fingered the cup in his massive hand and finished his drink. Then he stood and walked out, not looking back. Ben heard the car door open for him out in the street.

Curtis had been expecting the call on Ben and phoned soon after his boss left. The honeymoon feel of his morning with Amanda had not clouded his judgement and it was true what Carl had said. He did want to talk with the man, to confirm that he was in real danger.

Ben's excited voice did little to console him. "Man say you ave big problem. Like there people out for you or something. Best you meet up with him."

Amanda was by his side on the bed, stroking his back. Her flat seemed a long way from the world that was being discussed on the telephone. He took the details of the meet and hung up.

Ben was still talking into the hum on the other end of the line. "I gonna help you out, man, you wait. I know I owe you one on this."

The park suited him fine. This afternoon it was full of people, enjoying a break from the concrete and brick all around and he felt at ease in the open landscape, surrounded by strangers. Here he was a stranger too, not known as a hunted man by the others, and he strolled across the grass, enjoying the air.

The night before had reunited him with Amanda, made him aware of what she was to him, and he wanted everything back as it had been before. He was confident in Carl. Maybe he could organise a peace or some compromise. Though it was his only hope he was still in a positive mood. The girl had won him over this time and her touch pervaded his thoughts.

The car was over by a small lake in the corner of the park, Carl sitting in the back alone. He had sent the driver for a walk.

"Easy, Carl. Get your message." He climbed in the back next to him and spoke brightly, trying to show no worry.

"You look cheery for a man in your position. You must trust me, I suppose."

It had occurred to him that Carl could be bringing him in but Curtis was intelligent enough to know he had no choice. Dealing with his boss was the only option. "You gonna help me?"

"Yes, sah."

"Knew I could count on you there . . ."

"Help you with words, Curtis, that all. An' a way out maybe."

"How you mean?"

"You leaving for a while if you wan keep breathing."

"I can get away from town, yeah." This was a blow. Now he knew how important Amanda was to him again, the thought of leaving her for a while did not appeal.

Carl detected the swing of his mood.

"You think me is talking bout England, man? You gonna bawl bout sitting in the green an' pleasant land here? Think again."

"What you mean?"

"You travlin, that what I mean. You is journeyman fo a while. A good year, I feel."

Curtis let out a long sigh.

"Yes, sah. Away with you. You going Germany."

Curtis was staring at him in disbelief. "I can't leave England."

"Then you dead. Simple a that. Me can't cover you, boy, you have to go bury youself."

"Why there? I don't speak no rasclat German." His words sounded far away. He was retaining the look of someone involved in conversation but really his mind was drifting to Amanda's soft image, her body, the bond they had together.

"You have the choice here. Me ave people in Germany who can take you in. The market it a grow there. America they eat you up and anyway . . ."

"I can't do it."

"Only way I can help you an' that more than I should do. You know I like you, man, always thought you turn out good and in a way you have. You should a listen to me before though. This man too big, boy. You be alright for a while, then one time you out an' he find you. You a walkin' dead man. Here, take it." Carl pushed a packet across the seat and Curtis gingerly played with the edges of the paper. "You done play here, man. Is Bunny gonna fuck you too, I hear. Been stepping over the line. You should thank me, ya fuck." Carl was getting annoyed by his reluctance. He pulled the papers open. It was an air ticket and a list of names, slipped between some travel guides.

Curtis checked the flight time. It was for that evening. "An' money? I broke."

"That's your play, find some. Call me when you settle."

"But what do I . . ."

"Just find the people there, they handle it. Now go."

He wanted to ask questions, convince the man he was wrong and it would be safe to stay but he knew it was hopeless. The shot the night before echoed in his mind, the memory of Kimps begging with his tears. "I think it over."

"So long then, dead man. While you thinking, that all you is. Moving target, sah."

He backed out of the car and walked away. Carl watched him fade out of sight as he crossed the park.

Bliss was full of easy afternoon drinkers, chatting quietly or reading papers. He checked the faces. Though it was early, Ben soon saw Adam's frame wedged in a booth next to Petie and strode over.

"Him live. Me hear bout you adventure there, Ben."

"Hear bout Mike, then?"

"Yeah, but him get better the word. How's yourself."

"I'm sweet. Looking for a favour."

At this, Adam smiled and Petie shifted out of his seat, letting Ben sit down.

"Don't you buy a prospective customer a drink, then?"

"Get him a beer, Petie, an' me one too while you there. So this favour you talk about . . ."

"Yes, a loan. Big one, boy."

"What with your little escapades an' all I don't know bout you credit, boy. Might be a bit of a risk taking you on. An' anyway, thought you was minting your own money these days."

"We're owed the money for last night. That'll be . . ."

"How much you wanting anyway?"

Ben hesitated so as to add solemnity to his request. "Five."

"Cha, five hundred. Don't know there, Ben."

"No, Adam. I say five. Five thousand."

"Five grand, you kwashi." Adam was almost out of his seat, his voice soaring into the higher octave like an excited schoolkid. Petie looked over from the bar to make sure he was alright. "You out ya ras mind now. Thinks me can . . ."

"I know you can get it, Adam."

Adam showed his disgust for the remark. "Is no problem for I to give it to you. Problem is you giving me seven back."

"Seven to ras . . ."

"In one month."

"I a friend or what?"

"Well, them the rates, sah. Get it a Curtis if you needs it so bad."

"Need it from you."

"Then we shake."

Ben stared at the hand before him and the financial ruin it symbolised.

"An' you get the money now."

This was too tempting. Adam was expert at extending the carrot. Ben leapt for it and shook.

"Petie man, here sah."

Petie lumbered over, slamming a bottle down for Ben.

"Is a good thing. Me needs a drink."

"We giving Ben here five triple 'O'. Deal wid it."

Petie didn't blink but walked off towards the bathrooms at the rear.

"Just one minute, Ben, then you ave it. Time is . . ." Adam was checking his watch and concentrating. "So, thirty days from this time, sah."

"Thirty-one days a this month."

"Ah, but thirty the average fo the year, you see. I fair to all my client throughout the seasons.

"An' we shake now."

"Yeah, tirty alright."

Petie was back. He dropped a hand to Ben as though to shake but it was stuffed with notes. Ben shook and opened his hand to count the sum.

"Can't count in here, boy. This my office. You offend me."

"Yeah, Ben. You suggesting I'd burn you."

His eyes counted quickly, veterans of the cash rush, and he looked up at Petie. "Well, now you say it, this a ten short."

Petie dropped his head low, down to Ben's ear. "An' you know why, don't you?"

Ben stared up at the big man and smiled. "Course. That pay for the beers, innit."

They drank coffee together, not saying a word. To his eyes she looked more beautiful than ever and he had to set his mind on the parting, forcing himself to confront it. "There's no other way."

"I don't see the reason for it. It's so . . . at this time . . ."

"Amanda."

"It just isn't fair. I can see there's no point talking with you about it, even. Why now?"

"Because of what happened last night. There's no mystery. I killed a man and I have to go."

"You're so cold about it, like it doesn't affect you."

"So I have to cry before you think I sad? It my way, that all. Know no other."

"I know, I'm sorry." She came round the table and sat in his lap, kissing his neck.

"Maybe I can visit you. I could come over regularly."

"Another country too far for it to live between us. It bes we say goodbye, call it off. If I come back, then . . ."

" 'If' you come back?"

He moved her gently away and stood up. "This is serious, Amanda. Is the las time, probably."

She knew he wanted her but held off.

"It the bes way to say goodbye."

Now she joined him and they walked through to the bedroom.

When they had finished they lay together until time dictated he left. Shuffling round the room he dressed slowly, with her watching from the bed.

"Will you see Mike?"

"No. but I'll pass by Ben's and tell him to send my wishes. Have to say farewell to Ben."

"I'll come with you."

"You wan stand in the airport crying? We leave it like this, I walking out now. Watch yourself."

He left her. Without a last kiss or touch he walked out of the flat and down to his car. She knew his real feelings, how he wanted to stay. Their lovemaking had proved this to her. Curtis could only handle the absolutes in life. He was not a man for the long goodbye.

Ben was on his bed playing with the money. The notes were littered over his stomach and chest in a scruffy pile. "Money come, money go."

It was the least he could do, that he was sure of and he had no regrets borrowing from Adam. They owed him a grand anyhow and he was only in trouble on their account. He rolled off the bed and started to fold the notes, neatly placing them in his wallet. Out in the street he heard the familiar tone of his friend's car and strode over to the window.

Curtis parked and climbed out. He looked tired in the fading light and Ben watched him move slowly across the street, noting the frown. He hurried with the rest of the money and rushed down the stairs to the kitchen. Curtis was with his father.

"How ya keeping, then?"

"Reasonable, you know. An' you?"

"Life treat me the way I treat it so I can't complain."

"Curtis, what's been said then?"

"Don't think your father wants to hear our small talk, do you?"

It was a polite way of asking the man to leave and he obliged with a nod of his head. "I see you later maybe?"

"Some time, yeah. Ben, you have anything to drink?"

"No sah, just from the tap."

"Then we go an' have a drink, yeah? Could be a while afore I see you again."

"When you ave to leave?"

"Well, they ave a bar at the airport, I think. Put it that way."

"Let me get my coat an' I be with you."

The drive was relaxing. It was just after the rush and in the hot weather the traffic seemed lighter. Curtis didn't push it, he took it as a cruise, but they were soon out of town and gliding past green fields.

"You gone for a while, then?"

"I don't know, Ben. Long as it takes for things to settle, I suppose. Man say there a lot a things opening up out there for me to get into. Could be I like it an' stay."

"No sah. You a West Park boy wid the rest a us. We a team, man. I let you know soon as I get the word you can come."

"Oh, well cheers, Ben. That very kind of you."

Ben smiled at the sarcasm and turned to him. "I ave money fo you."

"Yah fuck. Ya dig some up fo me? Tell you the truth, B, I need it. Things not too good with . . ."

"Five grand." There was no clear sign of his shock but Ben could see he was impressed by the figure.

"Where you get tha . . . a ras, man, not tha fuck Adam."

"Matter where it come from? Money there to spend or give."

"Or pay back. How you going to make the pay? Him have you intrest on top, you know?"

"Me know, me no kwashi boy. There is the club . . ."

"Club fuck, you know that."

"Well . . ."

"Get real, Ben. Can't run a place where there been a

shooting, me know these things. Policeman know your face fo one thing."

"Me may try something new, another venue."

"Well, I'm not gonna tear you down, rasta. Not if you serious about the money anyhow. I in no position to argue right now."

"I have it for you, you hear me." He pulled the wallet out and passed it to him.

Curtis stuck it deep in his jacket. "Thanks, Ben. I feel you pay twice fo this to Adam."

"Don't worry youself all the time. Got to take life easy, let it wash over you in a tide, man. Oh, it ten short by the way."

"Ten short, you say, the money?"

"Yeah, that's for the beer."

"Wha beer?"

"The beer you gonna buy me when we reach, man."

The airport was alive with people. High walls of glass let the light flood the hall and after he checked in they found a bar, looking out over the runways. The planes were tiny toys off in the distance and Ben watched as a huge machine blasted into the sky on the long strip of tarmac.

Curtis was back with their drinks. "These bars overcharge, you know."

"Wha? With five grand you should be leaving a tip, not complaining."

"It the principle though. Ben. They shouldn't expect you to pay so much for a small glass a beer like this."

"You ave plenty where you a go."

They both laughed and stared through the glass.

"It's just a mircle they can get off the ground. I never been on a plane before. Almost envy you."

"You're not leaving what I am though, Ben."

"You mean Amanda?"

"What else? Think I'm gonna miss you, boy?"

"Thought you gone cold on her, that all." He was thinking

of the dance he had with her, how it was only a matter of hours ago. The night had been long. There was a tinge of guilt to his thoughts as well and he contemplated telling Curtis.

"Ben, I should tell you I may have wrecked your chance with Sophie."

"How that, then?"

"Well, we had a little ting going. It was nothing, just a mistake and it made me run back to Amanda. Crazy I have to leave now but I think you should try again. She might come round to you."

He was not sure how to react. It was as though he should be angry but he felt nothing. Maybe it was because this was the last time he would see his friend for some time. After a moment of thought he answered. "Cha. She nothing, man. I thought there was something a go on that day we went out. She acted funny, you know."

"You should start caring a bit more, Ben."

"Now you talk fuckrie."

"No sah. It worth it, giving a little."

"You gettin soft, man."

"No. Still have the same beliefs, just had a taste of something else."

They were quiet for a moment, sipping at the beer.

"So you go with her?"

"Go where?"

"You know what I say. Ya fuck now."

"Yeah. We did."

"So that mean the competition over, then." He turned back to the window.

"Wha you talk about?"

"Just something I had going with Mike, that all."

"You pissed off with me, then?"

"No. I told you. Gal nothin'."

"As you wish. Anyway drink you drink there. We ave time for another before the flight."

"Me alright."

"I'll go down, then." He finished the beer with one gulp and slammed it down on the table-top.

"What you doing about the car?"

"You can have it. Sell it an' pay Adam off before he sends the gorilla after you."

"I can't drive though. I can pick it up."

They left the table and walked towards the stairs for the departure lounge.

"I won't come down, man. Might watch you take off."

"Yeah. I'll be waving. Here." He gave him the keys and kept hold of Ben's hand. "This it, then. Time for a change but I be back, man. When I do we party, yeah? One year should see me kissing the ground outside the new club in West Park you'll be running. Till then."

"It's my fault you have to go. I don't . . ."

"Nobody fault. What happens, it like nature, man. You have to run when it good, duck when it bad. I'm the one who should have stepped in. You take it easy, Ben."

He took the stairs fast and was out of sight before Ben could shout a farewell. His suited figured had merged with the other passengers and Ben was left to wander back to the glass. He thought of the future, when he would see Curtis next. All the times they had shared filed through his thoughts and he remembered laughter, risks and excess. The last image he saw was the one from his dream, waiting to be saved. Curtis tracking the man, fearless in the dark. His presence pressing closer, remorseless. Could he set up a new club? There were too many obstacles this time though, so many problems. He wanted to be on top when Curtis hit town next though. The Chocolate Box success had tasted good, a bolt of power. He couldn't go back to ripping the hippies or rolling drunks. It was almost as though Curtis had expectations which he wanted him to live up to. Ben felt determined. He walked towards the underground link and thought of buying a magazine for the ride. His hand dug deep in a pocket and pulled out some change. It was not enough for a paper, let alone the ticket back. He sighed and stumbled off in the direction of the car. It was an inauspicious start but he was not depressed. It was just like the old days. There might be some change in the glove compartment.

JONATHAN BROOK is twenty-six years old and was born in Los Angeles, California. At six years of age his family relocated to Leeds, Yorkshire where he was soon installed in the local comprehensive and did nothing of particular note except learn to play the guitar and skank. As a member of an almost-known Ska outfit he toured the UK for a number of years, finding time to write reviews and music articles along the way. Moving to London in the late Eighties Jonathan did more of the same including studio work and US/Japanese tours for many an Acid Jazz band including the Night Trains and the Humble Souls. The closest he has ever come to any sort of stability has been his last three years' work with rocksteady superhero Desmond Dekker. BIG UP! is his second *Backstreets* novel and continues the action first introduced in SLACKNESS.

Also in the *Backstreets* series

SLACKNESS

"When Carl said big money Curtis knew what he meant. All his life he had seen the local players, the money men. He knew how much the car was, bought in cash, the suits and the flat, the trips back to J. Maybe this would give him the break he needed from Ben and the others who were still running around like kids . . ."

Curtis, Ben and Mike went back a long way. But coming of age means choices have to be made, paths chosen. In this, the first BACKSTREETS novel, the trio career hazardously around the streets of London and tumble headlong into their futures . . .